The Purloined Prognosticator

by

Nicki Pascarella

A Miranda Albright, Ph.D. Mystery,
Book Three

Cover Art by *Diana Carlile*

The Wild Rose Press, Inc.
PO Box 708
Adams Basin, NY 14410-0708
Visit us at www.thewildrosepress.com

Publishing History
First Edition, 2024
Trade Paperback ISBN 978-1-5092-5769-0
Digital ISBN 978-1-5092-5770-6

A Miranda Albright, Ph.D. Mystery, Book Three
Published in the United States of America

Dedication

To my editor Claudia Fallon,
thank you for taking a chance on a new author.
And triple kisses for being so patient with me.

Other Books By Nicki Pascarella

Troubles in Bellmount
The Curse of the Redhead
Rescuing Jellybean
Steamy Cairo Nights
The Duke Beneath Her Mistletoe

Chapter 1

The flames in Weston Westinghouse the Third's hazel eyes ignited a fire in my core. Clutching my hips, he pulled me to his hard body. His breath caressed my cheek, blowing a strand of my hair as he whispered, "I've missed you, Shortcake." He nuzzled my nose, and then his lips crushed mine.

"Knock, knock!" As usual, my mentor Dr. Lincoln Harrison used words instead of a physical tap to announce himself. He chuckled and his bespeckled eyes twinkled. "Miranda, are you daydreaming again?"

I shook off the remnants of my fantasy.

"Thinking about Weston?" he asked.

Seeing as how I was both turned on and humiliated, I fanned my burning cheeks. "Sorry. Do you need something?"

Lincoln Harrison was the psychology professor assigned to be my mentor at Bellmount College, where I taught English and Journalism. I was his off-the-record, behind-closed-doors, secret project. He studied my bizarre psychic abilities with the fascination of a mad scientist dissecting a prized lab rat. Besides experimenting on me, Lincoln was also my dear friend.

He propped his body against my office door frame and ran a hand through his Santa-like beard. "You might need to head to the newspaper office. Gibbons is up to his shenanigans again. There is some kind of standoff between him and Liza Smith. My money's on Liza."

Liza Smith was a talented journalist and the editor-in-chief of the Bellmount College newspaper. John Gibbons had barely passed English 101 and had written *Journalism with Doc Albright* in red crayon on his course selection card. The class clown enjoyed taunting me and we were stuck together for another semester. On the days he wasn't interfering with my attempts to impart wisdom to my young scholars, I found his tomfoolery amusing.

"Fudge. Not again." I grunted, then followed Lincoln down four flights of stairs to the basement of Sutton Hall.

John sat at Liza's desk, his hands folded behind his head, his dirt-covered sneakers propped on her notebook. Liza stood front and center, her hands on her hips. A fuming Michael Dunlap crossed his arms over his chest, and my three newest muckrakers gawked at the brouhaha.

"What did you do now, John?" I asked.

"Her royal highness is pooh-poohing my ideas. She thinks we can make the money we need with a bake sale. What are we, kindergarteners? We'll be lucky if we make five dollars selling cookies," John said.

In my overactive imagination, smoke oozed from Liza's ears, forming swirly tentacles above her head.

"Tell Dr. Albright about your asinine idea, John," she said.

"It's a great idea. I bet we can make hundreds of dollars and turn this hellhole into a cool crib." John brought his hand out from behind his head and swung it wide to present the "hellhole," also known as the

Bellmount College newspaper office.

Despite its lack of windows, it was an adequate space. The problem was the office furniture dated back to the 1950s, and the couch had housed a few rodent families over the years. Although the assistant to the dean had recently done her best to outfit us, she didn't have the budget to do more. My staff wanted a new couch, a microwave, a coffee pot, and a small black and white television VCR combo to watch the daily news. Keisha Brown, the aforementioned assistant to the dean, suggested the kids do a fundraiser.

Always a voice of reason, Michael Dunlap raised his hand. "Liza and I think we should sell coffee and donuts on Bellmount Bob Day. Missy agrees."

"Dunlap is voting with the girls 'cause someone stole his balls," John said.

Attempting to diffuse the situation, I slipped into my professor's voice. "Mr. Gibbons, language!"

I had moved to Bellmount a few months prior. Although I had spent past summers vacationing at my aunt's Victorian inn, I had not yet lived an entire winter in Bellmount. Therefore, I lacked a thorough understanding of the folkloric holiday. "Liza, tell me about Bellmount Bob Day."

She popped onto her toes. "If Bob emerges from his burrow and sees his shadow, it means five more weeks of winter. If he doesn't see his shadow, we'll have an early spring."

"Bob whispers his prognostication into his human handler's ear. He has been doing it for over one hundred years and has never been wrong," said freshman Dante Santiago.

"He is one hundred and ten years old and has a

wife and a dozen groundbabies," Missy Helmuth said.

Ridiculous! "Liza, do you think you can earn enough money selling donuts and hot chocolate?" I asked.

She glowered at her mutineer before gazing in my direction. "Dr. Albright, there will be hundreds of people there. It's a huge deal. Visitors from all over the state will show up at Pinkie's Steeple to find out if the groundhog sees his shadow. People stand around in the cold for hours to get a glimpse of him. If we sell a cup of hot chocolate and a sweet for one dollar, my calculations are we could make at least three hundred and fifty dollars. That won't buy us everything, but it's a good start."

"That sounds like a great plan," I said. "John, what's your idea?"

Enthusiasm bubbled from Mason Bitz and his gangly limbs. "I think Gibbons's plan is a winner."

John high-fived his buddy. He cleared his throat before mimicking a deep-voiced emcee. "The night before, I want to host a massive party at The Steeple. Tickets cost ten dollars apiece. All of the beer you can drink, a bonfire, dancing, and a Ms. Bob contest."

Liza groaned. "John, fill Dr. Albright in about the Ms. Bob contest."

John swung his legs off the desk, stood, and spread his arms wide, palms to the ceiling. "We have nominations for Ms. Bob. There is a bikini and snow boots contest and a Keep Me Warm Kissing Contest. The winner is crowned at midnight and helps the handler lift the groundhog from his cage." Keeping with the drama of his performance, he placed a hand on his hip, imitating a showgirl pose. "Miss Bellmount

Bob announces if spring will come early or winter will stick around."

I huffed. I'd been nominated as a Bellmount Harvest Princess a few months prior, and it had been the most humiliating moment of my life. It was even more embarrassing than my mentor constantly finding me all hot and bothered.

John puffed up his chest. "Can you imagine a beautiful woman in a bikini and furry snow boots delivering the news to the crowd? It will become a great tradition."

I drummed my fingers on the desk. "Sounds sexist and cold to me. Not to mention a lot of work."

"What do you think, Dr. Harrison? Don't you think having a big bonfire up on Pinkie's Steeple would be super cool?" John asked.

Lincoln ran a hand through his beard. "I think you would have to get a permit from the resort to have the party. You would have underage kids at the kegs, and Ms. Brown would skin you alive if you put a half-dozen half-naked women in a park in the middle of the winter."

"Ms. Brown would definitely kick someone's ass!" Keisha Brown bellowed from the hallway. The master eavesdropper entered the office, strutting like a queen. "I'll get you the tables, you can sign out one of the campus vans, and Nicole from the bakery will give you the donuts for practically nothing."

Liza clapped. "Thank you, Ms. Brown. You're the best."

"I guess it is baked goods and cocoa," I said.

"Boring." John sank into the chair, his bottom lip jutted out, and he pointed to the couch. "Get used to sitting on the mouse house, people."

"I will organize everything," Liza said.

"I'm sure you have it under control."

"Dr. Albright, from what I hear, Bellmount Bob Day is great," Missy called to my back "It's one of the reasons I chose to attend school here."

I stopped in my tracks and faced my crew. Maybe the event wasn't silly if it brought promising students to campus. Caught up in the contagious excitement, a surge of newfound energy shot through me.

"You are going to love it. The entire town feels so festive," Liza said.

"I'm sure I will."

After all, how bad could something "festive" be?

As long as nobody shoved a tiara on my head and I didn't stumble over a corpse, I was all in.

Chapter 2

Weston Westinghouse the Third stood in front of me, shirtless. His sun-kissed hair blew about as it dried in the breeze, and the river provided the perfect backdrop for his glistening muscles.

"Shortcake, run away with me," he said.

"Yes. Anywhere you want," I whispered.

He pulled me to him. "I lo—" Something in the distance distracted him.

I waved my hand in front of his eyes. "Say it, West," I begged.

"Doctor Shortcake, wake up!"

I opened one eye.

"Are you up?" someone asked.

I opened my other eye to take in the woman propped in my bed, leaning over me. She was only slightly larger than a child. A yellow plastic barrette held back one side of her light brown shoulder-length hair. Almond-shaped eyes that slanted upward appeared extra-large from behind the lenses of her thick glasses, and she had an adorable flattened nose. Cindi Westinghouse, West's younger cousin, sat on my bed, wide-eyed and bushy-tailed.

"Cindi, what are you doing here?"

She grinned. "You are up."

I sighed. "Not really. What time is it?"

The miniature Cindi Westinghouse looked at her

wrist. She used an index finger to trace shapes on her watch. Then she stuck it in my face. "Early."

I sat up, took her wrist in my hand, and double-checked the time. "You're correct. It is early. Five thirty a.m., to be exact. Why are you in my room?"

When Cindi grinned, her tongue slightly protruded. "I'm twenty-one today, and I have a job."

I rubbed my eyes, and the Shetland sheepdog curled at my feet covered his nose with both paws. "Happy Birthday!" I said.

"I am learning to make coffee. I get to say *hi* to people and do dishes. If I do good, I will be a waitress."

"That is awesome. Tell you what. Today, after you're done working, I'll take you out for a birthday lunch."

"Okay. Got it," she said.

"From now on, please wait for me to come down to breakfast. I like to sleep in on Saturdays."

"Okay. Got it," she said again.

I took her wrist-watched hand in mine. "When the little hand gets here," I pointed to the nine, "I will come down to the kitchen and say hi."

She held the watch close to her eyes and studied it. "Got it."

"I'm going back to bed now." My gaze settled on my bedroom door, hoping she'd get the hint.

"I like your dog, turtle, and hamster," she said.

I inclined my chin toward the annoyed Sheltie. "That is Spot." I swung my arm, indicating the cages on the top of my dresser. "The turtle's name is Princess Pickles. He is a boy. And the hamster is a jerky rat named Simon."

She giggled. "Your rat is bad." She perused my

bedroom. "It's pretty like a princess room."

My third-floor bedroom was one of two rooms that occupied the turret in my Aunt Edith's Victorian inn. It was romantic shades of white and blue floral patterns. My favorite part was the upholstered window seat that looked out over the west end of Bellmount. The cozy nook was framed by lacy white curtains and covered with throw pillows.

"Thank you. I'm going to go back to bed now. See you at breakfast, and when you get off work, we'll go to lunch."

"And we will see each other tomorrow," Cindi said.

"Tomorrow?" I asked. "Are you working Sundays too?"

She stared at me with a blank expression, so I rephrased my question. "Why will I see you tomorrow?"

"West is taking me to see Bellmount Bob and teaching me to ski for my birthday present."

My heart ached at the mention of my ex-boyfriend. West doted on his younger cousin, she adored him, and I missed him so much I could barely breathe.

"Cindi, why will I see you?"

She leaned her face close to mine. "I picked you to be my friend."

My heartbeat sped up. "What? Cindi, for real? Is West taking us both skiing tomorrow?"

She grinned. "And to see Bellmount Bob. He is the most *accure prognor* in the world."

Cindi meant to repeat the tagline, "The Most Accurate Prognosticator in the World." But it came out a bit jumbled.

"He's cute and has babies," she added.

She meant Bob, not West. To my knowledge, although adorable, West didn't have children.

Cindi studied her watch. "Edith says I have to be downstairs when the big hand gets here."

Before I could see what she pointed at, she crawled to the edge of the bed and headed toward the door.

"What time are we going skiing?" I asked.

"And to see Bob the most *accure prognor* in the world."

"Yes, and it is said like this—'The Most Accurate Prognosticator in the World!' What time?" Desperation filtered through my question.

She shrugged, then stopped in her tracks to stare at my window seat. A handsome filmy man stood motionless, studying her.

She closed her eyes tight and squished her face into a little ball. When she lifted her lids, she refocused and frowned. She clomped across the room, stopped a foot from my spectral visitor, and waved her hand in front of him.

The unfriendly ghost jutted his chin.

She closed her eyes again and squeezed her face even harder. When she opened her eyes, she fumbled with her glasses. "Ghosts aren't real."

Greg Grainey's eyes widened.

Moving in slow motion, she reached out her index finger and poked it through Greg's shoulder.

"Ouch!"

"Sorry, Mr. Ghost, but you aren't real." Then, brow furrowed and weighting her steps heavily, Cindi Westinghouse left me sitting in my blue turret with a confused poltergeist and my heart aching for her handsome cousin.

"What the hell is wrong with her?" Greg asked.

I pursed my lips. "You're a jerk! Nothing is wrong with her. She has Down Syndrome."

"Unbunch your panties, Crimson. That isn't what I meant. Why can she see me?"

I shook my head. "Wow, Greg. I don't know. Did you hear, though? She wants me to go on her birthday date with West."

"Yeah, I heard. I think it's a bad idea. You're just going to fuck, then fall for him again."

I hated when Greg was correct, so I sought moral support from my dog. "Spot, do you think it's true? Should I call West to check?"

Greg grunted, and a tired Spot whimpered.

I lay down, pulled my blanket to my chin, and closed my eyes. A second later, a knock on the door startled me. Assuming Cindi had come back, I called, "Come in!"

The door cracked a few inches, and Winona Westinghouse peeked into my turret.

I groaned. "Winona?"

My large-boned friend often forgot her herculean strength so she slammed the door behind her. It crashed, and she winced.

"Cindi said you were up."

"Not really."

An undaunted Winona sprang across my room. Greg, the perverted poltergeist he was, stared at her with lust-filled eyes. Unaware of the ogling, she sat on the edge of my bed.

"Miranda, last night Richard told me he loves me."

I sat up and let the blanket drop onto my lap. "Holy

guacamole!"

"Miranda, he's so handsome and so tall, and he's such a good kisser. I think I'm going to tell him I love him too. I also think I might—" She scrunched up her nose. "Ya know—" She leaned in and whispered, "—have sex."

Greg snorted.

I took my friend's hand in mine. "Winona, I know how you feel about him, but telling him you love him is a big step."

"I know. So is sex. I have only been with one other person and done some stuff with Greg Grainey."

Greg made a claw, wiped his fingers across his chest, then blew on them. *"Ruined her for all other men."*

I had not been frank with Winona about two things. It wasn't just that her ex-crush, the sex-starved ghost, sometimes crashed in my tower. I also didn't like her boyfriend, Richard, AKA Dinky, the DJ. His spiked hair stood on top of his head and his gaze wandered over everything with estrogen. Plus, according to West, he looked like he had stepped out of a music video.

"Winona, there is something I think you should consider. You know Officer Kline is crazy about you."

Douglass Kline was the only decent cop on the Bellmount Municipal Police force, and he happened to be as much of a sweetheart as Winona. The two of them could have enormous, air-headed, lovable children.

"Douglass is nice, Miranda. But Richard is so—"

"Is a fucking dick," chirped the wispy figure sitting at my window seat.

"—sexy," she said.

Yuck! I agreed with the ghost.

"Winona, after you guys get off work, I am going to take Cindi to lunch for her birthday. If you would like to join us, we can talk then. I'm exhausted. It isn't time for me to get up yet."

"Cindi told me you are joining her birthday celebration with West. Whatever you do, don't fall for him again."

"Yep," Greg said. *"Gotta agree with sweet-hips. You need off the Westinghouse meat train."*

I shot Greg a grumpy glower. "Winona, see you when I come down for breakfast and then later at lunch."

"See you later." She tiptoed to my door as if she hadn't already created enough noise to wake the dead. Although, in all fairness, her cousin Cindi was the one who had done that.

As the door closed behind her, my ghost piped up. "There were way too many Westinghouses in the turret this morning."

I burrowed under my blankets. "Well, considering there are at least five dozen of the buggers running around the county, only two of them have been here."

"From all of that writhing and moaning you were doing in your dreams, I'd say there were three Westinghouses in this room, and it isn't even six a.m."

I covered my burning cheeks with my hands.

"Unless you were having those little wet dreams about me?" The ghost smirked.

I flopped onto my belly and grumbled into my mattress, "Greg, stop watching me sleep."

Chapter 3

After breakfast, I walked into town and purchased a lovely embossed journal, a pen, and a gift bag. Later that afternoon, I presented them to Cindi while we perused the menu at Sandra's Cafe.

Cindi placed a non-menu order of a hotdog and fries. I ordered the gorgonzola, pears, and candied pecans over greens, and Winona chowed down on a Pittsburgh salad with extra fries. So much for the diets Winona and I had gone on before the holidays. As we ate, Winona filled me in on her escapades with Dinky the DJ, while I tried to convince her to give Officer Kline a chance.

Cindi was more interested in her new present than her meal or Winona's love life. She pushed her plate back, opened her journal, and wrote her name on the front page.

"What letters spell clues?" Cindi asked.

As I enunciated each letter, she took her time writing, and then held her script up for us to read.

Winona's chest swelled with pride. "Are you keeping a clue journal like me? You know I carry a notebook and write down details so I can solve crimes."

Winona was obsessed with about a dozen prime-time television shows. For the life of me, I had no idea why the Sherlock Holmes wannabe was more attracted to a punk DJ than a sweet cop.

Cindi looked up from her notebook. "I am a detective like Doctor Shortcake."

"I'm a detective too," Winona said.

Cindi pushed her off-kilter glasses into place. "But I am a detective like Miranda."

"What's wrong with me?" Winona's lips turned down at the corners.

Cindi hid her mouth behind her hand as if she was telling me a secret, then loudly declared, "Winona has a birdbrain."

Since I had just taken a sip, my iced tea squirted across the table, spraying Winona. My poor friend grumbled as she patted my spittle.

Cindi let loose with giggles that racked her body until her head shot backward. "Birdbrain," she chortled.

It was at that moment that Dr. Bradley Gordon entered the upscale bistro. Upscale in Bellmount, Pennsylvania was a relative term. However, Bear County residents changed out of their flannel to enjoy a meal at Sandra's. Every female in the establishment watched as the doctor waved, then strolled to our table to say hello.

Brad was my over-six-foot-tall pre-West ex-boyfriend. His thick dark hair, long black eyelashes that framed his priceless sapphire eyes, and dimples made women goofy.

"Hello, Winona," he said.

Winona batted her eyelashes. "Hi, Bradley."

Brad smiled at Cindi. "Hello, Cindi."

Cindi's lashes bounced up and down. "Hi, Dr. Gordon."

His voice deepened as his blue beauties stared into mine. "Hi, Miranda."

I tried to hold my lashes still, but they fluttered like feathers in a windstorm. "Hi. Brad."

"I'm twenty-one today," Cindi announced.

"Well, happy birthday," Brad said.

She flashed him her toothy grin. "I worked for Edith today."

Brad's eyes twinkled, and his dimples deepened. "Congratulations. Edith is my best friend, and I know she is happy to have the extra help. I bet you did a great job."

"I am twenty-one, so you can date me at the Polkamania dance," Cindi said.

For the second time that afternoon, my drink spurted out my nostrils, landing on Winona. Her wide-eyed gawk traveled back and forth between her cousin and the spectacular masculine specimen in front of us.

Without missing a beat, Brad took control of the situation. "Cindi, you are too young for me, and I can't date my patients."

"You dated Miranda," Winona said.

Brad cut his gaze to Winona and exhaled.

Cindi frowned. "But I'm twenty-one."

Brad pulled a chair up beside her. "Yes, and I am thirty-three. That is too old for you. You need to date a nice boy who is also in his early twenties."

Cindi's smile turned into a pouty face, her chin dropped, and her glasses drifted down her nose.

"Tell me about your picture. Are these clues?" Brad asked.

Cindi refocused her attention on her artwork and again slid her lopsided glasses into place. "Yes."

Brad winked at me; then smiled at Winona. She blushed. Okay, I confess, my cheeks caught fire.

He pointed at the notebook. "Tell me about this clue."

"That is Spot. He is a dog," Cindi said.

Brad nodded. "Spot is a great dog." He tapped the paper. "And this one?"

"That is Princess Pickles. He is a boy."

"How about this?" Brad pointed again.

"That is a bratty hamster." Cindi threw her head back and howled.

"You drew Miranda's pets? What mystery are they clues in?"

As the giggles over my rotten rat subsided, she said, "The Princesses Castle Mystery,"

Although I pretended to be a princess staring out over my kingdom, I in no way wanted other people to grace me with tiaras and titles. Still, Cindi's perception charmed me.

"Is that Miranda?" Brad traced a stick figure.

Cindi scrunched up her face. "No. That is Mr. Ghost."

Once again, my iced tea shot across the table.

Winona wiped my spit from her face, then turned her glower on her younger cousin. "Cindi, there is no such thing as ghosts. You know your mother doesn't want you talking about them, and it upsets Grandma Westinghouse."

Cindi's bottom lip jutted out, as she drew a big X over Greg Grainey.

Brad stood and shifted his weight back and forth while running a hand through his luscious locks. "Ladies, could you please excuse Miranda and me? We need to talk."

Neither of my lunch dates protested as I followed

Brad outside. Since I had left my coat in the restaurant, I wrapped my arms around myself, attempting to keep warm.

"Greg Grainey?" he asked.

I nodded. Like me, Brad Gordon had energy abilities. I could read minds and find psychic footprints left behind after tragedies. He could heal the sick and help with pain management using his skills.

Everyone in town, besides me, Lincoln Harrison, and the dead Grainey, thought that Brad was the average traditional doctor. However, Brad used a combination of scientifically proven medicine and his energy to heal. Since most people saw any form of energy capabilities as wacko superstition, Brad and I kept our abilities to ourselves. He had quite a bit of pride in his and saw them as a gift. I was ashamed of mine and saw them as a curse. Brad and I had been present at Greg Grainey's accidental death. Consequently, his trapped energy tormented us both, and his strange appearances rarely surprised us.

I leaned close to Brad's body heat. "Cindi saw him this morning when she came into my room to tell me it was her birthday."

He rested his thumb on his chin. "Her mother has brought her to me a few times because she wants me to cure Cindi of her talking-to-ghosts affliction."

"Holy guacamole. Cindi sees other ghosts? Do you think she is like us?" More precisely, I wondered if she was like a woman named Madame Alina, a psychic from the neighboring town of Greenport who could talk to the dead.

"Perhaps," he said. "And she is being told they aren't real and that she is misbehaving by talking about them. She has to be confused."

"Oh, Brad. We have to help her."

He stepped closer to me, and his voice softened. "You're cold."

I spasmed in an all-out head-to-toe shiver.

Brad took off his jacket and swung it around my shoulders. "I think you should talk with her. Be truthful and tell her what she is seeing is real. Explain that she has a special gift, but she can't talk to anyone about it but you and me. Maybe I could convince her parents to take her to see Dr. Harrison. He might also have ideas."

"I guess it would be better for me to talk to her. She has such a crush on you," I said.

He sighed.

"Every woman in this town has a crush on you."

He leaned forward so that his forehead was inches from mine. "Except for the girl I'm crazy about."

I have no idea what Brad saw in me because I was a nerdy bookworm. I had uncontrollable, wild red hair that knotted itself into something akin to macramé plant holders. Freckles splattered my nose like brown paint. I didn't hate my green eyes because they were the same eyes I saw when I looked at my cousin Liam and my Grandma Zoey's portrait. But my smile was too big, my skin was too pale, my breasts were extreme, and I was entirely too short.

But for some reason, a perfect Brad, smelling of dryer sheets and citrus, stood in front of me, warm and vulnerable, as his jewel-toned eyes begged for a kiss.

And Weston Westinghouse couldn't tell me how he felt. Sigh!

But West was under my skin. He was in my dreams and my fantasies. I heard his voice whispering sweet nothings and felt his skin pressed against mine. Memories of his aftershave haunted me.

Even if I allowed Brad to take me in his arms and make me his girlfriend again, it would be wrong. I knew without a doubt that West was the man I belonged with.

"I think she could also talk to West about it. He would understand. He knows about me," I said.

Brad's gaze drifted past my face as he stared into the distance. "If you think Westinghouse will help look out for her, it would be good for a family member to know. I will leave that to you, but I don't think her parents will understand. She isn't a lab rat, and I'm afraid that is what she would become."

I nodded.

"Edith invited me to her dinner party this evening. Will you be home?"

I nodded again.

"Will Westinghouse be joining you?" Brad held his breath.

"No." I bit my lip.

He placed his hand on my shoulder. "Let's get back inside so you can warm up."

We entered the cafe side by side. Winona quirked an eyebrow, and Cindi took a break from recording clues to smile at her crush.

I learned a lot at that lunch. Twenty-one-year-old Cindi Westinghouse was a powerful medium, had an eye for details, a natural knack for sleuthing, and good taste in men.

Chapter 4

Following lunch with Cindi and Winona, I helped my aunt fix a home-cooked meal of roast beef, gravy, mashed potatoes, green bean casserole, homemade bread with herbed butter, and pineapple upside-down cake. Aunt Edith's perfectly executed dinner parties were the cherry on top of her out-of-the-world cooking. My contribution was peeling the potatoes, setting the table, and mixing the cake batter. Meanwhile, Russ, the live-in caretaker and Aunt Edith's long-time romantic companion, dusted and vacuumed the guest parlor and polished the silver until we saw our reflections in the utensils.

Although Aunt Edith referred to the inn's front room as the guest parlor, I considered it a dining room. It was where the guests ate breakfast, and Aunt Edith held special dinners. Built-in walnut cupboards showcased antique china sets, and a sideboard housed coffee, tea, and baked goods from seven-to-seven daily. A mahogany table that comfortably accommodated ten opulently upholstered chairs took up the center of the room. Two smaller lace-covered round tables sat in front of the bay window that looked out over the town. Rich crown molding and a red floral damask wallpaper added to the room's elegance, and a chandelier dripping with sparkling cut glass hung from a gold ceiling medallion. If Greg ever knocked the nineteenth century light fixture onto the table while he was haunting the inn, the sheer weight of it would cause an earthquake on the hill that overlooked his beloved town.

Doctor Brad and Knight were the first to arrive. I had gifted the Lab husky mix to Brad after he treated me during a rash of injuries and illnesses. Both pup and doctor had jet-black hair and stunning blue eyes. Seriously adorable!

The second Knight saw Spot, he placed himself in a downward dog, his rump high. Then he wagged, smiled, and leaped on the Sheltie. Spot barked, and the two of them chased each other from one end of the foyer to the other—back and forth, and back and forth.

"I think they like each other." Brad kissed Aunt Edith on the cheek and handed her a bottle of wine.

My aunt lit up. "Thank you, Bradley."

Brad smiled at me, and his dimples appeared. "Twice in one day, Miranda." He hesitated for a moment before kissing me on the cheek.

My face caught fire. "Hi, Brad."

The doorbell rang again, and soon Liam, his nasty girlfriend Gina Schuster, Lincoln, and his wife Alice, filled the foyer. Aunt Edith and I took coats and ushered everyone into the library for drinks and hors d'oeuvres.

Russ popped the cork on the wine and poured a glass for everyone but me. Mostly a teetotaler, I had imbibed three times. The first time, I had gotten so drunk that West had to carry me home from the bar while I said filthy things to him. I had also chugged a glass of wine the night Greg Grainey died. The third time, I had kind of sipped whiskey with the ex-mayor of Bellmount during a sting.

The evening's conversation soon turned to our murdering ex-mayor and his replacement.

"Gina, how is your brother settling back into town?" Aunt Edith asked Bellmount Bitch Gina.

The Bellmount Bitches were a notorious group of mean women whom I despised. How my cousin had ended up falling for one was a mystery to me. Aunt Edith wasn't thrilled but would never stoop so low as to be a poor hostess. I also behaved hospitably during Gina's visits even though she made a point of sniffing at me like I was three-week-old leftovers.

"James loves it. His wife Cassandra seems a bit disappointed. She misses the city. Bear County is so boring and unsophisticated. Who can blame her? But Mommy and Daddy couldn't be happier."

Mommy and Daddy? For crying out loud! The demon woman was pushing thirty.

"Quite impressive. James ran unopposed," Brad said.

The Bellmount town council consisted of Aunt Edith, who had considered running for mayor but decided that the inn was her priority. Greg Grainey's daughter, Jessica, was also on the council. She'd declined the position because she worked long hours keeping her family's store running since her father's death. Good thing she wasn't interested because I hated Jessica more than I hated Gina. Jessica was Brad's ex-wife and queen of the mean girls.

Councilman Ian Patterson, a despicable wealthy coal mogul, was the most likely candidate for mayor. But he was too busy buying his way into Congress to take on mayoral duties. Then there was Pastor Smith, who you either loved or hated. Although I adored his daughter, Liza, I hated him. He was a holier-than-thou, cruel, Bible-banging chauvinist who claimed the lord didn't want him to be mayor. I suspected that was true because she probably agreed with me and thought him a blowhard. The final member was Brad Gordon, whose calling was to save lives. He would have made a brilliant, fair, and competent mayor, but he had no desire to campaign.

Aunt Edith failed in her attempt to talk West's father, Pop Westinghouse, into running. He was popular and had been the local bartender before bestowing the honor on West and taking over the kitchen at The Bear Claw Pub. He'd earned the name Pop because he looked out for his regulars. Pop declined, stating that he was happy running his business with his family,

Therefore, thirty-eight-year-old James of the old-money Schuster family had moved back to Pennsylvania from Chicago. His family had sold their lumber business a generation ago, but their ancestors had made so much money that they lived a life of luxury. No one knew why they chose to stay in Western Pennsylvania, although perhaps it was because their home was palatial. Winona whispered there were rumors the Schusters weren't quite as wealthy as they pretended, having squandered most of their fortune. Whatever the case, James Schuster the Second had stepped into the spotlight. Considering the lack of an opponent, his appointment wasn't that impressive, but Brad couldn't help himself; he was all diplomacy and manners.

"He will be a wonderful mayor. The Schusters have natural leadership qualities." Gina lifted her snotty angular chin into the air, the arrogant gesture making her even prettier.

I groaned into my ice water.

"Are they staying at the family estate with you and your parents?" Alice asked.

"Yes," Gina said. "There is plenty of room. They have an entire wing, and we have several outbuildings."

"How are your nephews fitting in?" Lincoln asked.

Gina preened. "Oh, Jimmy is doing wonderful. He is the starting center on the varsity basketball team, was asked to be on the student council, is president of the ski club, dating the head cheerleader, and already the most popular boy in school."

"Don't you have two nephews?" Aunt Edith asked.

Gina wrinkled her nose. "Yes."

"I recall James had twins, correct?" Lincoln asked.

When she didn't respond, Liam placed his hand over hers. "Chad misses his old school. He's struggling, but he's a great kid. I'm teaching him to swim at the community center."

Gina pursed her lips into a little bow. "Grandmommy ruined her rose garden because we had to put a wheelchair ramp in for Chad, and honestly, he requires so much attention it's ridiculous."

A room full of individuals gaped. Besides being a Bellmount Bitch and The World's Worst Aunt, the woman was also a witch who put spells on men. Why else would my handsome, intelligent cousin like her?

Aunt Edith cleared her throat. "Ding, ding! Let's move to the parlor. Dinner is ready."

On the way to the dining room, Gina made sure no one was looking and stuck out her tongue. No lie! Her tongue! Right in my face!

I swallowed my pride and clamped my lips tight.

After helping Aunt Edith and Russ carry the warm serving dishes to the table, I plopped into the chair between Brad and Alice. Gina monopolized the conversation, bragging on and on about herself and her family.

Greg Grainey popped in, eyed the spread, and frowned. My deprived ghost was often moody, having given up food and alcohol. No longer sleeping with numerous women added to his grumpy disposition. Good thing he had some sort of sensual energy relations with the nearby medium. This provided a small outlet for his hedonistic ways.

As Gina droned on about how beautiful the world thought her, Greg sauntered to me. "Damn, she's a cunt." He balked in her direction, then kissed me on the top of my head. "Boring dinner party. I'm gonna go feast on some Brooklyn muff."

I gagged.

Brad shot his ex-father-in-law a dirty look, as Greg disintegrated.

If the ghost had stuck around a little longer, he would have experienced a livened-up dinner party because moments after he left, the doorbell rang. Russ, Spot, and Knight trotted to the door to admit our visitor. They returned moments later, followed by West.

I held my breath and sat forward. Please let him be there to see me.

"I'm sorry to interrupt your dinner, Edith. This is my only break tonight, and I need to talk to Miranda about my cousin Cindi's special day."

I sat tall and emitted happy vibrations to Saturn.

"Of course, Weston. Cindi is very excited. Do you have enough time to join us for dinner?" Aunt Edith

asked.

West's gaze slid over the delectable spread and he licked his lips. "No thanks. I only have a few minutes."

Aunt Edith inclined her head toward the hallway, excusing me.

Goose pimples covered me from head to toe as I followed West into the foyer. When he reached the front door, he faced me. I stood in his space, looking up at him.

His jaw tensed. "Cindi adores you."

"Aww. I'm glad to hear that because I adore her too."

He studied his feet before looking back into my eyes. "She says you're her best friend, and she wants to invite you to our day tomorrow."

"She already invited me. I'd love to come. Is it okay with you?"

West's smile was akin to the sun coming out from behind a cloud. "Yeah. I wasn't sure you would want to come. We are skiing, then visiting Bellmount Bob. That rodent is a mean son of a bitch. Likes to eat human fingers for snacks, but Cindi is fascinated with him."

I laughed. "I think it sounds fun."

West brushed a strand of his dark blond hair from his eyes. It curled around his ears, landed mid-neck, and was its usual sexy mess. He hadn't shaved in a day or two. Dang, his five-o'clock shadow made me gooey.

"You ever skied before?" he asked.

"No, but Aunt Edith said I could borrow her ski pants and equipment."

West chuckled. "In other words, I'm going to have to teach you?"

"Don't you have to teach Cindi too?"

"No. Cindi is a good little skier. She sticks to the bunny hill, but she has mastered it."

"She told me you are teaching her."

"I taught her years ago. She still calls our trips lessons."

"Oh." I bit my lip and fluttered my lashes. "Do you think you can teach me?"

"Absolutely not! I think your backside is going to be freezing cold and covered in slush."

"West!" I slapped his shoulder.

However, he was correct. I had the athletic prowess of a slug frying on a hot patio.

Shielding his torso from my love pats, he chuckled. "We better pack the crutches,"

His unzipped jacket exposed exquisite pectorals beneath a thin white t-shirt. I broke through his shield to jab that oh-so-fine chest.

He wrapped his palm around my finger. "Shortcake, bring your insurance card in case we have to go to the hospital."

By the time I was four years old, West's teasing had made me aware I had tingly girl parts. At the age of twenty-five, I still giggled and blushed as I poked and hit at his hard athletic body. The next thing I knew, he had tossed me over his shoulder, and my head hung down his backside. I wrapped his perfect posterior with my palm. "West! Put me down!"

He laughed and spun in a circle as my arms and legs flailed about.

"West," I continued to call out as he hollered a helicopter-sounding *"Wrrr!"*

Crash!

I cringed.

West set me on my feet. A toppled wooden pedestal and half a dozen pieces of glass surrounded us.

"Shit!"

"Fudge!"

Spot and Knight sprinted from the parlor. Aunt Edith and Russ followed. My aunt stopped in her tracks to stare at her broken vase, and her hand went to her mouth.

"I'm sorry, Edith," West said. "Was it an antique?"

Everything Aunt Edith owned was an antique.

She nodded. "It was my mother's."

West righted the upturned pedestal. "Damn. I'm sorry."

The puppy charged toward the glass, his tongue reaching for a shard.

"Knight, no." I crouched to gather the glass.

Brad entered the foyer, calling his baby to him. He cradled Knight in his arms and took in the carnage. "Miranda, you're bleeding. We should clean you up and make sure you don't have any slivers in your hand."

"Shit," West said again. He squatted beside me and picked up the two largest chunks. He hesitated, then shook his head in frustration. He stood and handed Aunt Edith the pieces. "Gather it all together, and I'll try to fix it. If I can't, I'll do my best to replace it." He passed by me and opened the front door. "See ya, Shortcake."

I clutched a few pieces of glass in my hands as I followed West onto the porch. The wind whipped my hair in every direction, and the second my breath left me, it formed wispy condensation. "Do you want to take The Tank tomorrow?"

West stared at my bloody hand. "I bought a truck

last week."

"You did?"

"Yeah. I've been working long days and finally saved enough to buy a 1985 pickup. We can take it."

I leaned closer to West's warmth. "That is great. So now you have a motorcycle, a snowmobile, a dirt bike, and a truck." I have no idea why this fascinated me. I suspect it had something to do with an appreciation of West's interests being so different from mine. "What time are you picking me up?"

"After breakfast. Is ten okay? Pop gave me the afternoon off so we can take our time. We'll be home by dinner."

I stared at his lips. "Do you want me to pack something for lunch? After a few months under the tutelage of a master chef, I can both boil water and fry an egg with some amount of competency."

His gaze drifted to my mouth. Or perhaps it was my imagination, and it was just that my lips felt swollen and puffy.

"Nah. That's okay. Cindi likes to go to the snack bar at the lodge. She loves hot chocolate and hot dogs." He tilted his chin in the direction of the dinner party. "You better get back to your date."

"I'm not on a date."

West's brow furrowed. "Does Doc know that? Because I'm pretty sure he thinks he's on a date."

I beamed at the man I was crazy about. "West, I'm looking forward to tomorrow. I think the three of us will have a great time."

He nodded. "Cindi's really excited."

"Are you looking forward to it?" Please say yes!

"Yeah, Shortcake. It'll be fun." He grinned, and

my body felt as if it floated off the ground.

Shoving his hands into his jacket pocket, he descended the steps and navigated the snow-covered lawn. When he was halfway down the hill, he turned and waved.

I couldn't wave back because I was still holding onto sharp shards. "Oh, West. Stop pretending. I know you are crazy about me," I whispered to the wind.

Despite the broken antique in my hands, I dreamily strolled into the inn. I almost ran headfirst into Liam as he exited the parlor.

"Did Westinghouse leave?" he asked.

"Yes. He left a few minutes ago."

"Damn. I wanted to finish planning the Valentine's dinner party he is cooking for us."

Liam's gaze settled on the glass still clutched in my fingers. "Little cuz, you gotta give up on Westinghouse. You two are a disaster." He patted my shoulder as if his touch would help take the sting from his words. "You are like oil and water."

That was one too many times that someone had informed me that West and I didn't make a good couple. My shoulders tensed, and I growled from between clenched teeth.

"At least the person I like looks out for his family and takes them for hot chocolate. He spends time with them doing things they like, unlike your snotty girlfriend who—" I raised my voice a few octaves, mocking Gina's affected tone. "I'm beautiful and perfect, and boo hoo, my nephew's wheelchair got in the way of Grandmommy's roses." I made sure to make *Grandmommy* sound nasally. Then I stormed into the parlor.

Gina stood. "Liam, take me home now." She pointed at me. "I have had enough of her."

Apparently, she had heard my petty impression. I inwardly moaned.

"Gina, please stay for dessert," Aunt Edith said. "I'm sure Miranda didn't mean what she said and that we can work this out."

Gina stomped to the exit. Shoulders slumped, Liam followed her. The room was silent as I hung my head in shame, placed the broken glass on the table, and sat.

"My heavens," Aunt Edith finally said. "What a disaster."

Russ leaned back in his chair and rubbed his belly. If Aunt Edith had allowed it, he would have come to dinner in his baseball hat and overalls, and picked at his gums with a toothpick. Instead, he sat there in his dress flannels, sucking a piece of roast beef from between his teeth.

"Eh, I don't know, Edith. I thought dinner was delicious. The roast was just right." He sniffed. "And I gotta agree with Miranda. I don't know what Liam sees in her. She may be pretty, but she's a bitch."

Aunt Edith gasped and placed her forehead into her palms.

"Edith, I agree with Russ." Lincoln smiled. "About the beef being perfect. What's for dessert?"

Aunt Edith folded her napkin and got up from the table to fix coffee, tea, and cake. Alice trotted behind her. As soon as they left the room, Lincoln winked.

"Wow, this was like a dinner I once had with my ex-in-laws," Brad said.

I may have once again been the center of a scandalous evening, but, as usual, Dr. Bradley Gordon,

Dr. Lincoln Harrison, and Russ Jenkins were looking out for me.

And then there was Weston Westinghouse the Third, with his sensual grin, tight white t-shirts, and hazel eyes.

Chapter 5

I perched in the stairwell, gripping the balustrade, my heart jumping up and down to the ticking beat of the hundred-year-old grandfather clock. At three minutes after ten, West knocked on the door. I leaped to my feet and danced about, wiggling my hips and throwing my hands into the air. Good thing Spot was the only one who witnessed my absurd jig.

West carried my gear and placed it in the back of his new blue pickup truck between his and Cindi's. He explained that he kept Cindi's skis in his dad's shed so that her degenerate brother couldn't sell the equipment for liquor. Then he loudly sang out-of-tune country songs as we made our way to pick up Cindi.

We traveled across town to the river and drove about twelve miles into the middle of nowhere. I couldn't have found the house again if my life depended on it. The roads were curvy and veered off in every direction. We passed by farms, trailers, and state game lands. Eventually, we turned at an abandoned stone farmhouse where West's great-great-grandparents had lived when they first came to the United States from Czechoslovakia.

West's family name had been Zapadni, which meant westerly. His ancestors had translated it to English when they immigrated, settling on the very American-sounding Westinghouse. He came from a large family, most of whom still lived in the mountains. They had distilled moonshine until a decade ago. Pop and Uncle Will had hit it big by moving to town and opening a legitimate business. Grandpa Weston Westinghouse had passed a few years prior. Grandma Westinghouse intimidated the bejesus out of me; Winona told absurd family stories, and West adored both Winona and his younger cousin Cindi. Although I already knew much of West's family history, I soaked up the stories as well as his sultry country-boy twang.

"Shortcake, remember my family is backwoods. They can be a bit scary. Winona is the worst storyteller in the world, but she isn't bullshitting about what clodhoppers they are."

We passed by a half dozen rusted-out cars and trucks and pulled up to a filthy white ranch that desperately needed an updated roof and new siding. Not wanting to hurt West's feelings, I sucked up my shock upon seeing the derelict dwelling.

"It's pretty awful. Isn't it? I suppose it's why my mom took off and left Pop and me."

My mother had passed away tragically, and West's mother had abandoned him when he was a toddler. Consequently, we both avoided conversations that had to do with mothers. I had Aunt Edith, and he had his Aunt Polly and Grandma Westinghouse. So those were the matriarchs we usually discussed. The mention of his mother was rare.

"Cindi lives with your Grandma Westinghouse?" I asked.

"Yeah. Her entire family does. Pop and I used to. We moved into town when I was about four. We built my apartment above the pub right after I graduated." He put his truck into park and groaned. "Shit. Clive."

Cindi's older brother sat on the front porch with a bottle of beer in one hand and a plastic cup in the other.

"Whatever you do, don't make eye contact," West said. "It encourages him."

West exited the truck, and I followed.

"Nice wheels," Clive said as we approached the tilting front porch. He spat a wad of chewing tobacco into the cup.

I gagged.

"What the hell, man? It's Sunday morning. Why are you drunk already? I thought you were back in AA," West said.

Clive flicked his wrist. "Good thing for you, people like to drink. It's how you got that fancy new truck."

I tried not to make eye contact, but I accidentally did. It was similar to when I tried not to look at roadkill but focused on it anyway.

Clive whistled. "Damn, girl. You were a funny-lookin' kid, but you grew up super hot."

My face caught fire.

"If you get tired of my cousin, and want a real man, give me a ring."

The only reason any woman would give Clive the time of day was if she liked body odor, men with rotting teeth, or haphazardly done mullets.

"Give it up, buddy." West placed his hand on the small of my back and ushered me into the house. "Grandma! Hello!" he called.

Although the outside of the home looked like a pigsty, the inside had been scrubbed clean. The furniture was threadbare, the plaster was cracked, and the house smelled like cigarette smoke. However, it was tidy.

"In here," Grandma Westinghouse called.

I followed West into the kitchen. His grandmother had her back to us and was elbow-deep in sudsy dish soap.

West kissed her on the cheek. "Hi, Grandma. You remember my friend, Miranda?"

She faced me, a cigarette hanging from the corner of her mouth. She squinted and looked me over from head to toe.

"Hello, Mrs. Westinghouse. It's nice to see you again."

She wiped her hands on a nearby tea towel.

"Where's Cindi?" West scooped up a sticky bun from a package on the counter.

"Grab a plate, mister. We ain't animals here." She plucked a saucer from her dish drainer, dried it, and handed it to West.

West grinned, devoured a huge bite, and plunked the rest of his bun on the plate. "Could have fooled me. You have a drunk swine on your front porch."

Grandma flicked her wrist exactly like Clive had done. "Aren't you going to offer the girl a cake?" Her gaze traveled from the top of my head to my boots. "You are both too damn skinny."

West stuck his "cake" in my face. "Bite?"

I shook my head from side to side. I wanted nothing more than to take a bite of a pastry that had also touched West's lips, but Grandma Westinghouse stared at me with her assessing gaze. For the record, skinny wasn't the correct descriptor for either West or me. He was five-foot eleven inches of lean muscles and washboard abs. I was five-foot three, one-hundred-thirty pounds of bosom, curves, and red ringlets. Ironically, stick-skinny described Grandma Westinghouse to the tee.

West shoved the rest of the processed pastry into his mouth and licked his fingers. Something inside my panties tingled.

"Grandma, where's Cindi?" he asked again.

"In the basement, gettin' ready. Don't let her stick her fingers in that damn cage."

West chuckled.

"I'm serious. I'll wallop that handsome face of yours. Cindi cried for a couple of hours last time."

West playfully tickled her under the chin. "I heard you, Grandma."

Although she acted disgusted and shooed him away, her eyes twinkled.

The three of us turned to take in the newcomer who had ascended from the basement.

"Hi, Uncle Walt. You remember my friend Miranda?" West asked.

Uncle Walt smiled. "Yeah. The Marshall girl. Howdy."

"Edith Marshall is my mom's sister. I'm an Albright."

"Ah," Uncle Walt said. "Cindi do a good job waitin' tables?"

Besides waking me up before the crack of dawn, she had done a great job. "My aunt was pleased."

Uncle Walt shoved almost an entire sticky bun into his mouth and turned his attention to West. Wadded-up food mixed with his saliva as he spoke. "Don' wet Cindi feed that damn gwond hog." Once he swallowed, Walt winked at West. "You and your girl wanna borrow my camp?"

West groaned. "Uncle Walt, not to burst your bubble, but the camp isn't exactly a place to take a girl. Besides, Miranda and I are just friends."

My heart sank. We were friends, but we were also ex-lovers and soul mates. West was in denial.

A moment later, Cindi entered the kitchen, followed by her mother.

"Weston!" Cindi wrapped her little arms around his waist.

West hugged her back. "Hiya, Cindi Lou."

"Doctor Shortcake." Cindi embraced me.

I hugged her back. "Hi, Cindi."

Cindi kept her arm around me as she presented me to her mother. "This is my best friend, Doctor Shortcake, the detective."

"Hi. I'm actually a college professor."

"And a detective," Cindi said proudly.

"Aunt June, Miranda. Miranda, Aunt June," West said.

"You, the one that give her the clue book?" Aunt June asked.

I nodded.

"She loves that thing."

I beamed. Even though Clive was gross, the house was falling down, and Grandma Westinghouse intimidated me; I liked West's family. I couldn't imagine what their home had been like when Grandma Westinghouse had six sons, one daughter, a menagerie of animals, and Grandpa Westinghouse all running amok.

"We better get going," West said.

Cindi rummaged around in a pink backpack that sat

on a retro chrome kitchen chair. She removed something from the front pocket, handed it to West, and hollered, "Polkamania!"

West held up the cassette tape Cindi had placed in his palm. "Okay. You know the rules. Your choice for the ride there. Mine for the ride home."

Cindi clapped. "Polkamania!"

West shoved the tape into his pocket. "Let's go, little Miss Lou."

Cindi slid into her jacket, fumbled with the zipper, then took her time sliding both of her arms into the straps of her backpack. When I stepped in to assist, West glared at me. I backed off and stood patiently. Once Cindi had outfitted herself in her winter gear, West put his arm around her shoulder. I followed the two of them to the front door.

"Hey, Weston," Aunt June called. "Don't let that damn rodent bite her this time."

Cindi frowned and hollered, "It only hurt a little."

"You cried for two hours, and you had to get a shot," her mother yelled back.

Cindi huffed. "It didn't hurt that much, and I'm twenty-one now."

I couldn't help myself. I smiled, then bit my lip.

On the way to the truck, we passed by a lounging, gawking Clive. West helped Cindi into the cab, and she scooted toward the center of the seat. After giving me a boost, West's hands lingered on my bottom. The heat from his touch lingered.

West hopped in the driver's side. Before he could put the key in the ignition, Cindi reminded him he had her tape. He slid it into the player.

The sound that came out of the speakers was the

most unpleasant clanging I'd ever heard. If this was the folk music of West's ancestors, no wonder he couldn't sing. He put the truck in drive and headed toward the stone ruins. He stopped, turned the vehicle around, drove back up the hill, and rolled down the window.

"Hey, Clive. You better get in there. Grandma found your stash. Miss April's goin' up in flames."

Clive shot to standing so quickly that he spilled his cup of spittle all over his lap. "Shit!" he sputtered before taking off into the house.

West chortled as we headed down the drive a second time. I spun to take another glimpse of the shocking little house. Clive stood in the front yard, his middle finger held high.

I returned my attention to the pair beside me. Even though they were loudly singing the worst song I'd ever heard, a giddy joy overtook me.

Weston Westinghouse the Third was indeed the man of my dreams.

Chapter 6

Pinkie's Steeple sat three-quarters of the way up the highest peak in Bear County. At least a dozen evergreen-lined paths cascaded from the top of the mountain, past the resort, then down into the valley. It was as if an A-framed timber and stone lodge from the Swiss Alps had been transplanted smack dab in the middle of Western Pennsylvania. Smoke wafted out of the massive fireplace, and a few dozen people milled about on the snow-covered slopes. About fifty yards from the lodge sat a well-maintained red barn. Bellmount Bob, his wife Roberta, and a half-dozen baby groundhogs lived in this building.

My first lesson involved putting on skis. After about twenty minutes and a lot of trash talk from the Westinghouse cousins, I graduated to standing. I never mastered stopping.

Accepting that slalom racing while holding hands with Weston Westinghouse wasn't in my cards, I took off my ski boots, and West and I cheered as Cindi navigated the bunny hill.

Cindi's lips formed a straight line, and her jaw muscles tensed with concentration. When she reached the bottom, West and I clapped and *yahoo*-ed. Her toothy grin was visible from thirty yards away.

After numerous successful glides, Cindi clonked to us. "How many times?"

"Twelve," West said.

"I did twelve on my feet, and Miranda did three on her butt." She threw her head back and belly laughed.

"Hey," I grumbled through pouty lips.

The cousins hunched forward and clutched their ribs. They definitely shared genetics.

"Your turn, Weston," Cindi said.

"Okay. I want to hear some cheering."

"Then you better do good," Cindi said.

He ruffled her hair and bent low to look into her eyes. "I am the champ!"

"I am the champ!" Cindi said.

"Team Westinghouse," he yelled.

"Team Westinghouse," she chanted back.

Yep! Definitely the same gene pool.

West settled into a ski lift and waved goodbye. Cindi and I sat on a bench and talked about school. She proudly announced she could count money and make change. Eventually, a man swishing downhill in a bright blue ski jacket sidetracked us from our conversation.

I waved. "There's West."

We cheered as he passed by everyone and skidded to the side in a graceful stop. Glittering white sparkles dramatically flew into the air surrounding him.

"Again, Weston!" Cindi yelled.

"Again! Again, West!" I called across the white field.

Another run would give us more girl time and provide the opportunity to yell his name with passionate abandon without anyone questioning it.

Cindi and I chatted until we once again saw the agile man in blue crouched low, weaving in and out of the other skiers. This time he passed by us, disappearing into the valley below.

A few moments later, he appeared on the ski lift. Instead of riding it to the top, he dismounted and made his way to us. He lifted his goggles. "I am the champ!"

The Westinghouse cousins again proclaimed their dominance.

Once they returned to earth, Cindi tapped West's forearm. "Bellmount Bob now?"

"The barn doesn't open until one." West bonked my numb nose. "Besides, Shortcake needs to warm up. How about some hot chocolate and a hot dog first?"

Cindi's bottom lip jutted out, but she didn't argue. We loaded our equipment into the vehicle, entered the three-story lodge, and chose a cozy booth next to the fireplace. West and Cindi took off their jackets, gloves, and hats. West removed his glasses.

At first, I was too cold to remove anything. After a few minutes in front of the roaring fire, I peeled off my layers.

"What do you want for lunch, Shortcake?" West asked. "There's fancy food upstairs. On this floor, they have hot dogs, hamburgers, pizza, fries, hot chocolate, and cookies."

I didn't like "fancy food." Cheeseburgers and cookies were totally my speed. "Pizza, fries, and a hot drink sound perfect," I said.

"Can I be the waitress?" Cindi asked.

"It's a big order. You think you can handle it?" West asked.

"Yes. I am twenty-one and a waitress now."

West nodded and the two of them practiced the order a few times.

He handed Cindi a twenty. "You should get five dollars and some change back. Okay?"

"Got it," Cindi said.

"The hot chocolate could burn you. So you have to do one cup at a time. Do you want me to help you?" he asked.

Cindi pursed her lips. "No. Edith says I am a good waitress."

West's eyes filled with pride as Cindi headed to the snack counter.

"Even though I can't ski, I'm having fun," I said.

He kept his gaze on Cindi. "You're the world's worst skier."

"Hey!"

There were those sparkling eyes and lopsided grin. God, I'd missed West's playful taunts.

After Cindi reached the front of the line and placed the order, West relaxed and his gaze met mine.

"Damn. I feel bad about Edith's vase."

"Me too."

"She has to think I'm the biggest ass. I'm always screwing up around her."

"She adores you, West."

He shook his head. "Every time you and I are together, something bad happens."

"Because I'm a klutz." My laugh came out as an odd gurgling sound.

West's brow furrowed. I sighed.

"A few years ago, Cindi dropped the tray and spilled her hot chocolate. It happens. Winona does it all of the time. I've even done it once or twice over the years. But it shook Cindi's confidence." He exhaled. "Here she comes."

45

Cindi stared at the tray and stood still between each step. Once she reached us, she set two hot dogs and a burger in front of West.

"Good job," he said.

Cindi wiped the sweat from her brow and headed back to the counter. We sat in silence, concentrating with Cindi as she carried French fries and pizza to the table and placed them in front of me.

"Thank you," I said.

She released her breath and made her way back to the counter.

West's teeth gouged his top lip as Cindi clutched the hot chocolate. Without spilling a drop, she carefully carried it to me.

When she went back for the second cup, I stood. "I'm going to help her."

"No. Sit down and be patient. She wants to do this by herself and its good practice for her since she wants to be a waitress at the inn."

I smiled. "Doesn't she want to be a detective?"

He laughed. "She wants to be a waitress who solves crimes."

Once Cindi had placed three cups of drink on the table, I complimented her on a great job and West gave her a high five.

While we ate, they did impressions of me falling on my behind. I joined in, making a few self-deprecating jokes. The three of us were mid-rib-straining guffaws when Cindi sat straight and waved. She yelled a hello across the lodge, and a young couple approached us.

"Hi, Jimmy. I'm twenty-one now," she said.

"Cool," the handsome boy said.

"How old are you?" Cindi asked.

"I'm eighteen."

The blonde standing beside him nuzzled into his shoulder.

"How old is Chad?" Cindi asked.

"He's eighteen too. We're twins, so we have the same birthday."

Eighteen-year-old twins named Chad and Jimmy? This had to be James Schuster the Third, also known as Jimmy Junior. However, he seemed too friendly and genuine to be related to Gina.

"Where is Chad?" Cindi asked.

"He's at home today. I'm here with my friends." Jimmy smiled at the pretty girl beside him.

Cindi stood and extended her hand to the girl. "I am Cindi Westinghouse. I am twenty-one and a detective and a waitress."

The girl took Cindi's hand in hers. "I go to your school. My name is Abby."

"Hi, Abby. You go to Bellmount High School?"

"Yes," Abby said.

Cindi's brow furrowed. "How old are you?"

"I'm seventeen," Abby said.

Cindi nodded and pointed at West. "This is my cousin. His name is Weston."

West stood and shook Jimmy's hand. "Hi, man. Nice to meet you."

When West reached for Abby's hand, she blushed and giggled. Although he was ten years older than her, and she was with her basketball-star boyfriend, the teen was an awkward fool in West's presence. At least I wasn't the only one.

Cindi wrapped her arm around my waist. "This is

my best friend, Doctor Shortcake. She's a detective too."

"Miranda. And I'm actually a college professor." Our handshake ended with a volt of electricity shooting through him, into me, and stabbing at my heart. I immediately withdrew my hand because his touch burned my skin.

"Wow. It's dry out. Static electricity," the composed young Schuster said. "I guess we better go."

"We are going to see Bob," Cindi said.

"We're heading back onto the slopes. I'll tell Chad you said hello." Jimmy and Abby waved to Cindi and departed.

I leaped out of my seat and chased the teenager down. Once I caught up to him, the only thing I could think to say was, "My cousin Liam is dating your Aunt Gina."

"Cool. I'll tell Gina you said hi."

I searched for bare skin, but he had slid his hands back into his gloves, and the only part of his body that wasn't covered was his face. He wrapped his arm around his girlfriend's shoulders and walked out the door.

There were two issues with my encounter with the well-mannered young man. First of all, I hadn't said hi to Gina. In truth, I hoped maggots devoured her pretty eyes from their snotty sockets. Secondly, his touch terrified me.

I made my way back to West and Cindi.

"What the hell was that?" West asked.

I shrugged. "I don't know."

"Bellmount Bob now?" Cindi asked.

West checked out my half-eaten pizza and fries.

"Shortcake's still finishing her lunch."

Cindi squinted, then her face lit up. "Can I go by myself?"

"No way. You will try to feed that damn rodent, and he will eat your fingers." West opened his mouth wide and gnashed his teeth.

Cindi let out a squeal of terror at West's clicking teeth. However, the carnivorous groundhog didn't seem to faze her. "It only hurt a little."

"Cindi Lou, if you get bit again, your parents won't let you come with me anymore."

"I can go by myself. I'm twenty-one now."

West sighed. "You are an adult. Can you keep your hands out of the cage?"

Cindi bounced in her chair. "Yes."

"And keep your toes out of the cage."

Cindi threw her head back and howled, "Toes!"

"I'm serious, Miss Lou. No fingers, toes, lips, or face! No body parts near that damn beast. They carry diseases."

"Okay. Got it. No diseases." Cindy reoutfitted herself in her snow gear.

West motioned for her to come close. He took her wrist in his hand. "We will be with you in ten minutes. You go straight to the barn and wait for us. He pointed to her watch. We will be with you when the little hand gets here."

"Okay. Got it," she said.

Cindi swayed right then left, heavily weighting each stride as she headed to the door.

"Keep your body out of the cage," West yelled across the lodge to her back.

She faced us and loudly called, "Okay. Got it!"

West frowned. "She's going to stick her damn nose in there. I didn't say *no nose*."

"You said face."

"I didn't say *nose*."

I bit my lip and looked up at him through fluttering eyelashes. "Unlike me, you are a good cousin. I had a terrible fight with Liam last night, and Gina left dinner in a huff."

"What did you fight about?"

Since I didn't want to tell West that we had fought about him, I changed the subject. "You know Jimmy is Gina Schuster's nephew. His twin brother must be in Cindi's class."

"Seemed like a nice kid. Didn't act like a Schuster. However, his dad was always a decent guy. No idea how he ended up all right since Gina and her mother are bitches, and old man Schuster is a bastard."

Interesting. Perhaps James might make a decent mayor.

West stared into my soul. "Want to fill me in? Why did you chase a teenage boy across the lodge?"

I winced, then confessed. "You know how I pulled my hand away? It wasn't static electricity. His hand burned me. I wanted to shake it again to try to figure out why, but he had his gloves on."

"Maybe he's a superhero like you." West pilfered one of my fries and munched. "Come on. We better catch up to Cindi."

I glared at my soggy gloves and grimaced.

"You gonna finish that?" He pointed to my pizza.

"I think I'm finished. We better go find Cindi," I said, ignoring my healthy appetite.

He grabbed my slice and shoved large bites into his

mouth as we cleared the table.

There were less than four inches between us as we strolled to the barn. Since he didn't reach for my hand, and I was desperate for his touch, I did what any twenty-five-year-old woman with an advanced degree would do. I poked him in the shoulder.

West stilled and smirked. "What was that for?"

I shrugged and kept walking. West caught up to me. Master flirter that I was, I socked him in the shoulder.

"What the hell?" he said.

"That's for the time you pushed me in the river when I was holding Mrs. Dolly." And for making me ache for your touch.

West snorted. "You're a little late. That was twenty years ago."

I stuck my chin into the air. "Well, I'm still mad about it."

He wrinkled his nose. "That was one ugly toy. Scared the shit out of me. Looked like one of those demonic horror movie dolls."

I punched him with all my might.

Although his jacket and layers of clothing provided a suit of armor-style protection, he grunted and hopped away from me. "Oh, so that's how we're playing this?"

My taunts worked. West grabbed me around the waist. Unfortunately, he tossed me into a pile of snow. Fortunately, he leaped on top of me. I reached for his hat, planning to chuck it, but he pinned my hands to my side. I stopped giggling when West's breath blew across my ear. West stopped laughing when I arched my hips toward his.

"Damn," he said.

Tingles shot through me.

Wearing what felt like hundreds of pounds of clothing, West and I lay in a snow-covered, people-filled field and stared into each other's eyes until a loud commotion interrupted us.

"Someone help! There's so much blood!" a woman screamed.

West leaped off me and sprinted toward the barn.

Chapter 7

Although the massive barn was a newly constructed, aesthetically pleasing pine building that had been varnished to perfection, the scene that greeted me was gruesome.

Cindi stood behind a table in the back corner; blood spatter covered her face. From beside her, West's eyes were wild, his arms were raised, and his palms faced the ceiling in a questioning gesture. About a dozen people lurked under the beamed ceiling, mouths agape.

Certain that Bob had severed Cindi's finger, I gasped in horror.

I weaved in and out of a half dozen round tables and numerous cane chairs to reach Cindi. She held a knife in her gloved hand, and a bloody man lay face-up on the floor in front of her. If the repulsive red smears on the table and wall were any indication, he had tried to claw his way to standing.

"Someone needs to get me towels," West yelled.

"Towels!" I called to the entranced crowd as I almost stepped in a crimson puddle.

"He's dead," West said. "I checked. No pulse and dozens of wounds."

Cindi's cheek convulsed. "I helped."

I covered my mouth to stop another gasp.

"Tell me slowly, what happened first?" West

asked.

Cindi carefully enunciated her words. "I saw Bellmount Bob."

"What happened after that?"

"I said, 'Hi, Bellmount Bob. I'm twenty-one now.' I didn't put my fingers or toes in."

"Bob's cage is over there." West's voice rose an octave. He pointed to the opposite corner, where an eight-foot-long, four-foot-high glass-enclosed terrarium housing small rodents ran alongside the wall. Beside it sat a wire cage with one obese critter. "How did you get here?" He pointed at the ground in front of Cindi.

"I saw the ghost in the sky, and he said, 'Help me.' "

West's jaw clenched. "Cindi, this isn't the time to talk about ghosts."

"Let me try." I rested my hand on his shoulder. "Cindi, tell me everything the ghost told you."

West aggressively rubbed his chin.

Cindi swallowed. "He said, 'Help me.' So I did."

"How did you help him?" I asked.

Her voice soft, she said, "I took the knife out."

"No way." West shook his head. "She's not strong enough."

"Did you see who put the knife in?" I asked.

Her lip quivered. "No."

"You are a good detective," I said. "Is Mr. Ghost here now?"

Cindi perused the room. "No."

West turned his glower on me. "Don't encourage this ghost shit right now."

I took off my snow-covered gloves and used one to remove the knife from Cindi's hand. Placing the blood-covered object beside the dead man, I again called, "Where are those towels?"

"Did someone call the cops?" West yelled. "If not, someone needs to call the goddamn cops."

The barn door flew open, and windy wisps of snow followed a man as he rushed toward us. "What happened? I'm the manager, Jared Blackova."

"You need to call the cops. There's a dead guy in your barn," West said. "And we need some damn towels."

The manager's face turned red, his brow furrowed, and he blubbered something indecipherable.

"Don't just stand there," West yelled.

The distraught man departed the barn, the door loudly banging behind him.

I motioned for Cindi and West to move away from the putrid metallic-smelling corpse. I took off Cindi's glasses and used my other glove to wipe sticky smudges from her lenses.

Tears dripped from her eyes. "I didn't put my toes in the cage."

"I know, honey. It's going to be okay." I propped her glasses on her nose. "Did you see anything? Can you tell us what happened?"

She stared at me with big eyes and an open mouth.

"One question at a time," West said before pointing at the corpse that lay about five feet from us. "Who put the knife in the man?"

Cindi's nose twitched.

West rephrased his question. "Did you see who put the knife in him?"

When Cindi reached under a lens to wipe a tear from her eye, she smeared blood across her face. "No."

The manager returned with towels and a child-sized blanket. I removed Cindi's coat and mittens, wiped her down, and wrapped the blanket around her shoulders.

Blackova studied the profile of the supine man. "That's Phil Nowak. He's Bob's handler." He inclined his chin toward Cindi. "The girl do it?"

"What the hell?" Fury radiated from West. "No. She's the one who found the body."

"Then why's she so upset?" the manager asked.

West glowered.

"Because she found a dead man," I grunted between gritted teeth.

One would think that a man in the recreation business would have more tact and brains.

Cindi patted her runny nose. "Mr. Ghost said 'howdy.' "

"Is she crazy?" The manager used his index finger to trace circles in the air.

I clamped my lips together, so I didn't blurt, *She is a medium who has much more social etiquette and class than you, buddy.*

Thank goodness that Officer Kline of the Bellmount Municipal Police Force walked through the door before West beat the manager of Pinkie's Steeple to a pulp. I didn't care what happened to the despicable man, but I didn't want West to go to jail.

Kline headed straight to the corpse, checked for a pulse, and took a whiff of the death aroma. Then his heels clicked to us. "Hey, Westinghouse. Hi, Dr. Albright. Hiya, Cindi. An ambulance is on the way. Should be here in about twenty minutes." He studied the dead man and frowned. "Anyway, homicide and the coroner are also on the way, and the sheriff is right behind me."

West and I both groaned. Sheriff Schultz was the biggest nincompoop on a police force ripe with nincompoops.

A moment later, my archenemy entered. His gaze settled on me, and he scowled. The coatless sheriff puffed up his chest, hooked his fingers into his belt, and shuffled our way. He took in the scene with squinted eyes.

"I should have known this would involve the nosey redhead."

West bristled.

I waved my fingers in front of my nose. "Anyone smell manure all of a sudden?" Then I maturely pinched my nostrils while praying Homicide Detective Sergeant Sean O'Sullivan was on his way to save the day.

****

Lieutenant Bonnie Kramer, who oversaw the Bear County Special Crimes division, was about five foot six, with a scrawny build and shaggy brown hair cut close to her head. Her brown eyes were cynical and distrustful, her cheekbones were sharp, and every muscle in her body was pulled taut. I had met Kramer once before, and the two of us held no love for each other.

The Gestapo interrogating American POWs during World War II had nothing on Lieutenant Bonnie. I knew this firsthand because a few weeks prior, I had earned myself hours in a boxy room victim to her scrutiny. I couldn't quite add the lieutenant to my ever-growing enemy list because I had broken the law.

Besides, she was thorough in her investigative techniques, and most importantly, she was kind to Cindi.

The groundhog barn was a not-so-balmy fifty degrees, which was way warmer than the thirty-three degrees of the mountaintop air. So after we had waited for almost an hour for the coroner to show up, then an additional thirty minutes for homicide, Cindi and I shivered uncontrollably.

Lieutenant Kramer insisted that Jared Blackova find extra blankets to wrap us in. Unpleasant man that he was, Blackova threw a tantrum when instructed to send all of the tourists home for the afternoon. When he complained that the resort couldn't lose a profitable day, Kramer stared him down. She dismissed Blackova with an emotionless visage and the promise of a citation for hampering the investigation. Then she told him in no uncertain terms that he was to keep the hot drinks coming.

Kramer sat at one of the tables with West, Cindi, and me. Meanwhile, the coroner and Kline hovered over the hacked-up body, Shultz strutted around like he was the big man on campus, and Blackova pouted.

"Where's Detective Miller?" I asked.

Kramer leaned back in her chair and stretched her legs out in a confident-in-charge stance. "He retired."

Detective Miller had been sent to Bellmount to investigate the last few murders, and the man was useless, gray, and tired.

"It's about time," I said.

She pursed her lips and tapped her fingers on the table.

"Where is Sergeant O'Sullivan?"

West shot me a scorching glare.

The lieutenant's expression wasn't much more affable than West's. "He's working on another case. You're stuck with me." She shifted her attention to West. "Are you related to Wilt Westinghouse?"

West frowned. "Yeah. That's my uncle."

"Wag Westinghouse?"

West cringed. "My cousin."

"Which W's your dad?" she asked.

"Walt is Cindi's dad. Weston—everyone calls him Pop—is my dad. Cindi and I are cousins."

Kramer's gaze cut to Cindi. "Miss Westinghouse?"

Unaware that she had been addressed, Cindi continued to stare into the upper corner of the room.

"Miss Westinghouse," the detective said again.

Cindi's tongue slightly protruded from the side of her mouth as she gawked at something invisible.

West tapped her on the shoulder. "Hey, Cindi Lou."

My heart ached when she finally looked at him. Her eyes were a jumbled combination of confusion and fear.

"Lieutenant, she isn't used to being called Miss Westinghouse," West said.

"Ah," Kramer murmured.

"The detective is asking you a question, Cindi," West said.

Cindi's focus remained high in that corner for another moment before she looked at her inquisitor.

"Hi, Cindi. I'm Detective Lieutenant Bonnie Kramer, and I'm going to ask you some questions."

Cindi extended her hand. "Hi, Detective *Lutant*. My name is Cindi Westinghouse. I am a detective too."

The lieutenant didn't seem upset in the least over the mispronunciation of her name or Cindi's declaration of her identity. Interestingly, Kramer was slightly less intimidating when she smiled. "A detective, you say?"

Cindi pointed at me. "Just like Doctor Shortcake."

I cringed.

Kramer pushed her torso into the back of her seat and snorted. "Doc Sweetcakes is going to behave herself, keep her nose out of police business, and let us do our job. Right, Doc?"

I grunted.

"Lieutenant," West said. "Cindi left the lodge at about twelve fifty-five. I'm guessing she entered the barn around one sharp, about the same time it opened from the lunch break. Miranda and I headed to the barn a few minutes after. We heard a woman screaming that there was a lot of blood, and I ran in to find Cindi holding the knife. But she didn't murder the guy. She says she took the knife out of the body because she was trying to save him. But damn that'd be hard for her to do. Something else seems up."

Cindi fixated on the upper corner.

I ran through a list of reasons I might be able to pull her to the side and discuss the ghost situation privately. "Cindi hasn't been to the restroom in a while. Why don't I walk her over to the lodge? Come on, Cindi. Let's go find the bathroom," I finally said.

Cindi frowned. "I don't have to."

Kramer peered over her shoulder into the corner. "Cindi, what's up there?"

Just then, the coroner motioned for Kramer, so she excused herself. Once we were alone, I leaned close to Cindi. "Is the ghost still in the barn?"

West shifted in his seat and groaned.

Cindi took her time scanning the room. Fearful that the detective would come back before she answered, I asked again.

Cindi shook her head. "No."

"Shortcake, shit," West said just as the detective returned.

I forced a toothy grin and again tried to get Cindi by herself. "It's been a while. I better take her. We'll be right back." I stood.

"Sit down, Doc Sweetcakes." Kramer slapped a palm on my chair. "Hey, Cindi. How would you like to be my partner? You can call me Lieutenant Bonnie, and you can be Detective Deputy Cindi?"

While Cindi considered the offer, I squirmed like a sugared-up five-year-old. Eventually, a smile consumed her face. "Yes!"

Kramer rapped the table with both hands. "Perfect. Let's go for a walk and talk. I have to use the restroom. We can discuss the mystery on the way."

Cindi rummaged around in her backpack until she found her journal. The lieutenant patiently waited as she searched for a writing instrument.

"Can I see your book and pen?" Kramer asked.

"It's my clue book," Cindi told her.

"Could I draw something in it?" Kramer asked.

Cindi furrowed her brow.

"I'd like to draw your detective badge in there."

Cindi handed her precious possessions to Kramer, who sketched something before handing it back. Cindi looked it over, clutched it to her chest, then followed Kramer toward the door.

Once they were out of earshot, West snorted. "Fill

me in about the ghost in the corner."

I opened my mouth to explain, but nothing came out. I cleared my throat and tried again. Nothing. After a few inarticulate attempts, I blurted, "I think Cindi is like me." I bit my lip and waited for West's reaction.

"She can read minds with her superpowers?"

West adored Cindi. He would understand.

"She can't read minds."

"Then, what can she do?"

I aimed for my nonchalant voice. "She sees ghosts. She can talk to the dead." I flicked my wrist as if it was nothing.

West's eyes about popped out of their sockets as he rubbed at his chest. "And how do you know this? Can you see the ghosts, or do you feel them?"

"Neither," I said.

"So, you're just guessing?"

I exhaled and went for it. "West, I can only see one ghost, and Cindi can see him too."

West glared at me for an interminable minute. "And whose ghost do the two of you talk to?"

After hemming and hawing, I huffed, "Greg Grainey's."

"What the fuck? You failed to mention that that perverted murdering piece of shit is following my cousin around."

"He isn't following her around. He follows me around. And he didn't mean to kill anyone."

West tilted his head to the side and sputtered, "Shit!"

So much for the rekindling of our romance. West once again thought I was a freak.

Shultz took that awkward moment to waddle to us,

a toothpick hanging from the corner of his mouth. Knowing Shultz, he had retrieved the tiny stick from a trash receptacle. To cap off his slovenly appearance, his shirt had come untucked. "Looks like your little cousin's goin' to jail, Westinghouse."

West clenched his jaw and pounded a fist on the table. "Turn around and walk away, Sheriff."

A quivering Shultz did as told.

"Damn it. She will talk about ghosts and the detective will think she is mentally ill. They will lock her up and abuse the shit out of her. You should have told me sooner."

I reached for West's hand to comfort him. He didn't pull away. The problem was, he didn't respond to my touch at all. His ordinarily warm body was as cold as the room, and his fingers remained limp as Kline helped the coroner bag the body and carry it out the door.

It seemed an eternity before Cindi and Kramer returned. Kramer carried the notebook because Cindi used both hands to cradle a ginormous cookie wrapped in a napkin.

Kramer patted Cindi on the shoulder. "Good job, Deputy Detective Cindi."

Winona would die of envy when she heard that Cindi had beaten her to detective status.

"Mr. Westinghouse, Doc Sweetcakes, you are free to go now. I'll be in touch," Kramer said.

"You're gonna let a murderer go?" Blackova asked.

Kramer took a heavy step toward him. He backed up three steps.

"Let's get something straight right now." The

triggered detective glared at Blackova, then pointed at Shultz. "Cindi didn't murder anyone. First of all, the murder happened while she was in the lodge eating a hot dog. And second, whoever did it was hellishly strong."

Unfortunately, I called attention to myself when I shot Shultz a smug smirk.

"Let's get another thing straight." Kramer placed her nose six inches from mine. "Sweetcakes, stay out of my investigation. I'm not bullshitting. I'm not as laid back as Miller, and I'm not as horny as O'Sullivan."

West moaned.

I pulled my shoulders back indignantly. If I had been foul-mouthed and wasn't intimidated by her, I would have told Bonnie Kramer that my name was Doctor Shortcake and she could f-in' bite me.

As Kramer stood tall and fierce, no one in that room said a word except Cindi Westinghouse.

She looked at her watch and stuck it in West's face. "Dinner time. Grandma will be mad."

Chapter 8

I planned to meet my friend, Madame Alina, as soon as I got off work. We needed to make the twenty-minute drive from Bellmount to Pinkie's Steeple. Then Alina had to drive another thirty minutes to her home in Greenport before the forecasted sleet made the roads slippery.

Alina owned a mystical shop and advertised that she could read minds. Although it was a fraudulent claim, she could talk to the dead. It appeared she could also make love to the deceased if their energy was stuck in this plane. I knew this because, despite my hands over my ears and my vehement protests, Greg Grainey often filled me in on their sexual connection.

Before leaving campus, I stopped by Dr. Lincoln Harrison's office. He greeted me with his warm smile. "Hello, Miranda."

Since Lincoln was one of the few people who knew about my quirky abilities, his office was one of the places I could truly be myself. I placed my backpack on the floor, hung my coat on the back of a chair, and made myself at home.

"Uh, oh. What's going on?" Lincoln asked.

I filled him in on my previous day's excursion with West and Cindi.

Lincoln blew out a puff and took off his glasses. After cleaning them, he propped them onto his nose.

"That's better. So you were the one who stumbled on the corpse that I read about in the paper this morning? I think you might need to tell me the story again."

"Since when did smudged spectacles affect one's hearing?" I asked.

"When one mentors a young woman who keeps finding dead bodies, he requires heightened senses and lots of details," Lincoln said.

I didn't want to repeat the entire story, so I sighed and reiterated the most important parts. "Cindi Westinghouse sees ghosts. She talked to the murdered man."

"Is his energy stuck on earth like Greg Grainey's?" Lincoln tucked his neck into the collar of his shirt and searched his office for ghosts. Finding none, his gaze settled on me. "Is Greg here now?"

"No. And I have no idea if Phil Nowak's ghost is still around. Cindi told us he asked her to help him, said howdy, then left. I think she might have gotten the order of events confused. That's all she can articulate right now."

"And you say she has Down Syndrome?" Lincoln asked.

"Yes. She is young, very perceptive, and I suspect, terrified."

"And her parents think she is making up ghost stories?"

"Yes. She is getting into trouble for it. I explained her abilities to West, and he got upset with me for not telling him sooner. His anger isn't justified because I just learned about Cindi myself. I always seem to frustrate West." I paused to nurse my aching heart. Not that it helped. "Anyway, Brad thought you might have ideas about how we should handle this."

Lincoln ran a hand through his beard. "This is a tough one."

"Madame Alina, do you remember me telling you about her? She is driving to Bellmount to meet me. Then she, Greg, and I are going back to the groundhog barn to see if Phil's ghost is still there."

"That's a good idea," Lincoln said. "Let me get this straight. Bob's handler was murdered less than a week before Groundhog Day?"

"Yep. Any ideas about how we can help Cindi?"

Lincoln wrote something in the notebook he kept on his desk. "Interesting. I'm going to think this over. But first things first, I think you and Weston need to advocate for Cindi and tell her parents."

"West said they wouldn't understand. They're nice people, but so backwoods. I think they'd refuse to allow her to see West anymore. Brad pretty much said the same thing. Also, Brad believes her family could accidentally turn her into a lab rat."

Lincoln's eyes lit up. "A lab rat?"

"Lincoln!" I palmed my forehead and groaned.

"Interesting. Very interesting," he murmured under his breath.

I may have been exasperated, but the truth was, if Cindi were Lincoln's lab rat, he would take care of her in the same way he looked out for me, so she would be in good hands.

Just as Lincoln and I were saying goodbye, Keisha barged into his office.

"How come I wasn't invited to this party?" The assistant to the dean leaned against the door frame and tapped her foot. "I know you two are up to something.

What aren't you telling me?" When we didn't respond, she snorted. "Miranda, we need to go to the journalism office."

I gathered my belongings, thanked Lincoln, then followed Keisha into the hall.

****

Over the past few months, the Bellmount College newspaper had grown from one advisor and a staff of six student reporters to two advisors and a team of ten. Bodies filled the small room, and Liza Smith and John Gibbons were once again in a standoff.

"Dr. Albright, look at this!" Liza thrust a nine-by-eleven color poster in my face.

I took the paper from her, glanced at the content, and waved it in the air. "John, explain!"

"Dunlap still hasn't found his balls." Gibbons smiled smugly as if his declaration elucidated the bikini-clad woman with a dialogue balloon saying, *Vote for me to be your 1990 Ms. Bellmount Bob.*

Keisha grabbed the flyer, wadded it into a ball, and tossed it into the trash.

"Hey. I paid a lot of money at the copy place for that," Gibbons said. "Besides, five of us want the contest to go on while we're selling cookies and hot chocolate. If Dunlap wasn't pussy whipped, he could break the tie instead of voting with the girls."

"This isn't a damn democracy." Keisha stomped to John and lodged herself in his space. She placed her nose three inches from his. "It's a dictatorship, and I'm the queen."

Not to burst my best friend's bubble, but she was the new assistant advisor. I was in charge of all decisions concerning the running of the paper. Keisha, however, was still the queen of pretty much everything else in the world.

"How many of those posters have you hung?" I asked.

John huffed as Liza answered, "They're all over campus."

"And all over town," Michael Dunlap said.

I moaned. "John, I told you no already, and I meant it. Under no circumstance is there to be a sexist Bellmount Bob contest affiliated with this newspaper. You have one hour to remove every single one of those signs."

I hated to make my next threat because I enjoyed John's sense of humor and enthusiasm. Even though he was a lousy student, he was bright and had potential as a writer.

"I don't want to issue ultimatums, but if Ms. Brown or I see one poster, you are off the staff."

Keisha sliced her hand under her chin in an off-with-your-head promise.

John cringed.

"I have to go now. I have to meet someone." I turned to Liza. "Is everything else ready for Saturday morning?"

Liza's shoulders remained in line with her neck. "Yes. Ms. Brown has the van signed out, Nicole's Bakery has supplied the baked goods, and I purchased the hot chocolate and paper products. She stared at the ground before looking at John. "I asked John to cover the event with me and share a byline."

Michael Dunlap shuffled his feet.

My gaze slid from Michael to Liza to John. *Hmm*?

So there were no misunderstandings, I repeated my

directives. "Posters down, John." I scanned the room, making eye contact with each of my students. "Anyone who helped put them up, help take them down. One hour. See you all in class Thursday."

As I turned to leave, Gibbons muttered under his breath. "Thanks a lot, Dunlap. And you still aren't getting in her pants."

I halted, faced him, and growled.

John swallowed. "I didn't mean your pants, Dr. Albright."

After the odd exchange I had just witnessed, I assumed he had meant Liza's undergarments, but I didn't care who his inappropriate statement was referencing, I was twelve shades of angry.

Keisha tapped two fingers to her eyes and pointed those fingers in Gibbon's direction. "On you, buddy. On you like a hawk."

I searched for the clock. Crap monsters! Twenty minutes after four.

I raced out of Sutton Hall and leaped into The Tank.

****

A happy Greg Grainey sat in the front of The Tank with his translucent arm slung over Alina's shoulder. They made a lovely couple. Alina had big brown eyes and long curly hair that framed her exotic face. Greg's dark hair was stylish, and his teeth were polished to perfection.

Greg had a magnificent singing voice as a live man. Being an other-worldly phantasm added to his perfect timbre. He couldn't sing anything mesmerizing while I drove, or it acted as a lullaby and put me to sleep. Therefore, he sat between "his girls" performing an upbeat concert of Frank Sinatra, Elvis Presley, and Elton John songs. Eventually, Alina joined in, her nasally New York accent not quite harmonizing with Greg's perfect pitch. Their duet brought back memories of West and Cindi trilling along to Jimmy Sturr. For the second time in two days, I urged a vocal duo on with my enthusiastic cheers.

Unfortunately, their joyous crooning halted as we climbed the mountain. As the lodge came into view, Greg let out a resounding, "Shit."

"Is something wrong?" I asked.

Greg sat forward, practically plastering his filmy face against the windshield.

Dozens of cars and a full-sized Bellmount School bus were scattered throughout the parking lot. I put my car into park and stepped into the light flurries. Neither Alina nor Greg joined me.

I leaned against The Tank. "Are you guys coming?" I inclined my chin toward the barn. "Cindi found the body in there."

After hesitating another ten seconds, Greg climbed out. Alina remained in the front seat, chewing on her lip.

"Alina, are you coming?" I asked.

"Do yuh feel it?" she asked.

Greg shivered. "Fuck, yeah."

"Feel what? I asked.

"I don't know," Alina said, as she finally opened the passenger-side door.

They remained three feet behind as I hurried through the flaky precipitation to the double-swinging barn door. As I rushed into the groundhog abode, I met with an odd magnetic pull and a heat that knocked the wind out of me. Goose pimples traveled up my neck and along the length of my arms. The door closed behind me, but the pair still hadn't entered.

I shook off Alina and Greg's reaction and the uncomfortable temperature because it was a happy scene that greeted me. At least three dozen individuals visited with the groundhogs.

A man approached. He shivered despite his heavy jacket, gloves, hat, and long blue scarf. "Hi! Welcome to the home of Bellmount Bob, the most accurate prognosticator in the world."

"Hello," I said.

From behind me, the door opened, a wind gust knocked me half a step forward. A frowning Alina and a brooding Greg entered. They approached the cold-weather clad man.

Our greeter surveyed the olive-complexioned Alina up and down. "Welcome to the home of Bellmount Bob, the most accurate prognosticator in the world." He swept an outward arm to the people gathered around the groundhog cages. "It's always busy this time of year. Just a few days away from the big announcement."

"Big announcement?" I asked.

"Bob will announce if spring will come early or if we'll have five more weeks of winter. Bob is never wrong. He held out his gloved hand. "Howard Greene, Bob's new handler."

Both Alina and I shook his hand. Greg reached, passed straight through the man's grasp, and huffed.

At that exact moment, a young boy walked past, calling out, "Hi, Mr. Greene."

Greene smiled and waved back.

I peeled off my coat. "It's boiling in here."

"Hot?" Mr. Greene let out a *pfft* and shivered. "Oh, you're being sarcastic. I just sent a message to the manager letting him know the heat isn't working."

"I don't think the heat's gonna fix your problem," Alina said.

"Fucking broken gate of hell or something," Greg added.

I shook off my strange prickle. "Thank you. We're going to visit with Bob and his family."

"Be sure to come back this weekend for the festival," he said.

Without excusing herself, Alina joined the group watching the babies in the terrarium. I said goodbye and caught up to her.

As Alina and I stood among the visitors, I whispered, "Is Phil's ghost still here?"

She didn't answer. I didn't ask again because I sometimes needed silence to find an energy loop or read someone's thoughts and suspected she was the same way.

"I'm struggling a bit with my connections," she finally said. "But I don't think there are ghosts here right now."

The ill-tempered Blackova entered the barn and tramped to Greene. Their body language of tense shoulders, large arm movements, and wide stances indicated an argument.

Greg strolled toward them, positioning himself to eavesdrop on the conversation.

"Good ghost, Greg," I whispered.

Mr. Greene, the friendlier of the two, scratched underneath his hat, then greeted a couple who had just entered. Greg sauntered our way. Blackova noticed me and also headed toward us.

"Odd exchange," Greg said at the same time that Blackova asked, "What are you doing back today?"

I lifted my chin. "My friend wanted to see the groundhogs. I thought this was a public place."

Alina took off her coat, wiped her sweaty hand on her skirt, and extended it. "Hello. Your barn has bad energy."

Blackova squinted. "You a witch of some sort? Did Stone send you to ruin our big day?"

Alina pulled her shoulders back and huffed. In Blackova's defense, Alina had mysticism written all over her.

"Who is Stone?" I asked.

"Kip Stone is Jake's handler," Blackova said.

"Who is Jake?" I asked.

Blackova rolled his eyes as if I was an imbecile. "Creekfield Jake."

"I don't know who that is," I said.

"That damn fake rodent from Creekfield," Greg said. *"The beaver hasn't had a correct prediction in decades."*

"The Creekfield beaver," Blackova said. "He hasn't made a correct prognostication since 1944."

I threw my head back and guffawed. Even amid an oddly energized murder scene, I found competing rodents hysterical. The rest of the party gawked at me like I had sprouted beaver teeth.

"What's Squeaky the Squirrel's prediction rate?" I hunched forward and clutched my ribs.

Blackova shot me a hairy eyeball.

"Crimson, you're so citified. Fucking squirrels are stupid and can't predict a damn thing," Greg said.

I stopped laughing when my gaze settled on the table where I had seen Phil's bloody handprints. I leaned close to Alina and whispered, "Please distract the men."

A second later, she smiled at Blackova while using a curling finger motion. The sour-tempered man followed at her heels. Greg trailed after them, their locomotive picking up Greene. Alina and her admirers sat at one of the tables and she took Blackova's hand in hers. What I wouldn't have given to hear those fake fortunes.

Once I was sure that no one was paying attention to me, I took off my glove, placed my hand on the spot the bloodstain had been, dropped my mental barrier, then closed my eyes. It took a few moments for the image to take hold, but when it did, it knocked the wind out of me. I dropped to my knees.

Bob ate a carrot from my outstretched fingers, then something sharp stabbed my shoulder blade. I whirled to face large eyes peering from a black ski cap. I punched and kicked, but the pain continued to shoot through me, stabbing at my hip, chest, and face. Red spatter flew into the air. I collapsed onto the floor. Blood pooled around me, and I tugged with all my might, almost removing the knife. Caught in some sort of whirling vortex, up became down, and down became up. Then it all stopped. Someone grabbed my shoulders.

Mr. Greene shook me. "Miss, are you okay?"

It took me a moment to settle into my body. Since our skin touched, I attempted to read his thoughts to no avail.

"Shit, Crimson," Greg said.

I was too dizzy to move. Greene and Alina each put an arm around me, lifted me to my feet, then escorted me to one of the tables. Blackova studied me with pursed lips and squinty eyes.

"Panic attack?" Greene asked.

What a great cover.

"Yes, I think so. I remembered the body and all of the blood."

Jimmy Schuster was among the group of teenagers and the torrid gust of wind that sidled past us. I grasped Alina's forearm and pointed at Jimmy. Greg stuck his hands into his pockets and whistling, followed the teens out the door. After my breathing stabilized, Alina linked her arm in mine, and we exited the barn. Greg was waiting by The Tank.

"I found the energy footprint and experienced the murder," I said.

"The entire thing?" Greg asked.

"A lot of it. It was a terribly painful death."

"Oh, my God!" Alina said.

"Cindi was able to get the knife out because he had almost removed it himself. Phil couldn't see his killer because the guy had on one of those ski masks that covers your face."

We climbed into The Tank and closed the doors.

"I think someone or something interfered right as I was about to experience it from Cindi's perspective," I said.

"Somethin' in there was interfering with my energy too," Alina said.

"Shit," Greg said. "I have no idea why, but I didn't want to stay in there. Then I followed the kids out here and wanted nothing more than to be back inside."

"Hmm? By the way, what did you learn?" I asked.

"Not a damn thing. That bus is for the high school ski club. The kids were checking out the hog. Then they met up with a couple of other kids, got on a ski lift, and headed higher up the mountain. I also overheard the two stooges arguing over which one of them left the barn unlocked again. Then they both bitched about Kip Stone. Although who can blame them? Damn beavers don't even hibernate. Now a bear or a skunk, that would be legit. Blah, blah, blah..."

Interesting. Apparently, one of the men had left the door open the day of Phil's murder, allowing the early arriving Cindi to witness the disaster.

I interrupted Greg's rant. "That big handsome boy is the new mayor's son. He is radiating some crazy heat."

"So damn hot he made me feel like a marshmallow in a flame," Greg said.

Alina yawned. "I'm tired. I have no idea what your friend Cindi got herself into, but it isn't good."

"Yeah," Greg said. "Let's get the hell out of here."

He didn't need to tell me twice. I put the key in the ignition and stepped on the gas.

Chapter 9

Lincoln and I had a standing Tuesday morning session in which we drank tea and studied my telepathy. We told anyone who asked that we were discussing the college curriculum, then we locked his office door. Since we sometimes tossed around a few pedagogical ideas before Lincoln attached electrodes to my temples or shot an electric current into me, we weren't totally fibbing.

In addition, Aunt Edith insisted Lincoln treat me for post-traumatic stress disorder stemming from my mother's violent death. Occasionally Lincoln attempted to pry into my psyche but usually gave up, deciding it more interesting—although not any more productive—to focus on what it might take to make me move a paperclip using only my mind. Much to Lincoln's disappointment, I couldn't fly, disappear, or make an object levitate. I was a pretty pathetic psychic since I couldn't even read minds unless I physically touched someone.

A young girl with developmental disabilities who could talk to the dead was Lincoln's dream come true. Probably feeling as though he'd hit the jackpot, Lincoln enthusiastically agreed to meet Cindi. He sat behind his desk, his blue eyes sparkling, while I called the pub, asking to speak to West. It took some clever wording and a guilt trip declaring, you're the only one in your family who will understand Cindi's abilities, to convince West to agree. Eventually, he told his family that I was taking Cindi to the library, then he picked her up after the high school let out.

At four-fifteen on Tuesday afternoon, after a long day of lectures, I pulled in front of the inn and parked behind West's truck.

Looking in the rearview mirror, I groaned. I tried to neaten my hair, dabbed at a spot of smeared mascara, and dug around in my backpack for my lipstick. After tapping the red goop onto my lips, I puckered up and evened it out. Since I didn't have a tissue on hand, I kissed my lecture notes, took another glimpse in the mirror, and forced a smile. Yikes! Tired and pale.

Spot greeted me at the door, wagging away. While giving him his hello pats, I noticed that Aunt Edith's precious vase once again graced the pedestal. A crack ran along the front, and there was a chip in the rim that someone had painstakingly glued.

"West," I whispered before hanging my coat onto its hook.

I followed a loud clanging noise into the kitchen.

Russ lay on the ground, his torso under the sink, and West kneeled on the floor beside him, holding a flashlight.

"Hi." I perched on one toe, attempting a flattering side pose.

Since Russ's head was inside a wooden cabinet, he didn't answer. West grinned. "Hi, ya, Shortcake. Cindi's in the library."

"You did a great job on the vase," I said.

He wrinkled his nose. "It's not perfect."

"I think it looks great."

Speaking of great, West had shaved until his skin was silky-smooth and he wore a sexy musky aftershave.

"What are you guys doing?"

"Fixing the leaky drain," West said.

As if on cue, Russ reached his hand out, and West placed a screwdriver on his upturned palm.

"Cindi's excited," West said.

Not for long, since she would soon discover I was taking her to see a psychologist, and she had to keep it a secret from everyone but West and her doctor.

"Do you want to come with us?" I asked.

The sound of Russ's swearing almost drowned out, "Nah. Cindi wants to hang out with you. Some kind of girl thing."

Maybe we could have fun, despite the serious nature of our mission. "I'll make sure she has a good time."

Russ whistled to get West's attention. West took the screwdriver from him and refocused the flashlight that had traveled to illuminate my hip, back onto Russ's task.

"Do you want me to drive her home when we're finished?" I asked. "Although I'm not sure if I remember how to get to your grandmother's place."

"Nah. Pop hired some extra help, so I have a night off. I'm going to hang here and help Russ. So I'll take her home."

As Russ banged on something, I covered my ears with my hands and turned to leave.

"Besides, you don't want to be alone up there with Clive," West hollered to my back.

I shuddered at the understatement. "Okay. I'll see you later." I gave West an over-the-shoulder smile and called goodbye to Russ.

West waved.

Russ grunted. "Have fun." *Clang!* "Shit!"

Aunt Edith and Winona were in the foyer. Laundry baskets weighed them down.

"Hi, Miranda. How was work?" Aunt Edith asked.

"Good, but I have a ton of papers to correct tonight."

"You need to stop assigning so much work," Winona said.

Every once in a while, Winona said something brilliant.

"Cindi's in the library waiting for you," Aunt Edith said. "Do you think you'll be home for dinner?"

"Six thirty?" I asked.

Aunt Edith plunked down the laundry basket, placed her hands at the small of her back, and leaned back in a stretch. "Yes. Six thirty. Winona, how about you?"

"I have to train the new girl tonight." Winona stared at the dirty towels with contempt. "I had last night off and went to Richard's apartment." She looked into the distance, and her frowny face instantly turned into a dreamy-eyed, far-away look.

"West has off. Maybe he and Cindi could have dinner with us." I didn't even bother to hide my crossed fingers.

Winona's bottom lip jutted out again.

At a bang in the kitchen, Aunt Edith startled, placing her hand on her heart. She quickly composed herself. "I'll tell Weston to call your grandmother and let her know Cindi is staying."

"Grandma likes Cindi home for dinner," Winona

said.

"I'll send some banana bread and cookies home with Cindi, and your grandmother will be fine with it," Aunt Edith said.

Winona grimaced. "I don't know about that."

Meanwhile, joy bubbled from my belly to the top of my head. Spending the evening with West and Cindi made the prospect of my long night of paperwork less daunting.

Winona leaned in close. "Can I talk to you before you and Cindi leave?"

"Sure."

"Meet you in the library after I help carry the laundry to the basement," she said.

Aunt Edith squatted to pick up the basket of overflowing sheets and groaned. Winona grabbed a handful of fabric and tossed it on top of her towels.

"Aunt Edith, maybe you should hire some additional help," I said.

"Oh, my heavens," she muttered.

"Really, Aunt Edith. It's okay not to do everything yourself," I called before continuing my trek down the brown and rose-wallpapered hallway.

After sliding the pocket door open, I entered the Victorian library of stained glass, book-littered shelves, and dainty furniture.

Cindi's zippered backpack sat on the oak table alongside neatly arranged colored pencils. Her glass of milk was untouched, and one tiny bite was missing from her chocolate chip cookie. She furrowed her brow in concentration, and her tongue slightly protruded from a mouth coated with shiny lip gloss. A daisy barrette held back one side of her hair and a long string of pearls hung long over a rainbow-striped sweater. She didn't look up right away because she was making a notation in her clue journal. Once she finished, she studied it and put her pencil down.

"Hiya, Doctor Shortcake," she called in a voice much too loud for a library.

"Hi, Cindi. I'll be ready to leave in a few minutes. I'm going to talk to Winona for a sec."

Cindi got up from the table and wrapped her arms around my waist, pulling me close. "Got it." She grabbed her string of pearls and held them up. "Grandma says college girls are fancy."

I chuckled at Grandma Westinghouse's connotation of the word "fancy" and Cindi's enthusiasm. "You look beautiful."

"Thank you. You look beautiful, too." Cindi fingered one of my ringlets and grinned.

Winona entered just in time to hear Cindi say, "Winona wants to talk about kissing."

"Cindi!" Winona gaped in horror.

I laughed. "You can finish your snack and notes. I'll be ready in a couple of minutes."

"Okay. Got it." Cindi sat, sipped her milk, and nibbled on a cookie. Within seconds she was engrossed in her project.

Winona clasped my hands in hers and led me to the antique settee. We plopped down, and it creaked. We cringed in stereo, one of those, Oh no! the-chair-is-going-to-break-if-I-don't-stop-eating-Edith's-cookies cringes.

"What's up?" I asked.

She leaned close and in typical Winona whisper fashion, said much too loudly, "Richard and I did it."

Cindi kept drawing as she loudly declared, "Winona kissed Dick."

My chortle came out as a snort.

Winona gasped and looked over her shoulder. "Stop repeating what West says, or I'll tell Grandma."

Cindi shrugged. "Grandma said you kissed a dick."

Winona dropped my hands, and her voice raised an octave. "His name is Richard or Dinky."

Cindi pushed her glasses up a fraction of an inch. "Got it. Richard or Dicky."

Winona let out a disgusted puff.

"Winona kissed Richard or Dicky," Cindi said in a taunting voice as she made slurping sounds and kissed her wrist.

Winona clenched her fists. "Stop imitating West. Even though he's my favorite cousin, he's a jerk!"

Cindi crossed her arms over her chest and *harrumphed*. "He is my favorite."

Winona sucked her bottom lip into her mouth, and her eyes got very tiny.

I grabbed Winona's hand to refocus her. "The whole enchilada?"

Winona's face lit up. "It was so romantic."

I think I did an excellent job of hiding my revulsion. "Did you use protection?"

"Yes. Grandma would skin me alive."

I wiped the invisible sweat from my brow.

"I told him I love him." Winona gritted her teeth in an awkward grin.

Cindi packed up her backpack and tapped her watch. "It's been a couple of minutes. Time to go to college."

I hugged Winona. "I better go. Please be careful.

Remember, men can be jerks."

Winona's chin snapped back. "Just because West broke your heart doesn't mean Richard will break mine."

I bit my tongue and stood. "Come on, Cindi. Let's go."

Cindi slid into her jacket, then anchored both of her arms into her pack. She situated it on her back while Winona and I waited in silence.

Before leaving, I swallowed my pride. "Dinky is lucky to have you, Winona." I exhaled before following Cindi's pink backpack out of the library, past a wagging Spot, and past Aunt Edith examining her one-piece vase.

While grabbing my coat, I heard West laugh. I turned to find him standing in the foyer, pretending to make out with his wrist as Winona, hands-on-hips, glared at him.

Unless he wanted to be manhandled by a kiss-deprived redhead, Weston Westinghouse the Third needed to be careful with his puckered lips and sexy sounds.

****

Cindi crawled into the front seat of The Tank and looked around. "Hmm," she said. "Your car is big."

I rooted in the cushion for the seatbelt. "You're telling me. And he's ugly and brown."

Since I was absorbed in the elusive seatbelt search, I didn't quite hear her response. "What did you say?" I asked.

"Ugly is a mean word." She patted the dashboard. "Cars are not boys."

"Ah, ha! Found you, you little bugger." I held the

old metal clasp into the air like a trophy.

"Bug?" she called, her eyes as big as The Tank's wheels.

"Bug? Where?" I dropped the belt and jumped away from the car.

After realizing what had transpired, I chuckled as Cindi looked around the front seat for a creepy crawly.

"A bugger is something pesky and annoying," I said. "I was calling the seatbelt annoying since it hides in the seat cushion."

She nodded. "Booger."

"Bugger."

"Bugger," she repeated.

I retrieved the seatbelt and angled it across her torso.

Cindi pursed her lips. "I can do it by myself."

I handed it to her and she shoved the clips together. "They're hard to do." I reached in to help.

She stiffened. "Bugger!"

Since I wasn't sure if she had called me or the seatbelt a bugger, I closed the door leaving her to fend for herself. By the time I slid into the driver's side, she had hooked herself in and grinned proudly.

Since the drive to campus was short, I pulled onto the main street and got right to the purpose of our outing. "Cindi, you can talk to me about the ghosts you see. I know they are real."

"Ghosts aren't real," she said.

"They aren't real to everyone. But some people are special and can see them. You are one of those special people. I will tell you a secret, but you can't tell anyone."

"I have to tell Grandma."

"No!" I'm lucky I didn't snap my neck in two with the violent force from my shake. Once I checked myself, I calmly said, "You can tell Grandma other secrets but not this one. It is between you and me."

"I have to tell Mommy."

"Not this one. This one is between you and me."

"I'm not allowed to keep secrets, except with West."

Interesting! "What secrets do you have with West?"

Her thumb and forefinger zipped her lips.

Oh well. I'd pry the information from her another time.

"You can tell West this secret. And you can tell the doctor I'm taking you to."

"Dr. Gordon!" she called out enthusiastically.

I chuckled. "I'm taking you to see a different doctor, but you can tell this secret to four people. Me, Dr. Gordon, Dr. Harrison, and West."

"Dr. Gordon is my doctor."

"Dr. Harrison is a different kind of doctor. He is a teacher at the college, like me, and is the kind you see when you want to talk to someone."

"College girls are fancy."

I didn't have the heart to ruin her preconceived notion, so I agreed.

I repeated the plan, emphasizing all of the crucial parts. "Cindi, ghosts are real to some people. You aren't making it up. You can tell four people about the ghosts you see. Me, West, Dr. Gordon, and Dr. Harrison. Dr. Harrison is my good friend, and we are going to keep him a secret too. But this doesn't mean you should keep other secrets from your grandmother and mother."

The longer it took Cindi to answer, the more I felt my heart rise into my throat. What in the heck was I doing, asking her to keep secrets? I was indeed the Queen of the Buggers.

I parked behind Sutton Hall, and before exiting The Tank, divulged mine. "Cindi, I can see a ghost, too. You can't tell anyone because they will think I am lying and make fun of me."

"Making fun of people is mean. But Grandma says I can sometimes tease Winona," Cindi said between clenched teeth as she fought with her seat belt. Once she freed herself, she confidently declared, "Got it!"

****

Lincoln's beard didn't conceal the grin he sported when he ushered us into his office and offered us chocolate kisses and tea. Cindi passed on the drink but took a kiss. I didn't want to be rude, so I accepted a Godzilla-sized handful of candy and a cuppa. Cindi and I took off our coats, set our backpacks beside us, and sat across from Lincoln. Cindi looked around the room as I consumed chocolate.

"Hi, Cindi. I'm pleased to meet you. I'm Dr. Harrison, but I would like you to call me by my first name, which is Lincoln."

"Abraham Lincoln was a president," Cindi said.

He nodded. "Yes. That is who I was named after."

She reached across Lincoln's desk. "Hi, Lincoln. I am Cindi Westinghouse. I am twenty-one now, and I go to Bellmount High School."

Lincoln stretched his arm to meet her tiny hand. "It's nice to meet you. I hear you work for Edith. You know she is one of my best friends."

"Doctor Shortcake is my best friend. I am a

waitress at the Bellmount Inn and a detective."

Cindi bent to rummage in her backpack. She retrieved her journal, leafed through it, and showed Lincoln her deputy badge.

Lincoln nodded in approval. "Cindi, since Miranda is friends with both of us, she thought we could talk about the ghosts you see."

Her eyes clouded with confusion. My heart sank.

"Cindi, I talk to Lincoln about the ghost I see," I said.

She folded her arms across her chest. "Ghosts are not real, and I don't fib."

Lincoln nodded again. "I know you tell the truth. Most people can't see ghosts, so they think they're fake. Some special people like you and Miranda can see them. You are very special because you can see a lot of them. They can talk to you, too. The unfortunate thing is…" He scraped his fingers through his beard. "People who can't see them think you are fibbing, they don't try to be mean, but since they can't talk to them, they don't understand. It is best not to tell these people you see ghosts because they think you are telling big lies. But you can talk to Miranda, me, your cousin West, and Dr. Gordon because we know you are telling the truth."

Cindi rolled a pearl between her fingers. "I am in special classes at school, and my friend is special."

"Yes," Lincoln said. "Miranda tells me you help out your friends at school."

"I am brave."

Lincoln's eyes twinkled. "Do you see ghosts every day?"

Her brow furrowed.

"Did you see a ghost today?" I asked.

"No. Yesterday, I was talking to my friends."

"Where were you and your friends?" Lincoln asked.

She looked down at the pearls in her hand. "At school lunch."

Lincoln sat forward, his eyes wide. "Did the ghost say anything?"

Cindi sighed. "He asked me for my cookie."

"Was it the same man who was at the barn?" I asked.

She held her pearls in front of her face and stared at them. "No."

"Was he an adult or a student?" I asked.

Cindi shrugged.

"Do you know his name?" Lincoln asked.

"No. I told him, 'Ghosts aren't real. Go away.'" Cindi dropped her pearls to study her watch.

"Have you seen him before?" I asked.

"Yes," Cindi said. "He likes cookies. He asked my friend for a cookie too."

Lincoln leaned so far forward that he pressed his chest against the desk. "What did your friend do?"

Cindi squirmed in her seat and looked at her watch again. "My friend ate lunch and then went to see his friends."

"Did he see the ghost too?" I asked.

Cindi shrugged. "Ghosts aren't real. Can we go see the fancy girls?"

I sighed. "Sure, Cindi."

"Would you like to come to my house for dinner sometime with Miranda? My wife Alice is very nice and is a good cook."

Cindi sat straight and her jaw tensed. "I have to ask

Grandma."

I also stiffened. There was no way that curmudgeonly old woman was going to allow me to take Cindi to dinner with someone she didn't know.

"Do you remember what you learned during our talk?" Lincoln asked.

"Your wife Alice is nice, and I will ask Grandma if I can come to dinner."

I sighed again. Maybe the trip had been pointless. But a second later, Cindi said, "I am special, and I can tell you, and West and Miranda and my boyfriend Dr. Gordon about ghosts."

Lincoln choked. "It was nice to meet you. I hope you can come to dinner and we can become good friends." He didn't bridge the adolescent crush.

Cindi and I gathered our belongings and headed to the Letterman Campus Library to check out the fancy girls.

****

Russ, West, and Aunt Edith were gathered on the front porch when Cindi and I returned. Russ was perched on top of a ladder with his hand in the light fixture above the door. West held the ladder, and Aunt Edith stood, hands crossed over her chest. She waved as we climbed the steps. "Did you have fun?"

Cindi answered exactly as we had practiced. "Yes. We met Miranda's friend and saw fancy girls."

"Oh, good. Aunt Edith said. "Dinner is ready, so why don't you all wash up and meet me in the parlor." My aunt headed back into the house to put dinner on the table.

"West and Cindi, you guys can wash up in my room," I offered.

West grinned. "Sure, Shortcake. Be up in a minute."

"Come on, Cindi." I motioned for her to follow.

Once we were in my bedroom, I invited her to use the restroom first. West was only a couple of minutes behind us. He lightly knocked.

My heart missed ten million beats as I opened the door. His cheeks were pink from having braved the elements, and his hair was so disheveled it looked as though I had run my fingers through it for the past two hours. As I moved to the side so that he could walk past me, I shamelessly breathed in the remnants of his aftershave.

He headed straight for Simon and Princess Pickles. He tapped on my turtle's cage, sprinkling some food over top of him. "Hiya, little guy." He opened Simon's lid and tossed a piece of lettuce in front of him. "Hiya, Simon."

Simon hated every human he had ever met except for West. I have no idea why other than he seemed to enjoy that West teased me.

"Cindi is getting washed up," I said.

West inclined his chin to the bathroom. "How'd it go?"

"Okay. Lincoln explained that she has a special gift that she should keep to herself, although she can also talk to us." I had no idea how to bring up Brad's name without outing his abilities. So, I didn't.

West stared into my eyes. "Thanks," he softly said.

I crinkled my face until it ached.

"What's wrong?" West asked.

"Lincoln was trying to be sweet, and he invited Cindi to his house for dinner."

West took two steps toward me. "The problem being?"

"Do you think your grandma will let her go?"

West sniffed at something. My hair? The idea? Simon's cage?

"I'll take care of that. Grandma has to stop being so overprotective. We need to look out for Cindi, but she isn't a child. She needs to have friends."

The incorrigible boy, hell-raising teenager, and womanizing barkeep, had matured into a compassionate gentleman.

West moved half a step closer. "Grandma let her start a job, hang out with you tonight, and is letting her go home with her friend Chad after school tomorrow. It's a start."

I took half a step so that we were within arm's reach. I looked up at him and willed him to wrap me in his arms and kiss me until I saw stars.

Cindi stepped out of the bathroom and grinned.

West stepped back. "Cindi, go ahead and head downstairs. We'll be down in a minute."

"Okay," Cindi said as she exited the bedroom.

West cornered me against the bathroom door, looked down at me, and cleared his throat. "I'm gonna wash up." He navigated around me, headed into the bathroom, and clicked the latch.

I wrapped my arms around myself, sat on the edge of my bed, and breathed.

When the bathroom door opened, West headed straight to the hallway. "See ya downstairs, Shortcake." He waved to the turtle and the rat. "Don't let the redhead boss ya around, dudes." He smirked at me, then left me sitting on my bed, aching.

****

By the time I had pulled myself together and freshened up, everyone but Aunt Edith was seated at the table. My aunt had set out the white and silver china and filled the crystal goblets with ice water. I sat across from the cousins. Cindi's eyes held suspicion as she stared at a meatball the size of her fist. West sat behind a tower of spaghetti, smiling from ear to ear. Aunt Edith entered through the swinging door, carrying two plates. She put one in front of me, set the other at her place, and then sat at the head of the table across from Russ.

"It looks delicious, Edith," West said. "I haven't had your spaghetti in years."

"It was your favorite when you were little. You used to eat four plates. Tommy would eat three, and I was always afraid I was going to send you boys home with bellyaches."

West chuckled. "Nah. I have the appetite of a whale and the metabolism of a hummingbird."

I rolled my eyes, seeing as how I had the appetite of a whale and the metabolism of a sloth. Good thing for me, most of my calories found their way to my bosom. Unfortunately, the remainder found their way to my hips and behind.

Aunt Edith laughed and passed him the garlic bread. He placed two pieces on his plate, then offered the platter to Cindi, who wrinkled her nose.

"Edith makes the best garlic bread. Try it. I bet you'll like it," he said.

Cindi's face contorted into a ball of disgust as he dropped a slice beside her meatball.

"Our grandmother makes garlic bread with the store-brand loaf, without the garlic," West said.

Russ chuckled.

Once the bread and salad made their rounds, we dug in.

While West devoured food like the numerous times he had devoured me, he told Russ about his new truck. Aunt Edith's eyes were bright and the circles beneath her eyes disappeared. Cindi barely touched her plate. Besides looking terrified of the bread and meat, she stared longingly at her journal.

"Cindi, honey, why don't you put your book on the sideboard so that you don't get any food on it?" Aunt Edith said.

"I won't get food on it," Cindi said. "I don't make a mess when I eat anymore."

"Cindi, you gotta put it over there." West pointed at the wooden shelf. "Cause it's rude to have it at the table."

Cindi's bottom lip stuck out. "I am not rude."

"I know. You're polite. So put it on the shelf," West said.

Cindi struggled to push her heavy chair away from the table. Once she did, she placed her prized possession on the shelf. West helped her position her tiny body under the table before continuing his conversation with Russ.

Aunt Edith had prepared chocolate pudding with homemade cream for dessert. West ate two bowls before putting down his spoon.

"Yum," he said, looking at me with those same eyes he used when he thought I tasted delectable. "Edith, I haven't had a meal like that in years. I wouldn't mind a cooking lesson or two with you."

I sat forward. "You could come for dinner again.

Maybe the next time you have off work." I bit my lip before staring into my aunt's eyes. "Would it be okay?"

She cut her gaze to West, whose body stiffened.

My heart sank. Did their cryptic communication mean I was behaving like a love-sick fool and that West would gladly come to dinner—although not as my date?

"Weston, you know you are welcome anytime for a lesson or as a dinner guest," Aunt Edith finally said.

He grinned. "Thanks, Edith." He pushed away from the table. "Hey, Cindi Lou, we better get you home so you can get ready for school tomorrow."

Cindi fought with her big chair. "Thank you for having me for dinner. Grandma says Edith is a good cook."

West and Russ chuckled.

After Aunt Edith loaded the Westinghouse cousins down with baked goods and leftovers, they excused themselves and headed to the door. Like a silly infatuated teenager, I trotted after them, following them to West's truck.

Cindi hugged me. "Thank you for taking me to college and being my best friend."

"I'm glad we're friends," I twirled a strand of her hair between my fingers. "Maybe I can take you to see Lincoln in a couple of weeks."

"I'll ask Grandma."

West closed Cindi's door and turned to me. I attempted to pull my wildly blowing ringlets from my eyes so that I could watch as the wind whipped his hair about seductively.

"I had fun tonight," I told him.

"Me too."

I exhaled. "I miss you."

He tucked a ringlet behind my ear. "Shortcake," he whispered. "We tried. It didn't work."

"We could try again."

"Look, I've got stuff I gotta work through before I'm ready for a girl."

Both my gaze and my heart fell to my feet.

He ran a finger over my cheek and tilted my head so that I looked up at him. "You're the best girl in the world. But I'm not ready."

Was it my telepathy? That I wasn't sexy enough for him? That I was too weird? Bradley Gordon? Sean O'Sullivan? Was there another girl?"

West's voice still soft he said, "Damn. You're beautiful." He cleared his throat. "You better head in. It's freezing out here."

I retraced my path to the front porch. I was halfway up the stairs when he called, "Hey, Shortcake."

I turned and waited for him to finish his statement. After a long while, he said, "I'll see ya around. Right?"

I nodded.

It was a struggle to climb those stairs while carrying my ten million pounds of heavy heart.

A half-hour later, I curled up on my window seat with a cup of hot tea, a green pen, my stack of papers, and my thoughts.

Winona is correct. I assign too much work.

I will wither away if West never kisses me again.

Am I doing the right thing for Cindi?

Why do two of the Schusters glow and who killed Phil Nowak?

On and on spun my monkey brain. It took every ounce of discipline I could muster to mark up the first of the seventy papers in my pile.

Chapter 10

Combine Pennsylvania Dutch traditions with local Polish food and Czechoslovakian music. Mix in some mountain man Appalachian apparel, a hickish backwoods twang, and some rowdy drunkenness. Toss with a cantankerous rodent, and you have Bellmount Bob Day. The cold pre-dawn wake-up call being the cherry on top.

When my alarm went off at 4:00 a.m., I whimpered and Spot covered his nose with a paw. "I know, buddy. I'm sorry," I told my little companion.

Pulling the blankets over my head, I buried myself in their warmth for another ten minutes before crawling out of bed. I layered a tank, turtleneck, Nordic-patterned ski sweater, and two pairs of socks. After slapping a coat of makeup over my winter death-like pallor, I pulled my hair into a loose ponytail so that the wind didn't turn it into a mass of knots.

I left Spot in bed and tip-toed down three flights of creaking stairs. When I reached the parlor, I realized there was no need to silence my steps. Noisy tourists on their way to Pinkie's Steeple filled the room.

Aunt Edith had stocked the sideboard with hard-boiled eggs, fruit, muffins, coffee, and tea for the early risers. She invited everyone back to the inn for a traditional Bellmount Bob Day champagne brunch of almond waffles smothered in raspberries and faux-

Schwarzwurst sausages.

I grabbed a cup of coffee, a muffin, and a banana, and by four forty-five, had met up with Keisha and our team of reporters in the back parking lot of Sutton Hall.

Thank goodness that Keisha drove. She was surprisingly calm, navigating the almost standstill traffic. I was a jumble of anxiety, convinced that we wouldn't have our stand set up by five thirty. Other than mumbling hellos and John Gibbon's assurance that he had destroyed the Miss Bellmount Bob posters, my not-quite-awake students were relatively quiet.

As we got closer to our destination, there were hundreds of cars parked along the shoulder of the road. The weighed-down van moved slower than the walkers carrying their lawn chairs and picnic baskets. Occasionally Keisha pulled to the side to allow the school buses acting as shuttles to navigate around us as they traveled back to the main road.

The quiet dark of dawn met with a brightly lit parking lot. White Christmas lights hung on every available tree and surface. Food and souvenir stands encircled a large makeshift stage. Here and there, revelers warmed themselves at fires roaring within three-foot-high barrels. The booming band music vibrated the van windows.

We parked between two school buses. Our students unloaded the supplies and got to work. Outfitted with a stack of flannel blankets and two lawn chairs, Keisha and I set up an encampment about six feet back from our stand. From our vantage point, we could observe as Liza issued orders to the staff.

Within two minutes of set-up, a line of people waited for their donuts, muffins, and hot chocolate.

Breathing in the cold air, I soaked up the jubilation surrounding us. I wrapped a blanket around my shoulders and placed another across my lap.

Mason brought Keisha and me cups of hot chocolate. I cradled mine in my gloved hands and held it to my cheek as I watched the lively polka musicians perform.

I leaned close to Keisha. "This is unreal."

"I know. It's a lot of fun if you ignore the drunks and the cold."

Closing my eyes, I let down my shield in search of strange energy. I couldn't sense anything other than the dizzying excitement of the crowd. Not wanting to become overwhelmed, I slid my shield into place.

"Keisha, do you feel anything odd?"

"Like what?" she asked.

"Never mind." I took in a frigid breath and absorbed the festival—children running wild, foam cups of steaming drinks, and red cups of beer.

Goose pimples traveled up my spine as a handsome man, his hair sticking out from below a blue wool hat, strolled toward us. At first, he didn't see me, so I stood and waved. Once our gazes locked, West smiled.

Winona, Cindi, and Uncle Walt trailed behind him.

"Polkamania!" Cindi called out as she trotted to me. She wrapped her arms around my torso. "Hiya, Doctor Shortcake."

I steadied my hot chocolate and hugged her back.

She extended her hand to Keisha. "Hi. I am Cindi Westinghouse. What's your name?"

"Nice to meet you, Cindi. I'm Keisha Brown."

"Are you a detective like Doctor Shortcake and Winona?"

Keisha choked on the sip she'd just taken. "Nope. I'm just a sexy snoop."

Cindi threw her head back, singing out, "Sexy snoop."

I didn't find it all that humorous, but Cindi and Keisha guffawed. Cindi set her backpack on the ground and rooted in it. Meanwhile, the rest of the Westinghouses greeted us.

"Howdy," called out Uncle Walt.

"Hi," Winona said.

I'm the coolest man in the world oozed out of Weston Westinghouse the Third's pores as he said, "Hiya, ladies."

Keisha puckered up and sent West an air kiss. He tossed her one back. I scowled at Keisha.

"Ah, ha, bugger," Cindi said as she pulled her clue journal from her backpack. After taking off her gloves, she paged through the book. Then she struck a pose. One hand went to her hip as the other held out her badge. "I'm a sexy detective."

Keisha tossed her braids over her shoulder and grinned. "Damn straight, girl. We got it going on."

Cindi's brow furrowed for a second before her smile grew so wide that her eyes almost disappeared.

John Gibbons sauntered right into the center of our happy gathering.

Cindi's eyes lit up at the blond-haired, blue-eyed handsome nineteen-year-old. She held out her hand. "Hi. I am Cindi Westinghouse. Do you like polka music?"

John shrugged. "It's okay. I guess. Do you like it?"

"Yes," she said. "What's your name?"

He answered with a cordial, "John."

She held up her paper badge. "I am helping solve a crime. A man was murdered over there." She pointed to the barn.

John's gaze followed her finger. "Yeah. I heard about that. Bob's handler."

"Yes," Cindi said. "I am helping Lieu-ten-ant Bonnie solve the crime."

Wow! Cindi had been practicing.

Winona shuffled her feet and her bottom lip stuck out.

"Cool," John said.

Cindi moved into John's personal space and looked up at him. "Dr. Gordon can't dance with me because he is too old. Would you like to dance with me?"

West and Winona gasped, and Keisha chuckled.

What I wouldn't give to be as brave and spunky as Cindi around men I found attractive?

John took half a step back. "I have to run to the van and get more cups. Can I have the keys, Ms. Brown?" He faced Cindi. "I have to work, but maybe if her highness," he swung his finger toward Liza, "will give me a break, I could dance one song later on."

Keisha tossed him the keys.

"If I can get away, I'll meet you after the ceremony for a dance. Will that work?" John asked.

Stars danced about in Cindi's eyes. "Yes! Polkamania!"

"Polkamania," John called over his shoulder as he took off for the van.

Cindi watched him retreat then her gaze drifted. "Hi, Chad!" She waved.

Liam, Gina Schuster, and a man pushing a boy in a wheelchair headed toward us.

"Here come your cousin and the bitch," Keisha murmured.

I supposed Liam and I were still fighting because once he was within earshot, he said hello to everyone, ignoring me.

Cindi bent down and wrapped her arms around the boy in the chair. Then she focused on the handsome man behind him. "Hi, Chad's Dad. I am Cindi Westinghouse. I was at your house this week. Do you remember me? I remember you."

"Hi, Cindi. It's nice to see you again. We enjoyed your visit," James said with a smile.

How could this genuine man be Gina Schuster's older brother?

James and West knocked fists. "Hey, Westinghouse." James grinned at me. "Dr. Miranda Albright?"

"Yes," I said.

"Liam, is this your cousin?" James asked.

Liam nodded.

James Schuster held up a palm. "The woman who took down Reynolds?"

I hesitated before high-fiving him.

"I guess I better keep you on my good side." He chuckled.

Gina let out a very loud, "*Pfft.*"

I clamped my lips together.

The most beautiful woman I'd ever seen glided toward us. Her black hair hung down to her waist. Unlike my disheveled ringlets, her curls were strands of shiny silk. Her eyes were the same shade of green as mine, but her lashes were black. Like Jessica Grainey, her skin was unblemished, but hers seemed to glisten.

The dark-haired beauty, Gina, seemed plain standing next to this woman. She brought with her a rush of heat that should have melted all of the snow surrounding us. The gaze that settled on me could have baked my hide in the middle of that winter grove.

"Wow," Cindi said. "You are pretty like a princess."

"This is my mom," Chad said.

Interesting. Cindi had been to the house and met Chad's father but hadn't met his mother?

The woman studied Cindi with a haughty expression frozen on her face. She seemed to move in slow motion as she faced me. "And you are?"

"Cassandra, this is Liam's cousin, Miranda, the professor at the college," James said.

"Hi." I took off my glove and extended my hand.

Ignoring my greeting, she stared into the distance. "We should head to the stage now."

Chad's head moved from side to side. "Can Cindi stand with me on stage?"

"That doesn't sound like a good idea," said the gorgeous heater.

James put his hand on his wife's shoulder. "Honey, she can keep him company."

Cindi moved into James' space and looked up at him. "Chad won't be nervous if I go on stage and hold his hand. That's what we do at school."

Chad's up-and-down nod slightly quivered. "Yeah! I don't get nervous then."

"I think it sounds like a great idea, too," Liam said.

"Can I go, Dad?" Cindi asked.

Uncle Walt didn't even need to think it over. "Sure!"

Cindi clapped and hopped. However, her body didn't completely lift off the ground. Still, she had solved a huge problem. Cindi Westinghouse was going onto that stage to hold Chad Schuster's hand so that he wasn't afraid to face the onlookers.

Gina and her even more exquisite sister-in-law tied for The World's Worst Grimace. However, Chad and Cindi beamed.

"Keep your fingers out of the damn cage," West reminded her.

Cindi blushed, probably because he'd embarrassed her in front of her friend. She got over her frustration quickly and grinned.

"Got it. And my toes."

"And your nose, chin, and elbow."

Cindi shook her head as if West was insane for thinking she might put a body part into a groundhog cage. "It doesn't hurt that bad."

West growled.

"Cindi, you cried so hard last time," Winona said.

James Schuster chuckled. "Nobody will stick anything into the groundhog cage. I promise."

Cindi put her notebook into her backpack and slung it over her shoulder. "Please tell John I will be back for our date." Then she followed Liam and the Schuster family.

"Liam?" I called.

He stopped and turned.

"I'm sorry," I mouthed.

"Me too," he mouthed back.

I blew him a kiss, and he smiled.

"That woman is too damn beautiful for her own good," Keisha said, interrupting my moment with Liam.

West finally exhaled. "Shit. Gorgeous."

I glared at West.

"Yeah, but she's trouble," he said.

I forgave him for finding her alluring since he also thought her difficult.

Just then, Dinky the DJ's voice, came over the microphone. "Is everyone ready for Bellmount Bob Day 1990?"

Winona leaped up and down, her voice audible over the hundreds of cheers that rose from the crowd.

Apparently, the gathered mass at Pinkie's Steeple was ready for the prognosticating rodent to whisper his secret.

****

Dinky the DJ, had on more eye makeup than Keisha, Winona and me combined. He wore a long black coat, jeans, and a bright red scarf. His Mohawk stood three inches into the air while long stringy strands landed two inches below his shoulders. He was all gangly limbs, scraggly locks, and leather boots. Winona lit up as he took the stage.

Keisha looked from Winona to the DJ, to me, then rolled her eyes.

"How's everybody out there in the arctic tundra of WTFK-land doing?" Dinky called.

Cheers bubbled from the crowd, half of whom were inebriated.

"I'm DJ Dinky with WTFK, Bear County's one and only station, bringing you all the best in music and news. Thanks to Fat Jasper and His Merry Polkomania Band for waking us up this morning with their lively tunes!"

Uproarious cries came from the onlookers.

"Starting off our festivities, we have Mayor Schuster with his family. Please give them a warm welcome."

Enthusiastic cries greeted the Schusters. However, the rowdy crowd would have celebrated a worm on a rainy day.

A waving James climbed onto the stage, followed by his wife, parents, sister, sons, and Cindi Westinghouse.

I had every intention of focusing my attention on Cindi during her special moment. She grinned as she grasped her friend's hand. I spent a second of my attention on the handsome, articulate mayor as he said, "Good morning, everyone. It's great to be back in my beloved Bellmount."

However, most of my focus was on a beautiful woman and the mesmerizing vibrant red glow surrounding her. It took effort and concentration to look back at Cindi, who no longer smiled. Her eyes wide, she stared at Jimmy Junior, who emitted a light red aura from behind his brother's wheelchair. Meanwhile, James gushed about his amazing hometown, wonderful county, and amazing family.

I sidled to West, put my hand on his forearm, and leaned close to whisper, "Do you see anything odd on that stage?"

West ignored me, so I repeated my question. When he finally glanced at me, there was a faraway look in his eyes. "Damn. She's beautiful."

I grunted, returned to my seat, rearranged my blankets, and tapped Keisha on the shoulder. She continued to stare straight ahead.

I tapped again. "Hey, Keisha."

Silence!

"Hey!" I tapped harder. "You okay?"

She shook herself as if returning from a daydream and her long braids flew about.

"Have you seen Brad?" I asked.

"Bradley usually sets up in the first aid tent," she said.

"Where is the tent?"

Keisha swung an index finger toward the lodge, then stared back at the stage.

I perused the crowd to discover that most people eerily stared at the platform with wide-opened mouths and unblinking eyes. I shivered, then pushed through the throng, searching for the infirmary.

The farther I got from the Schusters, the less intense the focus on the stage seemed to be, and the more movement and noise there was. I eventually found the sick bay beside the entrance to the lodge. Brad and his assistant, Nurse Theresa, hovered over a man sitting on a cot.

"When this ice pack melts, you can use the snow to keep the swelling down," Brad told his giant-sized, full-bearded patient.

"And keep your hands out of the flames." Nurse Nasty waggled a finger three inches from the man's nose. "It isn't even six a.m., and you've had enough to drink."

I chuckled as he thanked the doctor, recoiled from the nurse, and re-entered the crowd.

"Hi, Brad," I said.

He smiled at my approach. "Hi, Miranda."

"Can I talk to you?" I asked.

Theresa's face twisted in disgust. "He is busy right

now."

Brad laid a hand on the nurse's shoulder, and her pinched expression melted. "Sure. Is everything okay?"

I willed my eyelashes to stay in place as I made my request. "Could we talk privately?"

"Of course." Brad followed me to a three-foot person-less space.

I shifted positions so that we both faced the stage. Unfortunately, the Schusters had departed the platform, and Dinky now instigated the crowd, singing out Fake Jake chants.

"Did you see James Schuster's speech?" I asked.

"No, I missed it." Brad inclined his chin toward his grumbling helper. "I was dealing with a drunk who thought he could retrieve singed kielbasa from a fire pit using his mitten, and a nurse who refuses to sleep until she rids the world of stupidity. Why?"

I moved closer so that we wouldn't be overheard. "The mayor's wife and son glow. Have you ever met anyone who glowed before?"

"Glow?"

"Red," I said. "Up on the stage, and face to face, they are furnaces. I'm not sure if anyone but Cindi and I have noticed. However, Greg and Alina sensed something that terrified them when we were here the other day. I think two of the Schusters are giving off heat." As an afterthought, I added, "Although the one who has put a spell on my cousin is an icy witch."

Brad laughed. "I'm sorry, Miranda. I've been so busy. I haven't noticed anything. I've met James and Chad. Chad has some health issues. Super nice kid. James has been to our council meetings. So far, I've been impressed. I wasn't expecting him to be so knowledgeable and impartial." Brad raised a brow and smiled. "You know, with his parents and icy-witch sister being who they are."

I bit my lip.

"Do you think they might have energy gifts like us?"

"I don't know. Maybe."

A crying child sandwiched by concerned parents approached Nurse Kane.

Brad placed his hand on my shoulder. "I better go, sweetheart."

Upon hearing Brad address me by my old pet name, I gasped. Unphased by his slip, Brad waved and made his way back to the tent.

I studied the retreating doctor's spectacular backside before fighting my way through the crowd. About fifty feet from my destination, I ran headfirst into my childhood friend, Tom Little.

Tommy wrapped me in an embrace, and I hugged him back. Tommy was precious to me because he had absorbed some of Liam and West's relentless teasing when we were children. He had also taken me on my first date when I was sixteen—if turtle hunting at the river actually counts as a date.

Tommy presented the smiling girl beside him. "Do you remember Trisha?"

I faked a happy hello.

"Hi, Randa," she said with a voice that was much too cheery. "When are you coming back to class?"

I wrinkled my nose. I would not make the same mistake twice. I had the misfortune of trying Perkypants's class once, and I didn't plan to ever participate in aerobic dance again.

Tommy chuckled. "Working out isn't Randa's thing."

Perkypants poked me in the bicep. "We need to get you in shape."

I stared at her finger as she repeatedly jabbed it into the sleeve of my thick coat.

Lincoln had once told me that he found me to be as energetic as the vibrating girl in front of me, adding that he thought I might be jealous that Tom had a new girl. I was pretty sure I wasn't jealous, so I'm not sure what possessed me to say, "I'll come back to class when you read a book. But it has to have words."

Tommy cringed as Perkypants called out, "I love this girl. She's a hoot."

First of all, Tommy's enthusiastic girlfriend was delusional. I was the only person in the entire world who found me funny. Second, Lincoln was wrong. Jealous, my foot. Perkypants was too perky! And thirdly, in four seconds, I would have to placate a chagrined Keisha as she pretended not to hold a torch for Tommy.

"You should say hi to Keisha, Winona, and West. Everyone is over there." I inclined my chin to the stand.

As Tommy, the sun-shiny drill sergeant, and I approached our friends, Dinky's voice became grave. "Let's take a moment of silence to remember Bob's handler, Phil Nowak."

The only thing audible for the next ten seconds was a crying baby.

The silence broke when someone screamed out, "Fake Jake killed Phil."

"Fake Jake, Fake Jake," the crowd chanted.

Perkypants was the only one in our group who

joined in. I knew it. The woman had the intelligent quotient of a mollusk.

Dinky gave the crowd a thumb's up. "I hear you, peeps. Beavers can't find their way out of a hollow log. So, let's get this thing going."

"Beavers bite," yelled the crowd.

"Beavers bite! Beavers bite," Perkypants jumped up and down and screamed next to my ear.

According to the Westinghouse family, groundhogs also bite, but pointing it out to the enraptured throng might be a death sentence.

Dinky's body barely moved as he emceed. However, the crowd's behavior matched the rise and fall of his theatrical voice.

"It's the moment we have all been waiting for. I'd like to introduce Bob's new handler, Howard Greene and the Fraternal Ring."

"Bob! Bob! Bob!" Echoed off the surrounding mountains.

The man I had met a few days prior walked onto the stage carrying a long thin scroll. He wore a top hat and tuxedo, and four men who looked like his clones pushed a crate on wheels into the center of the performance.

Mr. Greene tipped his hat to the crowd before taking the microphone from Dinky. "Welcome, everyone." He waited for the cheers to subside before continuing. "God rest poor Phil's soul. He was my best friend, so I can tell you; he would want us to go on with today's celebration."

"Woohoo!" and "Phil!" became the chants of the moment.

"With no further ado, let's proceed to the important

moment."

Two of the Fraternal Ring members unrolled the scroll and held it in front of Greene. He cleared his throat.

"On this February day in 1990, I do declare that I will uphold the greatest tradition in the state of Pennsylvania. I have been granted permission by these people that stand before me—" he swept his arm to encompass the boisterous crowd. "—to speak for the only true prognosticator, our very own Bellmount Bob."

The overzealous group of drunks off to my right might soon need Doctor Brad. After all, how much could humans screech and leap about chest-bumping before they required oxygen tanks?

Greene removed the lid from the crate. The crowd quieted in anticipation. He retrieved the rodent, held it to his ear, and nodded as the secret was whispered. He lifted Bob high. "Bob declares spring is to come early!"

"Woohoo!" I cheered. I couldn't help myself since blood had frozen in my arteries three months ago, and I needed to thaw.

Fat Jasper and His Merry Polkamania Band began to clang, and the mountain seemed to move as over a thousand people danced on Pinkie's Steeple.

When West grabbed and twirled me, I understood the appeal of the aggressive rodent to these rural people. Unfortunately, pirouetting in West's arms halted when someone tapped me on the shoulder.

"Hey, Dr. Albright," John Gibbons yelled over the noise. "Where's your friend? I promised her a dance."

West and I parted and looked toward the stage. No Schusters. West shifted his weight, stretched his neck to look over the crowd, then frowned.

"She hasn't returned yet, John," I said.

The music stopped, and the second half of his statement came at me as a shout. "Okay. I'll catch her later. I'm going to ask Liza to dance."

"Peeps, can I have everyone's attention? We have a super special surprise today. Are ya all ready?" Dinky asked.

"Ready," screeched Perkypants.

"You are going to love this, peeps. The first ever Miss Bob Contest," Dinky's animated voice promised. He swept his arms wide. "Ta-da!"

Three women dressed in fur coats and stilettos slinked onto the stage.

Keisha's let out a resounding, "Motherfucker!" as I covered my gaping mouth with a hand.

Like a leopard ambushing its prey, Liza Smith was upon us in an instant, her angry face in John Gibbons's space.

John shielded his body with upturned palms. "It wasn't me. I swear. I took down the signs. I have nothing to do with this."

As a song about peaches and cream and pouring sugar burst from the speakers, the heavily made-up women with hair teased to the moon strutted around, stopping here and there to pose provocatively.

Winona covered her eyes with her hands as she peeked through her fingers, and Uncle Walt grinned from ear to ear.

"It wasn't me," John said. "My girls would have worn bikinis and snow boots."

Just then, a voluptuous blonde opened her coat to expose a bikini-clad body. There was an equal mixture of gasps and cheers from the crowd.

"Shit," John muttered. Heading toward the stage, he called over his shoulder, "Dr. Albright, Ms. Brown, I'll get to the bottom of this. I promise."

The stripper-sounding music stopped. "Thanks to me, WTFK is the proud sponsor of 1990 Miss Bob. And thank you to Johnston Furs for loaning us these fine coats," Dinky said.

"Dingbat, your boyfriend is a dick," Keisha informed Winona.

Since children peppered the audience, watching a chauvinistic show, a gentler insult would not have sufficed. Ironically, any kiddies nearby were also privy to Keisha's language.

"We have a question for each of our beautiful girls," Dinky announced.

Winona collapsed into my chair and placed her head on her lap as smoke tendrils seeped from Keisha's ears. Meanwhile, Uncle Walt leaped about like he'd hit the lottery.

"Where in the hell is Cindi?" West asked.

"First up, we have Leyla."

A blonde waved to the audience as she strutted to Dinky.

"Lovely Leyla with the pretty yellow hair, how can you make Bear County a better place?" Dinky asked.

The girl leaned close to the microphone and, in a voice so high-pitched she sounded like a cartoon character said, "I would like to find a handsome man and be his bucket packer so that he can go to work and make Bear County the best."

"Boo hiss!" Keisha hollered.

I turned to West. "What's a bucket packer?"

He frowned. "Something is wrong. I don't see Cindi. I'm going to go find her."

As West walked away, Greg appeared by my side.

The absurd girl reveling in the spotlight kept rambling. "I'd pack him roast beef sandwiches and chips and pop." She curtsied, held her head high, and smiled as she took her spot. Placing one hand behind her head, and the other on her thrust-out hip, she settled into her pose.

"That twit just set women back a thousand years. Jumped right into the dark ages," Keisha grumbled. "A goddamn cavewoman."

"What's going on?" Greg asked with a confused squint. *"Shit! Is there a beauty pageant going on in the middle of Groundhog Day?"*

I nodded.

"Hmm," he said. *"I have no problem with beautiful women in furs and bikinis, but I like them to have a few brain cells."*

I sighed.

Dinky motioned for the second girl in line to approach. "Please welcome, Mindy."

I'd have wagered my raspberry-covered Belgian waffles that the only people who welcomed her were four sheets to the wind.

"Magnificent Mindy, how can you make Bear County a better place?"

Mindy looked out over her audience and used two fingers to make a V-shaped peace sign. "I want to save all the children and bunnies. I don't want any bunnies killed unless it is to keep people warm and make things like this." She caressed the length of her fur.

Yikes!

Most of the audience remained silent. It appeared that even drunks knew that making coats out of bunnies wasn't a popular conversational topic at a celebration starring a beloved rodent.

Dinky called the third woman with strawberry blonde hair to him, and she took her turn performing her pageant walk.

"She's my favorite," Uncle Walt said.

Keisha growled at him as Winona whimpered, "Uncle Walt." She dropped her head onto her cradled hands.

Dinky never had a chance to ask contestant three her question because a large woman with frosted hair and eyelids coated in garish blue eyeshadow, burst onto the stage. She smashed her bulk into Dinky and grabbed the microphone.

"Hello, Bear County," the new contestant hollered in a voice that was both high-pitched and raspy. "Vote for me for Miss Bob."

Gasps echoed off the surrounding mountains.

"Shit, that's a dude," Greg said.

The newcomer tore his coat open to reveal a hairy chest and a painted beer belly. Big red letters spelled out a crossed-out *Bob*. Underneath it, *Jake* was written in blue. The large man took a bow, then skipped around the stage, hugging each of the girls as they screamed and slapped at him.

"Damn Creekfield prank," Greg said.

I hope nobody noticed me nonchalantly whispering to my ghost. "Is the entire pageant a prank?"

"Nah. The girls are all Bellmount and tacky DJ. I think just the ugly guy in heels is Creekfield." Greg smirked. *"They got us good this time."*

Keisha waved her arms at the spectacle in front of us. "This nonsense has to stop. It gets worse every year."

The ridiculous situation continued its downward spiral when Shultz rode in on his white horse, determined to save the day. He stomped onto the stage, three police officers trailing behind him. The inept sheriff circled his arm like a lasso, setting the scene into action.

The officers chased the man in drag around as he wove in and out of screaming contestants. The big man belly-bumped Shultz hard, knocking the sheriff onto his behind.

Dinky helped Shultz back onto his feet, then the renegade made another round, stopping dead center. The big man flashed the audience his boxers while holding up a thumb and pinky and sticking out his tongue and belly. His protruding tongue flew about as he shook his head violently.

He was so consumed with his taunting that it afforded Officer Kline the advantage. Kline tackled, then sat on top of him.

The crowd cheered, and Shultz took the microphone from a wide-eyed Dinky. "If there are any more troublemakers from Creekfield out there, you best turn around and head home. Now!" Shultz flashed some teeth with his growl and handed the microphone back to Dinky.

The sheriff and the entirety of Bellmount law enforcement roughly picked up and escorted the prankster from the stage as the crowd chanted, "Fake Jake killed Phil."

"Is that guy going to jail?" I asked.

"Damn straight," Keisha said.

"Nah. I'm sure we did something shitty to ruin their ceremony too," Greg said. *"When I was eighteen, I spray-painted Beavers Bite on the side of Creekfield High."*

West made his way through the crowd to my side.

"Hey, Uncle Walt, I found Schuster and Liam behind the stage, but Cindi and his sons aren't with them," West said.

Uncle Walt scratched his head.

"Is the kid who sees ghosts missing?" Greg asked.

"She's probably with her friends," Keisha assured us.

My heart tripped over itself. West was correct and something was wrong. A week earlier, Cindi had witnessed a bloody murder scene, and we had left her with two glowing humans and a Bellmount Bitch while we watched pandemonium break out.

"Do you want me to help you look for her?" I asked.

"Yeah. Let's break into groups and search," West said.

Winona, Keisha, Uncle Walt, Tommy, and Greg jumped to attention.

West didn't have time to organize our search party because Dinky pulled himself together and returned to emceeing.

"What a crazy way to start our day. I, for one, can't wait to see what the rest of Bellmount Bob Day brings. Don't forget a traditional breakfast will be served at every restaurant in town, then make your way to the town hall to continue the party. Now, let's bring the star of our show back for a final bow."

The Fraternal Ring wheeled Bob's cage into the center of the stage. Mr. Greene took his place behind the crate, faced the audience, lifted the lid, and reached inside. He bent forward, his torso disappearing into the box for a moment. When he stood, he held something that wasn't an animal in his hand. He walked to Dinky and whispered into his ear.

Dinky relayed the message in that special way only he could. "Holy donkey dingles! Bob is missing!"

West took off in a full-out sprint, crashing into everyone that stood between him and that stage.

"Holy guacamole! Howard Greene is holding Cindi's clue journal," I said.

****

After five minutes of the sheriff publicly declaring his fury, James Schuster took control of the situation. With complete composure, he announced that the disappointed Bob fans should head into town and enjoy the rest of the day. Somehow James had a calming effect on the frantic throng, convincing them that the inept law enforcement had everything under control.

Not only were Cindi, a groundhog, and the Schuster boys missing, but John Gibbons had also disappeared. The newspaper staff, minus John, packed up wares and loaded the van. Liza frowned as she counted the money. Since I couldn't concentrate, I was useless. I even struggled to move half a dozen donuts from a paper plate into a box.

Tommy came to my rescue, placing a hand on my shoulder. "Randa, why don't you rest for a second? I'll help Keisha and the kids pack."

Keisha glowered at Trisha before smiling at Tommy. "Tom. I'd love your help." Keisha sugary sweet? Add another slash to the morning's oddities' tally.

The corners of the aerobics instructor's lips turned downward while Keisha's lifted. A clueless Tommy missed the exchange because Liza placed a large box in his arms and directed him toward the van.

Keisha winced at the donuts I had accidentally mangled. "Girlfriend, you haven't taken your eyes off the stage. I know you are worried about Cindi. Go check on West and Winona. We've got this."

I hugged my best friend, then made my way to where the Westinghouses, the Schusters, Liam, the Fraternal Ring, Dinky, Jared Blackova, and two police officers stood. The entire group focused on James as he spoke. Cassandra Schuster no longer emitted her eerie glow or gave off any heat. She appeared to be a beautiful but ordinary woman. I placed my arm around Winona's shoulder, and she leaned into me.

Shultz sniffed in my direction and cleared his throat. "We don't need your help, young lady. Best to be moving on." He swung two fingers and motioned down the hill.

Gina stuck her snotty nose into the air and agreed with Shultz. "We don't need you."

Liam bristled and let out a frustrated sigh.

Winona shifted her weight so that she no longer leaned against me and stood tall. "Gina, Miranda's family."

"Let her stay, Shultz," West said.

Shultz backed away from West and continued to sniff at me from a distance.

James Schuster got everyone's attention by raising a hand. "I think this will all be settled soon. Chad might have overheard that prankster and thought Bob was in danger. Chad loves animals and I can see him convincing Jimmy to save the groundhog. Jimmy dotes on Chad.

"They are great kids, so I'm sure they thought they were helping. Jimmy probably drove them to our house. Why don't Cassandra and I head home? Let us talk to them and straighten this out."

Shultz wiped a wrist across his nose, then stuck his thumbs into the waistband of his pants. "I'll go with you."

Cassandra's eyes grew wide as the boy's grandfather frowned and frantically shook his head.

"Edgar, I appreciate the offer, but Chad gets a bit nervous around people he doesn't know," the mayor said. "Police at the house might terrify him. Jimmy should have known better, but as I said, if something upset Chad, Jimmy would do whatever he could to fix it."

Somehow, the diplomatic James had placated the sheriff's fragile ego. Schultz nodded, not appearing upset in the least that his offer had been dismissed.

"Kidnapping Bob is a serious offense," Blackova declared.

Uncle Walt glared at the abrupt manager. "Cindi wouldn't kidnap nothin'."

"I think that while that lunatic ran around the stage distracting everyone, one of his buddies stole Bob. The kids might not have anything to do with it," one of the men in the Fraternal Ring said.

His penguin-like clones bobbled their heads up and down and mumbled.

"I think you are correct," James said. "Still, I

should head home to have a talk with the kids. Edgar, are your men still checking bags as people leave the mountain?"

Shultz gazed into the distance. "Yeah."

Since Kline was the only officer on the Bellmount Force with any kind of moral compass, and he was standing with us, I hoped the others were on the lookout for Bob. Unfortunately, I suspected the rodent was with the long-gone Cindi, Chad, and his glowing twin.

"One of my student reporters is also missing," I said. "A nineteen-year-old freshman. John Gibbons. Athletic build. About five ten-ish. Blond hair, blue eyes."

"Was he drinking?" asked Shultz. "Those damn college kids drink till they puke."

I put my hands on my hips. "No, Shultz. He was working at our food stand."

"Still coulda been drinking. Probably puking in a ditch," Shultz said.

I stomped to Shultz and jabbed his bulbous nose with my finger. West grabbed the hood of my jacket. I tried to break from his grasp, but West tugged and I jerked backward.

"A trouble-making fiery hellcat. I told you we shoulda sent her home." Shultz glared at me.

Gina snorted.

"Enough," Liam said.

Shultz crossed his arms over his expansive chest. I supposed he thought Liam, West, and Gina agreed and thought me a "hellcat." Perhaps they did, but he needed to wipe that smirk off his bloated jowls because West had just saved him from getting clobbered by a woman.

Still clutching my jacket, West held me in place.

"Hey, James. Why don't you let me go with you? Cindi would never run off without telling us. Something is off; I can feel it. And that was her book in the cage."

"Where's the book?" Officer Kline asked.

There was a lot of looking around, shuffling, and shrugging.

"See what I mean," West said. "Something's really wrong."

James placed three fingers on his forehead and rubbed—hard. "Westinghouse, do you know how to get to the estate?"

"Yeah," West said.

Shultz inclined his chin in the direction of a police cruiser that sat about thirty feet away. The *lunatic* peeked over the back seat, watching us.

"I'm gonna take that shit-for-brains back to the station and get some information out of him. Too bad I can't rough 'em up, but I'll probably have to exchange him if any of our fools caused trouble in Creekfield." Shultz waddled away.

Cassandra Schuster rolled her eyes.

James rested a hand on her shoulder. "Darling, you have to be from a small town to understand. Sometimes in the spirit of enthusiastic rivalries, we get carried away."

"But murder?" I asked.

"No. Murder is something entirely different," James said.

"I feel as though I'm living in a barbaric time warp," Cassandra said.

Although the town was a decade behind in popular trends, the conservative oligarchy was powerful, and I didn't quite fit in; I loved Bellmount with all my heart and would never allude to the quaint setting as a "barbaric time warp." Besides, I was almost two decades behind the times myself.

"Uncle Walt, you head home and see if Cindi shows up," West suggested.

Walt groaned. "Your grandmother will go ape-shit."

"Yep," West said.

Walt's shoulders caved forward. "West, call me right away if you find her." Then like a child receiving a devastating punishment, he skulked away.

The Schusters said their goodbyes and departed, Liam trailing behind.

About fifteen feet from us, Liam stopped and called over his shoulder. "Westinghouse, see you in a few?"

"Yeah, man. Right behind you," West answered.

"Little cuz, you want me to give you a lift home?" Liam asked.

At last, we had an olive branch. I popped onto my toes. "Thanks, Liam. I'm riding with West and Winona."

"I think I better go to the pub and tell Mom, Dad, and Uncle Pop," Winona said. "I don't want them to hear from someone else."

"I can take you home and then head back to the station," Kline said.

"No, I'll take her home," Dinky said.

Water leaked from Winona's eyes. "Officer Kline can drive me."

Dinky strolled to Winona and wrapped his arms around her. "What's wrong, babe?"

"I'm not feeling well."

Winona appeared to move in slow motion as she pushed away and turned her back on her boyfriend. He reached for her, but his arm froze mid-lift.

A terrifying timbre oozed from West's whistled, "*Whooweet.*"

Dinky faced West, and they engaged in a full-out stand-off.

After at least five seconds of eye bullets, West spoke. "Hey, man. She said she doesn't want you to take her home."

Dinky broke eye contact with West to watch Kline trot after Winona. "Why's she upset?"

I waved my hand in the air. "Your sexist fiasco, you nincompoop!"

"And her cousin is missing," West said, his handsome face twisted and distorted.

Meanwhile, Blackova grumbled something about "unholy disaster" and "murdering bastards" as the rest of the party dispersed.

West and I were halfway down the hill when someone called, "Hey, Dr. Albright."

We halted our descent and waited as John Gibbons charged toward us.

"Ms. Brown left for campus. Where have you been?" I asked.

"I was trying to figure out what was going on," John said between his raspy pants "That DJ organized Ms. Bob. I had nothing to do with it."

"I know," I said.

"Good." John rubbed at his heaving chest. "Also, did you know that the old groundhog dudes don't get along?"

"Old groundhog dudes?" I asked.

"You mean the Fraternal Ring?" West asked.

Gibbons nodded. "Yeah. And get this, the guy who manages the ski resort doesn't get along with any of them."

"That's interesting," I said.

"I also learned there were four other guys with the painted dude who ran around the stage. They got away when that officer took him down. They didn't expect our cops to do anything."

"Because our police department is mostly clowns," I declared.

"That's pretty much what they said," John said.

"You see my cousin Cindi?" West asked. "She's missing."

"Missing?" John stepped between West and me and whispered, "I thought you might want this."

I followed his gaze downward, where he clutched Cindi's journal close to his hip. "Oh, my. The cops are looking for that."

West ensured nobody was looking and stuck it inside his jacket. "Anyone see ya take it?"

"Nah. Everything was nuts. Nobody noticed me, so I grabbed it, but I didn't know she was missing. I just thought someone kidnapped the rat. The last time I saw Cindi, she was on stage with the mayor."

"Thanks, man," West said. "I owe you for grabbing her book. You need a ride back to campus?"

"Yeah. Liza is going to be pissed that I disappeared, and Dunlap is going to be all over my ass."

West smiled for the first time since we had danced. "Chicks and jealous dudes." He chuckled. However, a second later, his jawline tensed.

We walked the rest of the way in silence. I climbed into the cab of West's truck and sat between John Gibbons and Weston Westinghouse the Third.

Holy fudge. Glowing humans, a kidnapped rodent, a corpse, and three missing high school students.

For a small town in the middle of nowhere, Bellmount was chock-full of drama.

Chapter 11

Once West and I dropped John off at his dormitory, we were alone for the first time in ages. There were so many things I longed to tell him. For starters, I struggled to concentrate because he was always on my mind. There was the all-consuming way my body ached for his touch. And he made me laugh and cry and feel every emotion so strongly that it knocked the wind out of me.

Instead, I repeated for the umpteenth time, "I'm sure Cindi is okay." Too bad that the Cassandra and Jimmy Schuster glowing predicament left me an anxiety-filled skeptic.

West peered at me from his peripheral. "I hope you're right. It's just—" he grunted. "Look, Cindi wouldn't have gotten into a car with someone without telling her dad, Winona, or me. At least, I don't think she would have."

We rode the rest of the way in silence.

The Schuster estate sat at the end of a long winding drive. Bountiful snow-covered hedges lined a Tudor-style mansion that resembled something out of the Brothers Grimm. Two A-framed dormers with ornate stained-glass windows stood three stories high, and three stone chimneys rose into the air. The front door was a heavy oak, painted deep red. The structure sprawled every which way, with a wing jutting to the front on one side and to the back on the other. The out-of-place ladder that leaned against the side of the house did not detract from its beauty.

"Oh, West. It looks like something out of a fairy tale."

"Yeah," he said.

"Do you think they are as rich as people say? Winona doesn't think they are."

"No idea. I hear all kinds of shit from behind the bar. I've learned to block out most of it. And honestly, I could care less. I just want to find Cindi." He parked the truck in front of a garage large enough to house airplanes.

"How can anyone afford a house like this? It's even bigger than the Patterson estate, and Ian is the richest man in the county. One of the richest men in the state."

"Coal? Lumber? Oil?" West shrugged. "Exploiting the working class?"

I smiled at his profile. "You sound like Aunt Edith and Russ."

"Edith and Russ are two of the good ones."

I laughed. "Yes, they are. I love them." I sobered. "Hey, West?"

"Yeah?"

"Jimmy Junior and Cassandra glow."

He removed the key from the ignition and faced me. "What are you talking about?"

"They have a red aura around them. Cassandra's is intense and somewhat terrifying. Jimmy's isn't quite as bright."

West's brow furrowed. "Shit!"

"Well, they don't glow all of the time. But they

were glowing on stage. They also give off a lot of heat. At least I feel heat. I know it sounds like I'm crazy."

"Bat shit." He half-laughed, half-sighed. "Although, I believe you. Nothing surprises me anymore. Superheroes are crawling out of the woodwork these days."

"*Bat shit*?" I asked.

He ruffled my hair. "Stop pouting."

He deposited Cindi's journal in his glove compartment before we exited the truck and approached the massive building.

Turning in a circle, I took everything in before facing front, puckering up, and blowing a white puff. The misty cloud floated in front of a large inlaid medallion above the door. Brickwork resembling a maze spiraled inward until it formed a star with thin rays.

"The masonry is unreal. I've never seen anything like it."

"Yeah. Impressive as hell," West said. "But it doesn't quite match the rest of the brickwork."

I buried my chin into the collar of my coat. "I can't decide. Is it beautiful or spooky?"

Before West dropped the knocker, the mayor opened the door. "Come on in." He stepped to the side so that we could enter.

My skin prickling, we followed him through a grand foyer. Unfortunately, I had to lift my freezing chin from its warm spot in my collar to gawk at the oak ceiling timbers. Condensation from my murmur of wonderment traveled into the air, past intricately carved pillars. "It's freezing in here," I said.

Shit. How do I tell him?

Since the mayor's mouth hadn't moved, my filter was firmly in place, I couldn't read minds if I wasn't touching someone, and the house fueled my romantic; I shook off my overactive imagination.

We followed James into a steamy room of arching beams and stained glass. Liam stoked at the flames in the massive stone fireplace while the Schusters lounged in oversized furniture in shades of red, gold, and brown. Henry VIII himself could have perched in the throne-like chair that the oldest James occupied. When James the First stood, the rest of his family joined him. However, Cassandra and Cindi were not present.

A bead of sweat dripped down my forehead.

Mayor James placed a hand on West's shoulder. "I'm sorry. Your cousin didn't leave with my sons."

"What the hell? Then where is she?" West asked.

Whispers pinged off the high ceiling and stucco walls, echoing from all directions.

We are in trouble. Grandpa said, 'police.'

If we hadn't had to get rid of the help, I could offer them some hot tea.

Damn. What a mess. How are people ever going to trust me to be their mayor?

Where in the heck had the numerous voices come from since James was the only one speaking?

"I don't know where Cindi is. Neither do the boys," James said. "Chad got nervous when that man started running around the stage, so Jimmy brought him home."

"Yeah, but I told Grandma we were leaving," Jimmy Junior said.

The elder Mrs. Schuster's brow furrowed, and she frowned. "There was so much going on. I guess I forgot. I—"

Voices drowned out the rest of her statement.

Her memory is going. What am I going to do?

The police force here is such a disaster. They will never find the poor kid.

I hate her. Her hair is a mess. How can men like her?

"Shit," West said. "You told us you were going to look out for her."

The mayor ran a hand through his windblown hair.

West sighed. "When was the last time y'all saw Cindi?"

Jimmy Junior, the human heater, warmed his hands over the fire. "When we left, she was standing by the stage."

Sweat dripped in between my cleavage, and my head ached so much that I pushed the heel of my hand into my forehead.

Liam wrapped an arm around my shoulder. "Hey, little cuz, you okay? You look flushed."

I hate her and her stupid hair. Why do she and Liam have to have the same eyes? I wish he would stop defending her.

Where in the hell is Cindi? Fuck!

"Is there someone else she may have left with?" James asked.

West's jaw clenched and his eyes practically bulged. "No. Only family. Maybe Doc Gordon, Edith, Russ, or Miranda."

"What about her teacher?" James asked.

Miss Myers is a good teacher.

Liam's body heat singed my skin and the voices slapped at my brain with a violent vehemence. I flung my body into a chair, dropped my head between my thighs, and breathed.

I couldn't have stumbled into some sort of psychic footprint because those usually involved past events, and I heard present thoughts. I tried to articulate a question, but it came out a bit jumbled. "Was she, the teacher, there?"

Chad looked at Jimmy, and Jimmy answered. "She gave them hugs and told Chad and Cindi that she was proud of them. That was right before we left."

I hope some maniac doesn't hurt her was the last sentence I understood because words and phrases smacked at me like bombs dropping at the Normandy invasion.

Bellmount Bob! In trouble! Fuck! Hate her! Cookies and tea! Carrots! Something bad happened. Cindi! Roast beef! Embarrassed! Lieutenant! Big trouble!

Cassandra Schuster entered the room; the voices stopped, and the room spun. Nausea that started in my belly turned into a burning sensation that traveled up my esophagus.

I jumped out of the chair and retraced my path to the front door. The oak was so heavy it took me three tries and all of my body weight to open it. After descending the front stairs as quickly as my shaking legs allowed, I sprinted across the front lawn, trying to get as far away from the house as possible. I was a quarter of the way across the expansive front yard when I fell onto my knees and retched. As my banana, muffin, and coffee from breakfast made another appearance, I clutched my heaving stomach.

Fudge. I needed a new, less sensitive stomach.

West's gentle voice whispered from beside me. "Shortcake?" His hazel eyes studied me. His face had paled and matched the snow-covered mountainous vista behind him. "Are you okay?"

Liam and James stood behind him.

West and Liam lifted me off the lawn.

"Westinghouse, I'll take her home. I promised Mom I'd come for brunch today," Liam said.

Brunch! Dry heaves racked my body.

"That'd be great, man." West frowned. "I'm going to stop by Little's place and see if he can help me track down Cindi's teacher. Since his dad is a postman, he knows where everyone lives. Although, I have a feeling we may end up in Creekfield."

"You think someone from Creekfield took her as part of a prank?" Liam asked.

"Pfft!" James huffed.

West kicked at the ground, and snow flew into the air. "We have a missing rodent and a missing girl. I hope it's part of a prank because what else could it be? Although if those idiots scare her, I am going to beat someone's ass."

"Liam, could you please take me home?" I asked.

"Of course, little cuz. Come on. I've got you." Liam nudged me toward his car.

"West?" I called over my shoulder.

"Yeah?"

"We will find her."

He closed his eyes. When he opened them, he nodded. Meanwhile, Liam kept an arm around me, patiently waiting for me to finish my conversation.

"After I change clothes and take a shower, I'll come to the pub and help search. Will you be there?" I

asked.

"I don't know, Shortcake," West said, just above a whisper.

If I hadn't been nauseous, dizzy, and had half-digested chunks of banana stuck in my hair, I would have run to West and wrapped him in my arms. Instead, Liam escorted me to his fancy sedan. He didn't bother to cover the expensive leather interior with towels before encouraging me to sit.

I crawled into the front seat and swathed him with cousinly affection. "I love you and I'm sorry for hurting Gina's feelings."

"I know. I'm sorry. I love you too. I know I can be a pain in the ass, but you're like my kid sister. I just want to protect you."

I melted into the seat. Someone or something had sucked up my energy. Although exhausted and filled with dread, I smiled. "Let's never fight again."

"Agreed," Liam said before laying a smooch on my barfy-smelling head.

Chapter 12

Although guests packed the inn, and Aunt Edith was missing her morning staff and quite busy, she took time away from work to greet us. Spot and Russ followed her into the foyer.

Russ grasped Liam's hand in an enthusiastic handshake. "Hey, Liam. Glad you made it. We heard someone stole the hog."

"Yep. Crazy morning." Liam hung his jacket on the antique coat rack.

Aunt Edith hugged him. When she faced me, she did a double take. "Honey, are you okay? You look awful."

Since my neurons were slow to fire, Liam answered for me. "Miranda got sick to her stomach while we were at the Schusters. I think she's upset about Cindi."

Spot nuzzled against my calf, so I squatted to scratch his ears.

"What's wrong with Cindi?" Aunt Edith asked.

"You haven't heard?" Liam asked.

My aunt's voice raised an octave. "Heard what? Is she okay?"

Liam placed his hand on her shoulder. "Mom, Cindi disappeared about the same time as the groundhog."

Aunt Edith covered her gaping mouth with a palm.

"Do you think she's with Bob?" Russ asked.

"Nobody knows," Liam said. "We thought she might be with the Schuster boys, but they haven't seen her since right before they left the festival. She isn't with West, Winona, or her dad. The last time we saw her, she was on stage with the Schusters."

"On stage?" Aunt Edith asked.

I kissed Spot and stood. "She is friends with Chad and stayed with him because he was afraid of being on stage in front of the large crowd. It seems that Cindi comforts her classmates if they are nervous."

"Walt headed to the Westinghouse ranch to see if someone gave Cindi a ride home," Liam said. "Winona went to the pub to tell the rest of the family, and West drove to the Littles to see if Tom's dad knows where Cindi's teacher lives. Maybe she stepped in to look out for Cindi when things got crazy."

"Have the police been called?" Aunt Edith asked.

"Shultz and his guys were actually there," I said.

Russ huffed. "Well, that'll be about as helpful as fertilizer on the Sahara."

Aunt Edith stepped away to call into the guest parlor. "Please excuse me for a moment. Help yourself to the sideboard, and I'll have breakfast ready soon." Upon returning to us, she steepled her hands. "Walt and June must be beside themselves."

"West thinks someone from Creekfield took her as part of the prank," Liam said.

"Heard about that show." Russ shook his head. "Damn pranks get more absurd every year."

"The guests have been talking. Was there really a Miss Bob Contest?" Aunt Edith asked.

More like a Miss Boob contest.

I pulled my shoulders back and lifted my chin. However, I didn't feel well enough to climb onto my soapbox. "Yes."

"Honey, did you get ill because you think something bad happened to Cindi?" Aunt Edith asked.

"Well, I'm worried that the Sch—" Not wanting to sound doomsday crazy, I checked myself and started over. "Since someone murdered Phil Nowak and Cindi stumbled onto the murder scene, she may be in danger. She didn't see who did it, but the killer may not know that and may think she saw something."

Aunt Edith clutched her chest. "Oh, my!"

"Damn," Russ said.

"Shit," Liam said. "I didn't think of it that way. I figured it was part of the prank or an unfortunate mix-up."

I couldn't bring up my distrust of the Schusters in front of Liam. I also couldn't discuss my odd intuition with my family. Go figure—I needed to talk to Greg.

I stared longingly up the stairwell. "Aunt Edith, after I shower, I'll help you with the guests. Then I need to track down Winona and West to see if they had any luck finding Cindi."

"Mom, I'll help serve breakfast, then I'm going to head out to find Tom and West."

Russ put an arm around my aunt. "After breakfast, we can let the clean-up go 'till later and see what we can do to help. Hopefully, they'll have found her by then, but if not, we'll organize a search party. We need to find her before the storm hits."

"Oh, no. More snow?"

No one acknowledged my question, probably because I fussed nonstop about the frigid Western

Pennsylvanian winters.

"I'll call Polly as soon as I can get a free minute," Aunt Edith said.

We took off to deal with our tasks.

I opened my bedroom door to Greg's animated insults. "Shit, you look like hell." He grimaced. "Gross! Do you have puke in your hair? You look like you stuck your finger in a light socket. What's all over your jacket?"

After taking off my coat, I held it in the air and moaned. I peeked in my mirror. Greg was correct. My Medusa-hair looked like I had been in an electrical storm. I grabbed the soap and a washcloth from my bathroom and grumbled as I scrubbed at the crusty gunk.

"I'm glad you're here. Let me shower. Then I'll fill you in. Don't go anywhere because I want to talk to you." I waggled my finger in his face. "And stay out of my bathroom!"

"Give it a rest. I haven't walked in on you in a couple of weeks."

I slammed the door in his face and locked it. Not that a lock, or a pleading request, dissuaded my perverted spectral in the least.

****

Twenty minutes later, my hair smelled like strawberries and cream. However, it was still absurdly frizzy. Blowing it dry at warp speed hadn't helped. After applying a light coat of makeup, I dressed in stirrup pants, fluffy socks, boots, and an extra-long wool sweater. Then I sat at my window seat so that I could peer out the window while I talked to Greg and scratched Spot.

Greg held Princess Pickles in one hand, patting the top of his adorable turtle head with two fingers.

As usual, Simon was in a mood and sulked in the corner of his cage.

"Where did you go?" I asked. "You disappeared."

"I was looking for the kid. Didn't see her, so I popped over to Creekfield for a bit".

"Did you see her there?"

"It's almost an hour drive. I was only there for about fifteen minutes. Unless she teleported there, we wouldn't have been in town at the same time," Greg said in his Miranda-is-an-imbecile voice.

I grunted.

"Our prank was fucking hysterical. Someone dyed the beaver pink."

"That's awful. What if the dye makes him sick?"

Greg snorted. "Who cares? It's a beaver, for fuck's sake. They're stupid animals."

I would have asked if groundhogs were more intelligent than beavers, but I didn't have time to listen to Greg vent for the next three hours.

"Why were you decorated with upchucked food?" he asked.

I filled him in on the voices slapping at my brain, the spinning room, two glowing humans, and my ciphered energy.

He carried Princess Pickles back to his cage and gently lowered him onto the grass. "So they had to let the help go? I bet the rumors that old man Schuster spent all the money are true."

"Seriously, I tell you a horrifying story, and you are more interested in the Schusters' finances?"

Greg tapped on Simon's cage and stuck his tongue

out at the rat. "Yeah, I hate gossip. It's just that SOB was always such a snotty ass to me."

I popped off the window seat. "I have to go help Aunt Edith. Then I need to find Winona and West."

Greg made a circle with his thumb and index finger, poking his opposite index finger in the hole numerous times. "This isn't the time for doin' the bartender, Crimson."

"Oh, Greg. Don't be such a pig. West is a mess right now, I just vomited in front of half the town, and my friend is missing. Besides, West thinks I'm a freak."

Greg's chuckles defied reason since nothing about my morning was humorous.

I opened the bedroom door at the same time he said, "Hey, what happened to that book the kid carries around?"

"How did you know about that? And last time I saw it, it was in West's glove compartment."

"I know everything that goes on in this town," Greg said. "Well almost everything."

I halted mid-step. "Wait a minute." I closed the door. "Why would whoever took Cindi put her notebook in the groundhog cage?"

"Kid probably put it there herself."

I lifted a finger into the air. "Holy guacamole. Cindi left her journal as a clue."

"Maybe," Greg said.

"Not maybe. Most definitely."

I bounded down three flights of stairs, Spot at my heels, and skidded into the kitchen. I accidentally let the door slam in Greg's face. He walked through the oak and shot me a middle finger.

"I think Cindi left us a clue," I announced.

Aunt Edith placed a waffle on a plate and stared at me.

Russ grabbed a paper towel to wipe raspberry cream from his face. "Get going, kiddo. Edith and I have this."

Since my coat was wet and maintained its grossout factor, I asked if I could borrow a jacket.

"Yes," Russ and Aunt Edith said in unison.

"Mom?" Liam asked, his eyes as big as the Belgian waffles.

"You go too," Aunt Edith said.

Liam tossed a tea towel onto the counter, and the two of us grabbed coats and took off for The Bear Claw Pub, as a loquacious poltergeist clamored at our heels.

****

The Westinghouse establishment was less than a five-minute walk down the hill from the inn, and our families had been neighbors for almost three decades. As an outsider, I found it odd that there wasn't a signpost announcing the business. Perhaps a bar that served the best cheeseburgers and fries in the county, and was owned by the infamous family's charismatic branch, didn't need to advertise who they were.

Most days, the only adornment on the plain two-story brick and timber building was a cardboard sign tacked to the door that read *Open All Week*. The stairs running along the far side sent thousands of butterflies afloat because they led to West's studio apartment and decadent kisses.

However, our destination at that moment wasn't West's abode. Instead, Liam and I stood studying a newly hung paper sign. Thick black letters spelled out *Closed for Business*—a not-so-good omen for a place that remained open three hundred sixty-four days a year. Especially since during the winter festival, it should have been packed.

Liam opened the door that sat front and center and stepped aside, allowing me to enter before him.

The pub's interior style was woodland rustic. Round tables, copper camp lanterns, a long maple bar, and wildlife photos decorated the room. The Westinghouse family, Officer Kline, and the DJ gathered around the bar.

There was no joy in the voices that greeted us. Winona's shoulders slumped forward, and she rested her elbows on the bar. Dinky sat beside her, and Kline, a cup of coffee in his hand, and a huge frown on his face, stood beside Will.

Winona looked so despondent that I put my arm around her.

She forced a smile that disappeared the second Dinky placed his hand on hers. Hopefully, it had finally dawned on her that she was dating King Doofus.

"Find Cindi?" Liam asked.

"She wasn't at home," Walt said. "June and Mom will call here if she shows up."

"Was she with her teacher?" I asked, even though the somber faces provided the answer.

Will shook his head.

"West called about ten minutes ago," his Aunt Polly said.

Liam cleared his throat. "I hate to bring this up, but there is a big storm coming in tonight."

"Yeah," Kline said. "The sheriff put me in charge of finding her before it hits. He is still dealing with the Fraternal Ring and Jacob Blackova. The other guys are stationed around town making sure the tourists don't get rowdy and that there are no more pranks".

As soon as I blurted out, "Really? Shultz made a plan?" I felt terrible because it served as a reminder to the worried family that our "official" help was inept. I was still berating myself when West and Tommy entered.

"Anything?" West said as he took off his jacket and came around behind the bar.

The numerous "nos" triggered larger frowns.

"Shit!" West grabbed two plastic cups and filled them with water. He held one in the air, offering it to Tommy.

Conversations happened all around me, but my attention was entirely on West as he listened to his father, uncles, and Kline.

I waved my hand to get his attention.

He moved closer to me. "You feelin' better?"

"Yes. Just embarrassed."

"No need to be," West said. "It's been one hell of a morning."

"Can—"

Just then, Keisha strolled into the bar. She called "hello" to everyone, smiled at Tommy, growled at the DJ, then crammed her body between Winona and Dinky so that Winona sat sandwiched between Keisha and me.

Undoubtedly, Keisha had put space between the feuding lovebirds to prove to Dinky just how despicable she found his pageant.

Still waiting to see what I wanted, West tilted his ear toward me, his hands firmly planted on the bar.

"Can we talk privately?" I asked.

He motioned for me to follow him to the storeroom. He closed the door behind us and looked down at me with tired eyes.

"Where is Cindi's journal?" I asked.

"Still in my glove compartment."

"I think she left us a clue about what happened to her."

West inhaled—perhaps my fruit-flavored hair? He shook his head. "No, Shortcake. Stop."

"West, she is intuitive and perceptive. I think people discount her intellect."

"I agree with you. But leaving a clue?"

I sat down on a stack of crates and swung my legs as he sighed a million different ways. Finally, he grabbed my hand and pulled me to my feet.

"Come on." He dragged me into the hallway and out the back entrance to his truck, where we sat, our heads close together as we studied Cindi's journal. I pointed to the images on the first page, explaining that Cindi had sketched my bedroom, pets, and the visiting ghost.

West let out a dramatic groan at the mention of Greg Grainey.

Meanwhile, I concentrated on Cindi's less-than-stellar artistic ability. Not that I had excelled at beginner art.

West flipped through the pages. "Do you understand any of it?"

"Go back. I think that is a hill, and you are the blue person skiing down it."

Squinting, West held the notebook closer to his eyes. "You're correct. And the supine stick figure is you on your ass?"

After a chagrined "What?" I grabbed it back.

"See the ski pole sticking out of your gut, the long red hair all over the place, and the big frown. That's exactly what you looked like the entire lesson." West laughed for the first time in hours as I knocked at his shoulder.

I displayed the following page. "Do you see the similarities between this and the page with Greg and my pets?"

West flipped back and forth between the two sketches. "Yeah. What's it mean?"

"I'm not sure."

Intent on studying the details, I leaned forward at the same time as West and we bumped noggins.

"Ouch," I murmured.

"Shit!" West ran a finger over my forehead "Does it hurt?"

I bit my lip. "Not anymore."

His breath hitched and he pulled his hand away.

I brushed the barely noticeable red mark on his forehead as energy crackled between us.

Rap! Rap! Rap!

We jumped.

Someone plastered their face against the driver's side window.

I shoved the journal inside Russ's oversized jacket.

West wound down the window. "Hey, Lieutenant Kramer. I'm glad you came."

"Of course," she said. "My favorite deputy is missing. We need to get moving before the snow hits."

"Cindi likes you a lot, too, Lieutenant. Shortcake, I called the lieutenant from Little's house to ask her to help us. You know? Shultz being an imbecile and all."

As much as I disliked the intense woman, she was our best shot at having law enforcement assist us, and it was obvious she had a soft spot for Cindi. "Hello, Lieutenant," I said through a fake smile.

"Our family and friends are inside," West informed her.

I stayed put as West got out of the truck and escorted the detective into the building. Once they were out of sight, I placed the book into the glove compartment.

By the time I caught up to them, Kramer and Tommy were amicably clasping hands.

"Glad you're here, Bonnie," Tommy said.

"Damn good to see you too, Tom."

Tommie and Bonnie were old chums?

Kramer strategically placed a chair in the center of the room. She climbed on top of it and clapped three times. Once everyone was silent, she projected her voice. "Listen up. Cindi needs to be missing for twenty-four hours to fill out a missing person's report, so this is all off the record." She cut her gaze to Kline.

He held up his palms. "Shultz told me to find her, so I'm following orders."

Kramer gave him a firm chin down in approval. "Is anyone at her house?"

"Yeah," Walt said. "Her brother and mom are looking in the woods around our place, and her grandmother is staying near the phone."

"Good. We are breaking into groups."

The door banged, and Aunt Edith, Russ, and Brad Gordon entered.

The lieutenant stopped barking orders to look them over.

"They're cool," said West.

"Okay," Kramer said. "As I was saying, we're breaking into groups. Go where I tell you and report back here immediately after your area has been searched. We have about five hours until the snow starts, and in about seven hours, nobody's going anywhere without a snowplow." She pointed to Winona, Dinky, and Kline. "You three are heading back to Pinkie's Steeple with me. I want every inch searched. Aunts and uncles, you are staying here. Keep the coffee coming and stay near the phones." Her hand swept to Keisha, Tommy, and West. "You three are driving to Creekfield and checking out the town. Head to the town hall first because the mayor has resources he is offering." Then she addressed Aunt Edith, Russ, and Brad. "Get a photo of Cindi and ask around town."

"What about me?" asked Greg.

"And you?" She glared at me, and her cheeks puffed.

I crossed my fingers, hoping that I was assigned to Keisha, Tommy, and West's group.

I waited.

"Fine! Then I'm going with Gordon," Greg announced.

Brad grimaced.

I bounced on my toes.

Everyone waited with bated breath.

I squirmed about.

"Doc Sweetcakes. You go home, curl up in bed and keep yourself out of trouble."

"Hey!" I stomped my foot.

For a group of despondent people, they sure could chuckle.

149

For the record, I appreciated in-charge females—even those that called me Sweetcakes and scowled at me. After all, liking and appreciating are not the same thing.

Chapter 13

It only took a lot of eyelash-fluttering and a couple of over-the-shoulder hair tosses to convince West to ignore Kramer and take me with him. I climbed into the front seat beside him, muttering under my breath, "Piece of cake."

Unfortunately, a disgruntled dead man pushed in beside me, forcing me to scoot closer to West. "Ugh! Greg, close the door!"

"La tee da da. I can't hear you," sang the passive-aggressive ghost with his fingers in his ears.

West hopped down and strolled around the back of his truck to shut the passenger side door.

"I know you can close a door since you slam them around all of the time, and I thought you were going with Brad," I said.

Greg removed his fingers from his ears to flick a dismissive wrist. *"He's in a mood. I think he needs to get laid. Come to think of it, you are acting bitchy. Maybe you also need to get laid."*

I was still giving Greg an earful when West slid in behind the steering wheel.

"He's probably in a bad mood because he hates the ground you glide on. And don't be a pig," I said.

Although I was talking to Greg, West responded. "I don't hate you. I'm upset about Cindi, and you're the one that's in my space." He secured his seatbelt. "Hey, are you reading my mind again?"

"No. Greg is sitting right here. I'm talking to him." I poked Greg in the shoulder. "And he is the pig."

"Ouch," Greg said dramatically—as if he could feel pain. *"Do you want my assistance finding the kid or not? Because I'm a huge help with this kind of stuff? I can move quickly, teleport—"*

West leaned across me and waved a hand in the space Greg occupied. The end of his fingers passed right through the grumbling ghost. "Is Grainey here now?"

"Yes. Wait. Back up. West, are you having piggish thoughts?" I fought with my lips, but they didn't cooperate and formed a stupid grin.

Greg chuckled. *"He's a man. Isn't he?"*

"No. It's just—Hey! It's not my fault. You're the one that's practically on my lap," West said.

"Because Greg is sitting in my spot."

"You can sit on my lap, Crimson."

I groaned.

West stuck the key in the ignition, and the engine turned over. "Does Grainey take up space, or is he like a fluffy cloud?"

Since both things could be true, depending on the human, Greg happened to be annoying, I said, "Yes."

Greg leaned close and shouted into my ear, *"Does Westinghouse just pretend to be a cocky ass, or is he really this much of a stupid bastard?"*

Since I ignored him, Greg folded his hands over his chest and stuck out his bottom lip.

"Why did you convince Little and Keisha to cover for us, and where are we going?" West asked.

"Greenport. We're going to see my friend Alina," I

said.

"Yum." Greg made a gross slurping sound.

"Why?" West asked. "Is she a superhero who can find missing people?"

"Yes. Pretty much."

West cut his gaze from the road to me. "What?"

"She's a medium like Cindi. I thought she might be able to sense Cindi or help us decipher the clues."

"Plus, she gives good head," Greg said.

I rolled my eyes.

We rode in silence for the next twenty minutes. West was probably thinking about "superheroes" and finding his cousin, and Greg was most definitely thinking about the delights that awaited him in Alina's store. I had a case of monkey brain. Everything from the stack of papers that needed to be graded, to the missing girl, to West's hip presently squished against mine crashed about in my mind.

The silence broke when West tapped *play* on the cassette player. "How about some music?" His normally out-of-tune singing voice took on its sexy drawl as he harmonized with Garth Brooks.

What a fascinating discovery. West wasn't a discordant crooner. However, he usually sang at the top of his lungs, distorting his voice. Not that I could have passed beginner choir class.

"Terrible." Greg huffed and popped the tape out.

West stopped singing. "Hmm." He pushed the cassette in and amplified his voice as he enthusiastically belted out something about whiskey and beer.

Ironically, I'd never seen the bartender singing about inebriants take even a sip of alcohol.

Greg popped the tape out again.

Annoyed, I shot Greg a side glance.

West held the steering wheel with one hand and retrieved the tape with the other. He held it up so that he could check it out while keeping his eyes on the road. He shrugged, pushed it into place, and once again pressed *play.*

West hadn't even started to sing when Greg swore and hit *eject.*

West frowned. "Grainey, if you touch my tunes again, I'm gonna break your goddamn ghost fingers."

"Westinghouse, you sing like someone shoved elk balls in your gullet," Greg shot back.

"Be quiet, Greg," I said.

"What did he say?" West wanted to know.

"Nothing," I said.

Greg leaned across me. *"I said my cock is three times bigger than yours!"*

I glared at Greg. "You're disgusting."

"What did he say, Shortcake?"

"Nothing," I said again.

"If you have shit you wanna say, man up and say it to my face," West said.

"Your shaft is fucking pint-sized," Greg yelled across the front seat.

I was just about to tell Greg what he could do with his supposed ginormous man-sized thingy when Alina's storefront came into view.

"There," I pointed. "See the sign that says Madame's Brews and true Psychic Readings: Palm's, Tarot, and Medium."

West parked his truck in front of the magical, mystical shop. Thank goodness we arrived before a fistfight broke out between the arrogant ghost and the cocky bartender. My heart may have been with Weston Westinghouse the Third, but he didn't stand a chance against the ruthless invisible phantom.

****

Three women in their early to mid-thirties stood at Alina's counter sniffing herbs and teas. Alina waved to us as we took our place in line.

Greg gawked at the women's behinds, shifting positions to take in the best view. As the women leisurely discussed the aroma that came from each container, I squirmed like a hyperactive toddler who'd consumed a few juice boxes. West swung his arms and shuffled his feet.

Greg patted one of the women on the rear, and she turned to face us. He winked. *"Hello, gorgeous."*

She smiled at West. Hi," she said as she nudged the woman beside her. Then all three arranged themselves so they could gawk at West.

How rude and presumptuous. Why would they assume that West wasn't my boyfriend? Flirting with another woman's man in front of her was brazen even for love-potion-shopping-bimbos. Besides, West was in love with me. The fact he didn't know it was beside the point.

A woman with long, brunette hair spoke. "You're the bartender in Bellmount."

"Yeah," West said, still shuffling his feet.

"You make a sexy Sex on the Beach."

Greg grunted and my lips vibrated.

West's gaze traveled from his feet to the girls' faces, and he graced them with his deadly grin. "Ya do say?"

As the girls giggled, I shot them with shrapnel-laced eye darts.

"Come by next weekend, and I'll make ya'll the best daiquiri you ever had," West promised.

Greg reached around one of the girls and pinched her behind. She looked over her shoulder and brushed her hand over her rump.

I punched Greg in the shoulder.

"Ouch!"

All three girls looked down their noses at me. They probably thought I was insane for punching at air. Besides being tactless, they were ungrateful since I was defending their honor against a sleazy specter. Sigh!

"Excuse me, ladies. I'd be super appreciative if y'all could finish up." West winked at the brunette. "Drinks on the house next time you visit my bar. It's important I talk to the lovely proprietress." He inclined his chin toward Alina.

The girls fluttered their lashes before turning forward to complete their purchases.

"Remember, de man of your dreams is very close," Alina said in her fake exotic accent. "And you, play hard to get," she told the brunette who liked skanky pink drinks.

Yeah, right. That's like telling Spot he can't chase squirrels.

Once she bagged their purchases, they passed by us, giggling and waving at West. As Greg watched their backsides retreat, West focused on Alina.

Once the door closed and the bells on the front door tinkled, Alina came out from around the counter and wrapped her arms around Greg. He jammed his tongue in her throat and caressed her rear. She kissed him back, running her hands up and down his back.

Although West's lips distorted into a grimace, his eyes widened with fascination. He leaned toward me and whispered, "Is she gettin' busy with a ghost?"

I fought a gag. "Yes."

"I think I can see his outline. It's kind of a white light," West said.

As Alina's foot slid up Greg's leg and over his hip, his ethereal form took on a more corporeal look. Her long skirt lifted, revealing a calf. Greg pulled the fabric higher and reached under it, exposing a good portion of her thigh. Alina's head tilted back as she moaned.

"Is it just me, or is that kind of sexy?" West asked.

I leaned away from him and shot him my are-you-insane look? However, West wasn't wrong. Alina was sensual and lovely, and something was fascinating about the way Greg became more life-like when she touched him and filled him with her energy. Even though I wasn't sure how I felt about the entire voyeur thing, everything seemed sexy with my aching body inches from West.

"Hey, you two." I waved my hands about until they stopped groping each other and looked at us.

Alina ran a hand over her mouth and fluffed up her skirt. She clinked toward us, held out her bangled wrist, and her voice took on its nasally tone. "You must be de man who's stolen our girl's heart."

My face burned scarlet, crimson, vermilion, and ruby.

West remained emotionless. Had he even caught the statement that made me want to climb into a bomb shelter for eternity?

"My cousin Cindi is missing. Can you help us find her?" West asked.

"Is this de young girl who can see de dead?" Alina asked.

"Yes," I said.

Alina brought a hand to her mouth. "Oh, my!" She traveled a circle around her shop, flipping the sign on the door to closed, blowing out a few candles, then motioning for the three of us to follow her up the stairs to her apartment.

****

West, Greg, and I sat around Alina's country-chic mint kitchen table amongst her flowered trinkets while she poured three cups of hot tea and arranged a plate of maple leaf cookies on a lace doily. I hadn't eaten since my early breakfast, and since I hadn't kept it down, I was starved. I devoured one of the treats in three bites. Alina continued to move about her kitchenette as we talked.

"Tell me, what's goin' on?"

After West repeated a detailed version of the story, I placed the book on the table. "Alina, she kept this journal. I think she left it as a clue."

Alina set a plate of quartered ham and cheese sandwiches front and center, then sat with us. She slid her round-framed glasses into place and picked up the book.

Meanwhile, I shoveled a mustard-covered square into me as she leafed through pages. Self-conscious about my appetite, I handed West a sandwich before I scarfed another. Greg scowled as West inhaled his snack.

Finally, Alina took off her glasses and set them on the table. The bright red nail of her index finger settled on her chin, and she stared into space.

I turned to the sketch of my bedroom. "These are my pets, and this is Greg. Do you see how she repeats these images on this page?"

Alina studied both pages. "I would say that this is the murder scene. She's drawn another ghost and de groundhogs. Your bedroom also shows animals and a ghost."

Eureka! "Of course," I said.

She pointed. "I think this is blood, and this is de knife."

"Oh." West leaned over to examine his cousin's art. "That makes sense."

Alina looked from me to West, replaced her spectacles, then turned her attention back to the book. "You can see she repeats de ghost in various pictures."

West and I abandoned our chairs to come around behind her.

"Is Phil Nowak's spirit following her around?" I asked.

"It better not be you, Grainey." West shot an intimidating glower at the precise spot Greg sat.

"Fuck you!" Greg gave West the middle finger.

"Perhaps it's this recently murdered man. Or maybe it's different ghosts," Alina said.

"Shit," West said.

I displayed the picture of us skiing.

Alina smiled. "I think there is also a hill in this other drawing." She held the notebook up. "There might be a house behind it."

Greg drummed his fingers on the table. *"Mountains, ghosts, animals, blood, knives, and skiing with Crimson and the pretty boy. What does it all mean?"*

Alina leafed through again, settling on the last drawing. "I don't know, but I think this is a crescent moon."

"It looks like it is on the building instead of above it," I said.

West did a double-take and grabbed the journal. "Wait a minute. I think that's an outhouse".

"An outhouse?" I asked.

"Where poor people shit," Greg said.

"I know what an outhouse is," I growled. "I just didn't know they still existed."

West held the drawing with one hand and traced it with the index finger of the other. "There is an outhouse at Uncle Walt's camp."

"Maybe the kid got scared, hijacked the rat, and is hiding out at her dad's camp waiting for you to come and save her," Greg said.

I repeated Greg's statement for West.

"How in the hell would she have gotten herself to the camp?" West asked.

"West, do you think the Schuster boys took her there? Chad is terrified they are going to get into trouble, and I think it is because they are lying about something."

"Damn," West said. "It's in the boondocks. There's no running water or electricity. She will freeze to death in a few hours without a fire."

"Would they have had time to take her there and get back to their house before we arrived?" I asked.

"We were talking to the cops at Pinkie's Steeple for a good forty-five minutes. If they rushed, maybe. It's about twenty minutes outside of Bellmount, close to Foxfield."

"But why would they take her there?" I asked.

"Who are these Schuster boys?" Alina asked.

"Do you remember the boy at the steeple who walked past us and radiated heat?"

Alina shivered.

"He and his twin brother are the mayor's sons," I explained. "They both seem like nice kids, but something is off. Chad is super sweet and has Cerebral Palsy. Jimmy Junior glowed on the stage today. Although as far as I know, I am the only one besides Cindi who noticed. He seemed to…" I searched for my words. "Alina, I think the crowd was hypnotized."

"I saw it. They fucking glowed," Greg agreed.

"I wasn't hypnotized," West said.

"Westinghouse, you looked like a fucking horny zombie staring at Cassandra," Greg said.

"They glowed?" Alina asked.

"Their mother glows too. Do you know why that might be?" I asked Alina.

"My great-grandmudder told a story of glowing fairies in de old country, and my grandmudder told tales of an iridescent German witch. She claimed she followed her around. Of course, my grandmudder hit the bottle to block out de spirits that followed her." Alina shrugged. "So, I don't know."

"Wow, in Transylvania?" West asked.

"Yes. Romania," Alina said.

Greg stood, reached for the ceiling, and stretched. *"You mean Brooklyn, sweetheart."*

I chuckled as Alina glared at Greg.

"Did I miss something?" West asked.

I'd explain that Alina exaggerated her exotic roots and hailed from New York at a more appropriate time.

"West, should we head to the camp to see if Cindi is there?" I asked.

"Yeah," he said. "But Grainey isn't going with us." This time West's scowl was wasted on an empty chair because Greg was leaning against the wall, deep in thought.

While West visited the restroom, I pinned Greg with my best pleading eyes. "Could you head back to Bellmount and let Brad know we are going to the camp? Ask him if he can call Aunt Edith and Pop so they don't worry. Tell them to say that we called his cellular phone to let him know. I'd prefer that nasty Kramer doesn't find out."

A sulking Greg didn't answer.

Alina slid to him and kissed him on the cheek. "Gregawhy, you will take this important message. Then tonight, you'll return to my bed and keep me warm."

Fortunately, when West again joined us, he had no idea that Greg smirked, claiming himself the superior male specimen.

West picked up Cindi's journal and grabbed another sandwich. "We have a long drive, Shortcake. First back to Bellmount, then to the camp, and it's gonna be damn cold. And you better use the bathroom before we go."

Alina packed our leftover lunch and cookies into a paper bag while I took West's suggestion.

After hugging us and pushing us out of the shop, Alina poked her head out the front door. "Be careful, my dears. Glowin' humans are a bad omen." She caught a snowflake on her tongue. "And de storm has come early."

Chapter 14

West's typically contagious energy was subdued. Although he pressed *play* on the cassette player, he didn't sing or whistle. He kept his eyes focused on the road, and as the pace of the snow quickened, he lowered the volume. By the time we reached Bellmount, we traveled at a snail's pace, and he had turned the music off.

Although happy to be near him, I couldn't take the silence another minute. I studied his long lashes and his muscular jaw. Oh, those lips. "West?"

"What's up, Shortcake?"

I mustered courage. "I know today isn't the best time to discuss this, but I need you to know something."

Just as I finished speaking, we entered a snow squall. The flakes hindered our visibility so much it was as if a white bed sheet wildly waved in front of us. West leaned forward to peer out the windshield.

On second thought, I couldn't open a can of worms amid horrific driving conditions.

A couple of minutes later, the snow lightened, and West sat back. "Is there something you want to tell me?"

"Never mind." I waffled as my index finger drew circles on the dashboard. "Yes! I enjoyed our dinner earlier this week, and I hope you can come whenever you have a night off. Don't worry. I don't expect you to be my date."

Since that wasn't what I had intended to tell him, and I did indeed want him to be my date, I swallowed and tried again. "Are you going to ask someone to be your date for Liam's Valentine's dinner party?" I held my breath.

"Nah, I'm cooking and I want to concentrate on the meal."

What kind of idiot discusses emotional matters in a two-and-a-half-ton vehicle skimming atop frozen water?

Me, apparently. "I need you to know that the kiss with Sean was because we were undercover and almost got caught. It seemed like the right thing to do at that moment. And it was before you and I were dating."

Call me *Idiot* with a capital I.

"I'm sorry, West. I know I should let it go, but it eats at me that you might not know what you meant to me. What you have always meant to me." Like a filterless fool, I kept blabbing, providing a flimsy excuse. "And I thought you were with another girl that night."

West sighed. "O'Sullivan told me. And I remember that night. I waited for you to come to me."

"Oh, West. I'm so sorry."

There was sadness in West's eyes when his gaze left the road to peer at me.

When he looked forward, he slammed on the brakes. The truck skidded, and the back end swung forward. Although my seatbelt held me in place, West's hand shot out to stop me from crashing through the windshield. The vehicle completed its fishtail in slow motion.

Once we came to a stop, I steadied my breath as my heartbeat flooded my eardrums.

"Are you okay?" he asked.

As if West wasn't aware of the Jack in the Beanstalk-sized oak illuminated by the headlights, I panted out, "We almost hit a tree."

"I can't see a damn thing through this snow." He exhaled and drummed his fingers on the steering wheel. "There's a flashlight in the glove compartment."

I willed my hands to stop quivering. However, they didn't behave, and I struggled with the coordination it took to open the glove compartment and hand him the light.

"Stay here." He left the key in the ignition, then exited the truck.

Despite the poor visibility, the headlights occasionally bounced off his bright jacket as he moved about. A few minutes later, he climbed into the cab and shivered. "It's a whiteout. I can't tell if I'm even driving on the road."

"How far is the camp from here?" I asked.

"The road sign up ahead indicates that we are about three miles away. Your seatbelt on?"

I nodded.

"We're going to go slow, and you are going to have to help me."

I held my breath and pointed out trees as West and I made that treacherous three-mile drive.

By the time we pulled in front of the cabin, daylight had faded. Snow had piled on the pitched roof, chunks of stone were missing from the unkempt fireplace, and the peeling door frame had long ago been painted barn red.

Once West turned off the headlights, we found ourselves in a disorienting darkness. Even the moon had disappeared behind the black sky and white wisps. I shoved Cindi's journal and our leftover lunch into my backpack. West switched on the flashlight, and we trudged through knee-high snow.

He kicked at a snowdrift about a foot from the door. Once his toe encountered what he was searching for, he bent down and brushed at the spot until a rock appeared. He retrieved a key from under it.

When he opened the front door, two feet of snow tumbled onto the planked floor. In the illumination provided by the Flashex, wet splotches the size of footprints appeared.

"Has someone been here recently?" I asked.

West pointed the light into every corner. "Cindi," he called into the dark.

No one answered.

"Shit," West said. "No one here."

"It's kind of cozy." I followed him into the center of the room, where I reconsidered my statement. Uncle Walt's camp was only thirty percent cute and seventy percent a hovel.

West cringed. "There's no water or heat. Mice call it home, and let's not even discuss the spiders."

I jumped and grabbed hold of him. "Spiders!"

"Yeah." He grinned. "As big as baseballs."

Unfortunately, if there was an arachnid about, West was more likely to pitch it at me than protect me from it. I shuddered.

Rustic and threadbare don't quite capture the state of the single-room building. The sparse furniture included a wooden table, two falling-apart cane chairs, a rocking chair with the tip of a rocker missing, and an old dresser. A patchwork quilt in shades of blue, brown, and gray covered the bed that had been pushed against a sidewall. Along the back wall ran a wooden cupboard, and on top of it sat a metal dish tub. Orange and yellow curtains concealed the cabinets' contents. Mugs, plates, and various odds and ends littered the shelves that hung one foot below the ceiling.

While standing beside a rusted kerosene heater that looked as if it had been pilfered from a landfill, West exhaled. "Let's check the outhouse."

I wrapped my arms around my torso and followed him back into the winter storm. West started the truck so that the headlights illuminated our view.

An outhouse that had probably been built out of scrap wood during the Great Depression sat about fifty yards behind the cabin. The rotting corners didn't quite match up. The carved moon stood front and center and provided an untoward peephole.

Even though I had no intention of ever relieving myself in the scary box, I was fascinated, never having seen an outhouse before.

"They smell like holy hell," West said. "I'd much rather find a tree."

I wrinkled my nose in horror.

"Plus, spiders jump on your head, and rats bite your ass."

I stopped walking and brought a hand to my mouth. Meanwhile, West vibrated with mirth.

"You're teasing me." I slapped his shoulder.

He snorted. "Nope. Rats and spiders love outhouses."

I performed something akin to a kegel, deciding

right then and there that I'd rather hold my bladder until the end of time.

"Cindi Lou!" West called.

No one answered.

Once we reached the yucky little building, West knocked below the crescent shape. "Hey, anyone in here?" When there was no answer, he pushed on the door.

I held my breath. However, there were no humans, vermin, or eight-legged creatures in attendance at that particular moment. I didn't wait around long enough to inhale the malodor.

West spent a moment in the abomination before making his way to my side. "Someone recently did their business." He grimaced. "Although, I have no idea if it was Cindi. If it was, and she tried to walk home, she'd never make it in this weather."

"How far of a walk is it?"

"Six, seven miles."

Not wanting to add to West's misgivings, I sucked up my gasp.

"Does she know the way to her house from here?"

"I doubt even under normal circumstances. And no way with this visibility."

I placed my hand on his shoulder. He didn't pull away, so I let my hand rest on him until he said, "Let's walk around."

West and I spent forever stomping about in those woods, calling out Cindi's name and looking for footprints. Our search halted when I fell into a snowdrift, twisting my ankle. West didn't tease me for my clumsiness. Shocking! Instead, he helped me stand.

With each step I took, pain shot from my foot to

my calf.

West stopped short. "You hurt yourself, didn't you?"

If I wasn't worried about Cindi, in terrible pain and cold and wet, I may have stared forever at West in the soft ray of the flashlight—pink-nosed and gorgeous, with the snow blowing about him. "I'm okay."

We marched onward.

Three grunts from me later, West again asked, "Did you hurt your ankle?"

I glared at my foot submerged in snow. "Yes. And the snow is so deep I'm having trouble lifting it." My out-of-shape thighs also burned.

West put an arm around me, absorbing some of my body weight, and we headed back the way we came. The more the snow came down, the more difficult it became to pick up our footprint trail.

About ten minutes later, the camp came into view. Thank goodness, because I was trying to decide if I would rather sit down and freeze to death or keep going despite the shooting pain.

Once in the cabin, West lifted me and carried me to the rocking chair. He lit a green kerosene lantern, set it beside me, then built a fire.

I peeled off my jacket and gloves.

After he had the fire roaring, West pulled off my boots and gently explored my ankle. He sighed, then rooted around in the dresser, tossing a pair of thick socks, a towel, and flannel pajamas onto the bed. "Dry off and put these on. I'm going back out to look for her."

As cold as I was, I didn't want to stay by myself. "I'll go with you."

"No. You need to dry off, warm up, and keep your ankle elevated. Plus, you have to keep the fire going."

I protested as he pulled one of the chairs in front of me and helped me prop my foot on it.

"Look," he said, "you're going to slow me down. Plus, I might need the smoke from the chimney to find my way back here. We almost got lost earlier."

I resigned myself to the broken rocking chair.

He inclined his chin to the fireplace. "You think you can keep it going?"

"Yes." Years ago, I had helped Russ build backyard bonfires, so I knew how to stoke a flame.

"Change your clothes and keep the fire going. Other than that, keep your foot up." The door slammed into place behind him.

As soon as he was gone, I limped to the bed and stripped off the wet leggings. Walt's pants were so big that I couldn't keep them on my hips, so I laid them on top of the quilt. I donned the flannel top, which hung to my thighs, and slid my feet into the socks. Carrying the lantern, I gingerly poked around the cabin. After placing our leftover lunch on the table, I rooted through the cabinets and added a box of graham crackers, fruit cups, and a jug of water to our meal.

I peeked into a red cup inside the metal bin and gagged. Spittle and chewing tobacco.

Since the nightshirt was long, I slipped out of my soaking wet panties and laid them on the hearth. Placing the kerosene lantern beside me, I sat in front of the warm fire studying Cindi's journal. The longer I waited for West to return, the more my anxiety increased.

About thirty minutes later, West burst through the

door, startling me.

No Cindi.

He shook the snow from his body and shivered. "Fuck!" On his way to the fireplace, he shed his snow-covered layers.

"West, I think that Clive was the one who was here."

He held his hands near the flame and rubbed them together. "What makes ya say that?"

"There is fresh chewing tobacco in a red cup in the dishpan."

West grabbed the lantern and left the warm fireside to check out the contents of the gross cup. He lifted the curtain to peer under the faux sink.

"Empty whiskey bottle and fast-food wrappers. Uncle Walt never leaves trash, and Clive is a hog."

"Was he here looking for Cindi?"

"He didn't have the clue like we did. Knowing Clive, he was looking for a place to hide out and be lazy."

"West, I have a feeling the Schuster boys dropped her here with the groundhog. I bet somehow Clive got a phone call, found out she was here, and now she is back at home, safe and sound."

West tapped a palm on the counter. "Yeah. I bet you're correct. It's gonna be a rough drive so let's head out." His gaze settled on my panties, and a grin spread from ear to ear.

Even though West had seen me numerous times without underclothes, a scorching heat singed my body. "They are wet from when I fell."

Using his thumb and index finger, he picked them up. His eyes gleamed, and his smile was wicked.

"Soaked panties. Sexy!"

Finally, West was again flirting, but there was nothing sexy about putting on my wet clothes. I groaned.

West tossed them onto my lap. "Why don't I warm up the car while you change? That way, you won't freeze to death. I'll pack up our sandwiches, and we can eat them on the way."

"Okay," I said, despite dreading the feel of squishy underclothes.

West filled my backpack. It took me forever to lift my body from the rocker. First of all, it was finally warm. Second, putting my body weight on my injured leg made me want to scream. I had just lowered my propped foot onto the ground when the door banged open.

"Shit! Shit! Shit!"

My heart tripped over itself. "Is it Cindi? Is she okay?"

West rubbed his forehead. "I never turned the lights off."

"Oh, no. The headlights?" I asked, knowing full well that was what he meant.

West sat and dropped his forehead into his palms. "I screwed up. The battery died, and nobody knows we're here."

"Greg knows we're here," I said.

"Great," he said, sarcasm oozing.

Yeah, great. Greg Grainey was probably tucked into bed between his pretty paramour and a warm crocheted afghan blanket.

****

Fifteen minutes and an unfortunate outhouse

experience later, West wore Uncle Walt's pj bottoms, I still wore the flannel top, and we were sitting at the table partaking of dinner by kerosene lantern light. Our clothes dried all around us. West used a plastic bag and snow to make an ice pack, insisting I prop my foot on the rocker. The leftover sandwiches, cookies, syrupy peaches, and company made a satisfying meal. The graham crackers, not so much.

I had just taken a chomp off the end of one of the crackers when West asked, "Where ya get those?"

I smiled. "The cupboard." I'd done an excellent job of foraging for food, considering our circumstances.

West narrowed his eyes.

"Your uncle won't mind, will he?"

He looked into the box and cringed.

I dropped the cracker. "What's wrong with them?"

"Nothing." After sealing the box, he carried it to the counter, lifted the curtain, and deposited it into the trash can.

"West! Tell me!"

He grimaced. "Nothing."

"Tell me this instant," I demanded.

He sat across from me, rubbed his nose, and snorted. "Umm. Mice."

"Mice! Yuck!" I spit onto my paper towel a few times, then scrubbed my tongue with my fingers. "Augh! Yuck! West!"

He chuckled. "Don't you know, you never eat open food at a camp. Unless you're craving mouse turds and ants?"

"That's disgusting. How could you let me eat it?"

"I thought maybe Alina had sent them. Plus, you were shoveling food in, and I didn't have time to stop you."

I considered vomiting in his lap.

He opened one of the fruit cups and popped a maraschino cherry into his mouth. "Here." He held a peach in the air.

I shook my head.

"These are fine." He slurped down the one he held, then used his fingers to spoon out another. "Come on. They're good."

I scowled. "Just like the worm you convinced me to eat when I was four."

West threw his head back and laughed. "You gotta get over that."

"Never." I crossed my arms over my chest and pouted.

West looked into my eyes, bit off the tip of a peach, and placed the fruit close to my lips. "I promise. It's okay."

The things I let Weston Westinghouse the Third convince me to do when he stared into my eyes, got close to my lips, or spoke softly.

I licked at his peach.

His breath hitched.

I took a tiny bite.

He tossed the rest of it into his mouth.

I bit my lip.

"There," he said. "All better. Nothing gross in your mouth. Just peaches and sugar."

And hopefully, some of West's saliva. He was correct. I was all better.

He finished off his fruit, refilled a plastic cup with water from the two-liter jug, and handed it to me. "You really think Cindi's back home?"

"Yes." Afraid of the outhouse, I sipped sparingly. No full bladder for me. "I'm certain that she was afraid that the groundhog was going to get hurt, so she convinced the Schuster brothers to help her get Bob to safety."

West grinned. "That's a Cindi move."

"You think there is enough wood to keep us warm tonight?"

"Yeah. In the morning, I'll walk to my grandmother's. It will take me about two and a half hours. I'll get Uncle Walt to drive me back here with jumper cables. You'll be home by late afternoon."

A twinge of anxiety hit me. I would lose the time I spent Sunday mornings preparing lectures and correcting papers. The pang only lasted for a moment because I was about to spend an evening in a secluded cabin with the man who consumed my fantasies.

West's gaze focused on the flames.

"Penny, for your thoughts," I said.

"I'm thinking about pizza. Man, what I wouldn't give for some pepperoni and extra cheese." He licked his lips.

"I have a twenty in my backpack."

"On our way home tomorrow, you're buying me pizza."

I batted my lashes. "What have you done to earn pizza?"

West gathered up our trash, tossed it into the receptacle under the counter, and brushed his hands together. "I did the dishes."

"That took three seconds."

He puffed up his beautiful bare chest. "I'm also going to help you over to the fire and make sure you stay warm."

Oh, the many ways that Weston the Third could raise my body temperature.

"Fine. If you keep me warm, I'll buy you a pepperoni pizza

He stood, then waved his hand inches from my face bringing me back to the moment. "Don't forget the extra cheese." He removed the ice pack, tossing it into the dishpan. After lowering my foot onto the floor, he pushed the rocking chair in front of the fireplace. He helped me to stand, then swung his arm under my thighs and lifted me.

"Quadruple cheese and I can walk."

"Let's be clear. You can limp."

I wrapped my arm around his neck and enjoyed the five-foot sojourn from the table to the fire.

West lowered me onto the rocker, then retrieved the lantern and Cindi's journal before pulling a chair close. He sniffed. "Ya smell like Uncle Walt before he showers."

So much for the romantic ride in my prince's arms.

He bent forward and took a whiff of his thigh. "Of course, so do I. I wonder when these pajamas were last washed?"

"Augh," I groaned. Although West smelled like he always did—yummy!

He leaned close to me. We leafed through the book, studying each page, and theorizing.

"Wait," I said. "Go back."

West flipped a page.

I pointed to a sketch that fascinated me. "I think that is a lunch table. And that is a ghost."

"Maybe. What does *CKIE* spell?"

I tapped the book. "I bet it means cookie. I think that is the ghost who asked Cindi for a cookie at school. She told Lincoln and me about it."

West narrowed his eyes. "A ghost at school?"

I nodded.

"Why'd she draw red shit on this kid?" He pointed at a stick figure that was covered in scribbles. "Is that blood?"

I placed a finger on my chin and thought. "Perhaps it's Jimmy Schuster. I think she sees the same red glow that I see."

"What's it mean?"

"Cindi told us that she had a friend at school that was special. I thought she meant Chad because he is in classes with her. I wonder if she meant Jimmy and was referring to some sort of telepathic ability."

West shifted in his seat, stretched out his legs, and wriggled his toes. "I don't get it."

"Lincoln and I told her she is special because of her telepathic ability. She told us she is in special classes at school. I think she used the word correctly in both cases, but Lincoln and I misinterpreted it."

West handed me the journal before throwing another log on the fire. "Gross." He flicked his wrist, and whatever he had found distasteful flew into the air.

When a withered spider, the size of Jupiter, landed in my lap, I screamed, dropped the journal, and jumped out of my seat. My injured ankle didn't support my weight, so I stumbled backward, careening over the rocker. "Fudge," I screeched as I landed on my butt with a thud.

West was by my side in an instant. "Are you okay?"

I flailed my arms about. "Where's the spider?"

He tried to pick me up.

"Where's the spider?" I called out again.

"It's dead," he said, pulling me from the ground.

I pushed on him attempting to get as far away from the defunct arachnid as possible. I hopped on my good foot to the bed, plopping down on the mattress. "If it was that big dead, how big was it when it was alive?" I whimpered.

West chuckled. "Big ass. Probably had thirty long hairy legs. Are you okay?"

I glared at him. "Of course, I'm not okay. You threw a spider on me. I don't have an ankle, and now my tailbone is broken."

West laughed so hard he had to brace himself to stay upright. "I didn't mean to throw it on you." He chortled. "You still have an ankle. You didn't break your ass. It's probably just bruised."

I slapped my thigh. "Stop laughing!"

West sat on the bed beside me and tickled under my chin. "Want me to double-check to make sure your ass is in one piece?"

At that moment, the only thing in the world that I wanted more than for West to "double-check" my body was for him to stop laughing, so I huffed at him.

The next thing I knew, his fingers played itsy bitsy spider as they crawled up my thigh. Since I even hated imaginary bugs, and I had a serious panty issue, I swatted at him.

He ignored my protests and continued to tickle me until I gave up fighting and giggled.

He laughed as we wrestled about for a minute. Unfortunately, he stopped touching me, and his lips formed a straight line. "I'm sorry, Shortcake. I shouldn't tease you. You went down pretty hard. Are you okay?"

I had vomited my guts out and been forced to use an outhouse in front of an Adonis. I had spent the afternoon filled with anxiety over Cindi, glowing humans, and treacherous roads. I had fallen and injured my ankle. I had shared a cracker with a mouse, had a gargantuan tarantula thrown on me, was freezing cold and underwear-less. I had bruised my tailbone and suffered massive insults from Bellmount Bitches, intense detectives, and sleazy cops. And worst of all, I smelled like a deodorant-less Uncle Walt.

I smiled. "I'm okay, West."

That was the God's honest truth. As long as I was sitting beside Weston Westinghouse as he studied me with compassionate eyes, I was one trillion percent wonderful.

Chapter 15

West tossed the spider remnants into the flames, and to placate me, did a quick search of the camp, promising to escort any rodents, bugs, or dead things into the great outdoors. His carrion hunt unearthed fly wings, a ladybug shell, and a fermenting apple.

Since we needed to ration the kerosene, he extinguished the lantern, and soon we were back in front of the fire warming ourselves and talking about life. He listened to me ramble on about the new semester and the book I was reading. Then he told me a story about Pop slicing his finger while cutting a potato. His excitement over his upcoming cross-country motorcycle trip was contagious. Since he was reading *Treasure Island,* we compared and contrasted my contemporary read, *A Prayer for Owen Meany*, with Stevenson's classic.

As our evening wore on, I tried to hide my yawns. Eventually, West caught me in the act.

"It's been a tough day. Why don't you get some sleep?" he said.

"I'm not tired." I wiped a water droplet from my eye. "I want to stay up a little longer and talk."

He ruffled my hair. "You need sleep. After we get this mess straightened out, we can talk while we eat that pizza."

"Promise?"

"Yeah," he said. "I'll tell you what else. Next time I have off, I'll take you and Cindi for ice cream, and we can talk to her about why she can't steal animals, run away, and hide out at the camp."

I was exhausted, so with the promise of future time with West, I limped to bed. Balancing on one leg, I hovered beside the bed and grimaced.

"What's up, Shortcake?"

I showered the quilt with contemptuous glares. "Do bugs and mice get into the bedding?"

He chuckled. "If there is anything in those blankets, it froze to death two months ago."

I crossed my hands over my chest and shivered. "Can you check?"

He smirked.

"Please," I pleaded, using my pretty-please-with-sugar-on-top voice and prayer hands.

West wriggled his toes. "Of course." He stretched his legs, then stood. "The things you convince me to do."

I rolled my eyes. "The things I convince you to do? Are you kidding?"

For the next thirty seconds, we engaged in a full-on squinted-eye standoff that ended with us both smiling.

"I'm susceptible to bug bites. Remember how bad my rashes were when we were kids?" I reminded him so that he didn't think me too fussy. "That's why I don't like them."

"Yeah. You used to get those bloody welts all over." He made a yuck-face, chucked a log into the fireplace, and joined me beside the bed.

The fire illuminated the edge of the mattress closest to the center of the room. The far end was dark and probably hid a dead bug or two.

He pulled the blanket back and rubbed the sheet. "No critters. Now lay down."

"Aren't you going to sleep?"

"I'm up late because of work all the time, so I'm going to stay awake and keep the fire going." He patted the mattress. "Come on. I'll keep an eye out and make sure nothing bites you while you're sleeping." He distorted his face and gnashed his teeth. "Unless I get hungry for scaredy-cat blood. Then I might take a big old bite out of your neck."

Pretending to be offended, I flicked him a dismissive wrist. The truth was he could nibble anywhere he wanted.

He tapped the bed again. I sighed and took my time crawling onto it.

Since my hair caught under my back and in my armpits, I lifted my head, gathered the ringlets together, and arranged them on the pillow so they fanned out around me.

West leaned over like he meant to tuck me in. Instead, he hopped onto the mattress, chanting, "The itsy bitsy spider climbed up Albright's spout." He tickled me until my body convulsed.

My giggles and swats only encouraged his shenanigans. I wriggled under him like a squirmy puppy until he stopped his taunting to hiss.

Uncle Walt's shirt had risen, reminding us that my underwear still sat on the hearth. I pulled the nightshirt into place. West scooted to the edge of the bed and sat with his back to me.

"Sweet dreams, Shortcake."

Covering my exposed parts had to be instinct

because fantasies starring the two of us naked bombarded me nonstop. I wanted him to wrap his arms around me, whisper scandalous things into my ear, and kiss me senseless. I certainly didn't want him to turn his back to me or leave that bed.

He stood.

"West?"

He glanced over his shoulder.

The effect my D cups had on him seemed to be my best chance of luring him under those covers. I bit my lip and undid a button.

He did a double-take and faced me. His eyes widened, and his lips parted.

I undid the next button.

His exhale sparked a tingle in my nether regions.

I undid the last two buttons and pulled the shirt open, exposing my entire body.

"Fuuuuuuck," he puffed out as he moved closer and hovered over me. "You look like a forest nymph." His husky voice sent my heart to my feet.

"Really?"

"Yeah. With your hair like that. And your pale skin and green eyes. Or, like a siren who lures a man to his demise."

Even though I had arranged my hair for comfort and not seduction, I embraced my full-out temptress.

"You aren't playing fair, beautiful."

I brushed a hand from my neck to my hip. "What's not fair?"

West's breath blew across my cheek. "Using your body to confuse me. I'm trying to behave, and I'm looking at those luscious breasts."

His statement triggered my undulation and a moan.

"Why behave?" Even though West hadn't touched me, my traitorous hips again lifted off the mattress as I emitted a guttural, "Ohh."

Talk about *unfair*! I intended to taunt him, but wherever his eyes settled, I came alive, then writhed.

Propping on his side, he lay beside me. The firelight dappled across his muscular shoulders and lit up the amber specks in his pupils. The man in front of me was so spectacular that I forced myself to take in air.

He twirled a ringlet. "What do you want?"

"You, West," I panted as my breasts took their turn rising off the mattress.

"What do you want me to do?" he asked, his words caressing my ear.

"Everything. Please," I begged.

He traced a decadent figure eight around my breasts, eventually settling back in the center. "I miss fucking you."

Liquid trickled between my thighs. "Deep inside me," I pleaded.

West tugged the nightshirt off me, threw it across the room, then placed his finger into my mouth.

I sucked it in, devouring his decadent masculine tang that I craved.

"Is this what you want deep inside you?"

"Yes." And so much more. I moaned and wrapped my tongue around his finger.

His other hand journeyed its way down my body, stopping to roll each nipple between his fingers. Then it traveled south, resting between my thighs. He parted me. "How about here? Deep inside your pretty pussy."

I ached to cry out, but the finger in my mouth

muffled my response. I wrapped my hands around his neck, pulling him to me. West filled every inch of me as his tongue took over exploring my mouth, and his finger continued searching my aching insides.

After kissing me until I couldn't think, he made his way to my ear to purr, "You're so wet."

Shame over my animal-like reaction to him caused me to say, "I'm sorry."

"Don't be sorry. I want to fucking drown in it."

"Oh, God!"

His other hand caressed, kneaded, and danced its way down my body, eventually spreading me wide to assist in the exploration of my insides.

Capturing my gasps in his mouth, he absorbed them, mixed them with his moans, and sent them back.

I tickled, then tightened. "Right there."

"Right there, beautiful?" He rubbed at my pleasure spot.

"Yes!"

He traced another circle.

My body buckled. "Yes!" I cupped his ear to confide, "I'm on the Pill now."

"Mmm," he growled. "I'm going to worship your sweet pussy until you explode. Then I'm going to come deep inside you."

"Yes. That's what I want."

His lips left my ear to paint a trail down my torso. Each kiss ignited a spark, making me vibrate. Once he reached his destination, he peeked at me from between my thighs. I gasped at his wicked grin.

"Right here?" His finger again teased my special spot.

"Ohh!"

"Yum," he said right before his mouth took over.

I tossed my arm across my forehead and closed my eyes as West's magical tongue flitted in and out of me. He knew exactly where to lick, where to suck, and when to nibble.

When a new tingle caused me to spasm, I threaded my fingers into his hair to keep myself grounded. My hips bucked, and I pushed his face tight against my pelvis.

West moaned inside of me, sucking harder.

Consumed with the tight little ball that sat beneath his lips, I begged, "Don't stop."

With his mouth and fingers both inside me, I kaboomed! "West!" I cried as waves of pleasure rolled over me, rocketing me to the moon.

A wet-lipped, heavy-lidded West crawled up my body. His smile mischievous, he ran a hand across his mouth, wiping away the evidence of our scandalous lovemaking.

I reached for the waistband of the pajama bottoms. Athlete that he was, he hovered above me, ridding himself of the pants in record time.

"Do you see what you do to my cock?" He guided my hand to his swell.

I wrapped my hand around it. "Yes."

"Fuck!"

I shoved West's offering inside of me before I withered away to nothingness from raw need. He sucked in a breath and pushed into me so hard my body heaved, and I howled.

Four thrusts later, I begged, "Harder," as I scraped my fingernails down his back.

He kissed me before slamming his hips against

mine. I wrapped my arms around his neck and my legs around his waist, meeting his thrusts with an equally violent force.

"I'm going to come," he grunted.

"Deep inside me!"

His jaw tensed, and his eyes rolled back. He grew and grew until he exploded. "Miranda!" he roared into the rafters.

At last! That thing I craved more than air. He came and I milked. Every female inch of me sucked that liquid in, pulling it into my core.

I clamped my mouth closed, fighting to keep an impending *I love you, West* tucked inside of me.

****

I lay beside West, a boneless, heaving mass of mush. I rested my head on his chest and listened to the repeating, *thump-thump, thump-thump*.

"I won't read your mind," I told him. "I promise. I just want to cuddle."

He peered into my eyes as he brushed my out-of-control hair to the side. Oh, please let him say something wonderfully romantic.

"When ya go on the Pill?" he asked.

Not the earth-shattering proclamation I'd hoped for. "Before Christmas. So that we could do things like this."

He pillowed his head on his forearms and nestled his body into the mattress. "That was fucking wild."

"Amazing!"

"Are you hurting?"

"No," I shook my head. "It felt heavenly."

He chuckled. "I meant your ankle and your ass because you're a klutz."

I didn't have an ounce of indignation left in me, so I ignored his teasing. "No. You made them all better."

He exhaled a soft sigh and pulled me to him. "Sleep tight, beautiful." He kissed the top of my head. "Don't think that fucking me gets you out of buying that pizza."

My head bobbled up and down on his torso as he chuckled.

The flames flickered, casting golden patterns on the wall as West's heartbeat played an intoxicating lullaby. Eventually, I closed my eyes and fell asleep with a grin plastered across my face.

Chapter 16

I awoke two times during the night. The first time I was cold, and the fire was dying, so I nestled myself against a sound-asleep West's warmth. The second time, he lounged in the rocking chair in front of a roaring fire with Cindi's journal in his lap. I fell asleep before I could call him back to bed.

When the sun peeking through the window woke me, West was staring into the flames with a faraway look in his eyes. The scene in front of me was so perfect that I didn't want to disturb it. With the intensity of a creepy voyeur, I held my breath and studied his profile. His hair was matted and stood in the air, he'd developed a five o'clock shadow overnight, his cheeks were flushed, and he was again wearing pajama bottoms. Even West's messy morning look made me gooey.

An electric current surged through me, screaming, *West kisses.* I positioned my body in what I hoped was a seductive pose, grimaced because a pain shot through my buttocks, then pulled the blankets down, exposing my body. "West," I whispered.

He faced me and stood. One side of his mouth twisted upward to form a crooked grin.

Holy guacamole! That bare torso. How often did he have to shave to keep his chest smooth, and how many women had run their hands over it? Shaking my green-eyed monster to Alpha Centauri, I smiled back.

He stalked across the room and was about to pounce on me when I screamed and pulled the covers to my chin. A wide-eyed West stopped dead in his tracks and searched the room.

"Greg," I screeched. "Why can't you learn to knock?"

"That would ruin all the fun." Greg flashed me a smart-alec grin. *"Damn, you have a nice body."*

"Ack," I sputtered. "You scared me to death. I hate when you do that."

"What the hell, Grainey? Get lost," West called to the air.

Greg shot West a middle finger, then faced me. *"You'd think you two could dial back the fuck fest until we find the kid."*

"What are you talking about? Isn't she at home?" I asked.

"What's he saying? Is it about Cindi?" West asked.

"She's still missing," Greg said. *"What made you think she was at home?"*

West frowned. "What's going on?"

I held up a hand to quiet West. Being the intermediary in ghost conversations required the diplomacy of a prince, the patience of a saint, and the firmness of a prison warden. "We thought Clive had found her, then taken her home. The battery died in the truck, and we got stuck here overnight. We haven't heard anything."

"Shit," West said.

Greg sat on the edge of the bed like I wasn't naked, and West wasn't a foot away. *"Clive? That stupid bastard couldn't find his way out of a three-foot maze."*

He cut his gaze to West. *"Pretty boy flood the engine or leave the lights on?"*

I slapped my hand on my thigh. "Greg, just tell me what's going on."

Greg bobbled his translucent head. *"Apparently, nobody has seen the kid since she got off stage. Just disappeared. Schuster called a press conference for today at eleven at the town hall."*

West paced from the bed to the fireplace and back again.

"No leads at all?" I asked.

"Nothing," Greg said. *"And everyone is looking for you and King Cocky."* Your aunt is worried, and Weston senior is fit to be tied."

West halted his frantic movement. "What did he say?"

I sighed and shook my head.

"You want me to let Gordon know you are stuck here and see if he'll bring some cables?" Greg snickered. "Or you want me to leave you here with your sex toy."

I scowled and used Winona's favorite expression. "For Pete's sake, get us help."

Greg chuckled, then disappeared.

"He's gone," I said.

West plopped on the edge of the bed in the same spot Greg had just occupied. "Tell me what's going on?"

I pulled my legs up to my chest and wrapped the blanket around me. "Clive didn't find her."

"I got that part," West said.

"They don't have any leads or clues, and they are looking for us."

West's sigh was so heavy that I felt it in my core.

"I guess I better head to Grandma's and have Uncle Walt give us a hand. You stay here and keep warm."

"Greg is getting us help."

West narrowed his eyes. "How's he doing that?"

I knew what Greg was up to, but I didn't know how to break the news to West, so all I said was, "We better get dressed."

We spent the next few minutes in silence as West tossed my clothes onto the bed. Then lecherous thoughts consumed me as I watched him dress. *Not the right time,* I scolded myself.

As I fumbled with my bra, West made a guttural noise that tickled my skin. I clasped it, and then self-conscious about cellulite, I faced him. Hooded eyes watched as I pulled my sweater over my head. Crawling across the bed, I let out a whimper when my weight pressed into my ankle.

"Are you hurting?" he asked.

Pain shot through my hindquarters, and my foot ached, but it seemed selfish to complain in our current circumstances. "I'm okay."

"Fibber."

I faked a smile as I slid into my panties and leggings. I parked on the bed and was about to put my socks on when he stopped me.

"I'm going to make you another ice pack. Be back in a second." He grabbed the plastic bag from the dishpan and went outside.

As soon as the door closed, I cradled my head and moaned. Something was very wrong, and I had misled West into thinking things were okay, then seduced him. Saying I felt guilty was an understatement.

"Hey, Crimson, you okay?" Greg asked.

I looked up to find his ethereal form standing in front of me.

"This is bad. Isn't it?" I asked.

"Yeah. How does a kid just disappear?"

"She didn't just disappear," I said. "So where is she, and is she okay?"

Greg shrugged. "They are arranging a four-county search party at the press conference. Kramer is going ape shit. Anyway, Gordon is on his way to get you two."

"Thanks."

"I think I'm gonna head back up to the Steeple to poke around."

I nodded as Greg disintegrated.

"Hey, Greg, I called to the air.

He reappeared. "What?"

"My student, Mason, said something is up with the Fraternal Ring. Can you check them out?"

"Something besides being a bunch of geekified nerds with a rodent hang-up?"

"You are impossible." I huffed. "I don't think they are getting along. Also, those Schuster boys are up to no good, and there is something very odd about their mother."

"On it." Greg clicked his heels and disappeared a moment before West came through the door carrying my makeshift ice pack.

West helped me to the rocking chair, propped my foot up, and secured the ice in place. His energy heavy, he sat in the chair next to me. "Hey, Shortcake. Why did you tell me Clive found Cindi and that she was safe? Did your superpowers mess up?"

How had I screwed up so badly? I turned the last twenty-four hours over in my head, trying to make sense of it. I struggled to look him in the eyes. "I don't know. I was sure the Schuster brothers had dropped her off. Since Clive had also been here, I think I jumped to a conclusion."

West stared into the fireplace.

"I'm sorry, West. I really thought that was what happened. Maybe it was wishful thinking."

He retrieved the journal from the table and leafed through it. "She didn't leave us a clue, did she?"

"I don't know." I closed my eyes briefly before saying, "Brad Gordon is on his way to get us."

West's eyes narrowed, and his jaw tensed. "How does Doc know where we are?"

Anxiety-infused butterflies sucked up my air. How could I explain that Brad could communicate with Greg? I shrugged.

"Out with it!"

I stood, pain shooting through my entire body.

"What are you doing?" West asked.

"I hurt. I want to stretch out on the bed." I needed to get away from him before I got all emotional and said something like: Don't you understand that I cheated on Brad with you because you are the man who has always possessed my heart? Or, why can't you get that the kiss with Sean meant nothing because we were undercover, and it was before you and I were an item? And then there was the worst thing I might say: Brad is like Cindi and me.

"Okay," West said. "But put a pillow under your ankle."

I took my soggy ice bag with me, leaned against

the headboard, and stretched out my legs.

A minute later, West joined me and lifted my foot, placing it on a pillow. "Something bad happened to her. Didn't it? She's such a good kid. One of the best people in the world. And she's so damn innocent."

"We'll find her," I promised.

He collapsed beside me, laying his head on my lap. I rubbed his temple in what I hoped was a comforting motion.

"I'm glad you moved to town, but weird things have been happening ever since."

My breath hitched.

"I know it's some sort of coincidence. It's just making love to a woman who can read my mind, ghosts popping in and out of the room, people who can talk to the dead, a heroic doctor who seems to show up whenever you're in trouble." He swallowed. "There are murders every other day, and Cindi disappeared into thin air. It's a lot for an unsophisticated country boy like me to digest."

"I know," I whispered. "I don't understand any of it either, and you're not unsophisticated; you're perfectly charming."

"Am I losing my mind?"

"You're the most rational person I know, West."

As soon as the words left me, my heart crashed. How could I ask so much of the man I adored? My world tormented me. I hated my abilities and all of the headaches that came along with them. Asking West to help carry my burden was unfair.

A dagger lodged in my heart. Two decades ago, I had fallen for a boy who vibrated with energy and had a zest for life. Unfortunately, I was slowly siphoning that carefree joy from this grown man.

I kissed West on the forehead, then ran my fingers through his hair. If I truly cared for him, I had to let him go. However, while we remained at that cabin, he was still mine. Therefore, I cradled Weston Westinghouse the Third on my lap, telling him that everything was going to be okay.

****

About thirty minutes later, West opened the door to a fresh-scrubbed Brad and a chatty Greg. West and Brad greeted each other with a nod. Unfortunately, since I had moved to town, their friendship had become one of impersonal gestures.

"Gordon didn't know how to get here, so I rode with him. I'll help with the car. Then I am heading to Pinkie's Steeple," Greg said.

How in the heck could Greg help the guys get the car started? As usual, Brad remained stone-faced as Greg stood beside him, making a hundred absurd declarations. Perhaps Greg just wanted to play the part of the charismatic man's man that he had once been.

West leaned one muscular arm against the door frame. "Doc, how ya know we were here?"

I pushed off the bed and hurried toward the awkward little group.

Brad scratched his head.

Greg poked a finger into West's bicep until West looked at his arm and swatted. Finding nothing there, West focused back on Brad, waiting for an answer.

The annoying Greg poked West again. *"For fuck's sake, Gordon. Do I have to fix everything? Tell him that Alina called you."*

Brad sought reassurance from me, so I nodded.

"Alina called me," Brad said.

West squinted. "Doc, how do you know Alina?"

"Miranda, how did you hurt your leg?" Brad asked.

West pursed his lips. "How'd you know she hurt her foot?"

"I didn't know it was her foot." Brad sighed. "I thought it was her leg because she hobbled over here, cringing in pain."

I cleared my throat. "I twisted my ankle. West has been taking care of it. I also fell and hurt my bu…my lower back." Better not to reference my hindquarters with the three men gawking at me. Fake chuckling, I waved a hand. "You know how klutzy I am. I fell in the snow, then tripped over the rocking chair."

Brad stared West down as if it was West's fault that I had fallen both times. Greg smirked as his gaze traveled back and forth between my ex-boyfriends.

"I think she sprained her ankle," West said. "It's pretty swollen, and her ass is bruised."

As usual, the stupid blood vessels that sat too close to my skin heated. So much for thinking West's hiss as I dressed was because he liked my booty. He'd simply caught a glimpse of my injury. Although maybe he had been a little turned on since his tongue had made a brief appearance.

Brad grabbed the doorknob. "Let's get your truck hooked up. Then while it's charging, I can check out Miranda's injuries." He pointed to a chair. "Off your foot until I look at it."

"Put your ice back on it," West said.

"Go fix them a turkey pot pie," Greg said between his maniacal chortles.

Greg's reference must have been a huge insult

because Brad grunted at Greg as the three men left me alone with my injured body and whirling thoughts.

****

After the guys got West's truck running, Brad checked my injuries as West and Greg watched. He wasn't able to infuse me with any of his healing energy since West stood behind him. Diagnosing me with a severe ankle sprain and a bruised tailbone, he wrapped my ankle with an ace bandage.

West and I put out the fire, closed up the cabin, then drove on the snow-covered backroads to his grandmother's.

A swollen-eyed Aunt June greeted us at the front door. A disheveled Uncle Walt ushered us into the kitchen, where Grandma Westinghouse stood at the stove with a pinched expression and terrifying, angry eyes. She waved a spatula in the air.

"Where in the hell have you been?"

West ducked under her kitchen weapon and wrapped his arms around her boney body. "Grandma, I was out looking for Cindi and my truck died. We had to stay at that pigsty of a cabin until Doc Gordon fetched us. Miranda fell and hurt herself. The night was an unholy mess."

Unholy mess? The night had been incredible. Well, besides the dirty cabin, smelly pajamas, mouse droppings, dead arachnids, freezing temperatures, and missing cousin. Okay. Maybe it had been somewhat disturbing. However, the chemistry between West and I had been like a ten trillion dollar firework display.

"You two had anything to eat?" Grandma asked.

"Last night Miranda shared a cracker with one of Uncle Walt's vermin," West said.

Grandma, Aunt June, and I cringed.

"Ah, hell. That won't hurt ya too much," Uncle Walt said.

I crinkled my nose and grimaced.

"Sit down," Grandma said. "Eat something, then go home and get yourselves cleaned up. You both look like hell. Then head to that thing the mayor is doin'."

I didn't require a mirror to know that my hair looked like I had spent an hour inside a cyclone and then stuck my finger in a light socket. "Is that the press conference?"

"Yeah. More search parties," Uncle Walt said.

Aunt June dropped her head into her hands and sobbed.

"Pull yourself together, June," Grandma said. "You aren't gonna find her blubbering like a baby."

I put my arm around June until Grandma shot me an intimidating glower and pointed at one of the chairs. I gingerly lowered my bruised rear as she piled eggs, greasy home fries, toast dripping in butter, and black coffee in front of me.

"Grandma, Miranda likes cream and sugar," West said.

Grandma Westinghouse's cigarette hung from her mouth as she carried a pan of bacon to the table. "That cream and sugar 'ill kill ya."

West got his finger slapped for reaching a fork into the sizzling bacon. He ignored it, stabbed anyway, and shoved a piece into his mouth. He grimaced as steam escaped through his lips. Instead of admitting his mistake, he chewed and swallowed before getting up from the table to retrieve the sugar bowl and a carton of milk from the refrigerator. Whistling as he prepared my drink, he created the perfect coffee-to-sweetener-to-dairy ratio.

I guzzled caffeine and shoveled in food as we talked.

"Why was Clive at the camp yesterday?" West asked, his mouth full of egg.

Uncle Walt propped himself against the sink cradling his cup of coffee. "He was out in the woods looking for her. He did a pit stop. He's out looking right now."

West frowned but didn't mention the empty alcohol bottle. Since we'd had sex several scandalous ways while at the camp, he couldn't be too critical of Clive.

"So nobody knows a thing?" West asked.

Grandma ran her cigarette under the tap before sitting at the head of the table. "I don't know how in the hell the three of you lost her?"

"Mom, it was packed," Walt said.

"She's probably been kidnapped by a drug lord or the mafia." June slapped her palm on the table, then took off toward the basement. Before slamming the door, she yelled, "How can you people be eating breakfast when my child is in a ditch somewhere?"

June's comment made me reconsider my plate of food. I sighed and spread grape jelly onto my toast. I'm not proud that I kept eating, but after a light dinner and a night of physical exertion, my stomach gurgled. The Westinghouses ignored the hysterical mother.

"You're a fool, Walt," Grandma said. "You'd lose your asshole if it wasn't in back of your prick."

Unfazed by the insult, Walt sat in June's seat, guzzling coffee.

Grandma leveled her judgmental gaze on West. "I'd expected more from you and Winona. You know that damn rodent probably bit her, and to protect it, she's hiding it somewhere."

Interesting. The intimidating matriarch might have a sound theory.

"Grandma, I'd give my life before I'd let anything bad happen to her," West declared.

Her angry lines softened. "You're a good boy, Weston. But you're too damn skinny." She pointed a spindly finger in my direction. "And your girl's so pale she looks like she saw one too many ghosts."

West's fork teetered halfway in, halfway out of his mouth. I wondered if it was the reference to me as "his girl," my unkept appearance, or the fact that I had seen "one too many ghosts" that made him gape.

"But Weston, skinny or not, you're the one that's gonna find Cindi 'cause you're the only one of these boobs that won't let me down." Grandma narrowed her eyes at Walt.

West rubbed the stubble on the chin as he looked at me—hopefully not examining my pasty complexion too closely since it had been twenty-four hours since I'd applied makeup. He put down his fork and pushed his plate back. "Shortcake, we better get going. I want to shower before I head to this meeting." He stood and placed a kiss on top of his grandmother's teased gray hair.

I took one last gulp of coffee, shoved a bite of lard-covered root vegetable into my mouth, then stood. "Thank you for breakfast, Mrs. Westinghouse."

She had that same look in her eyes that Lincoln got when he was trying to read my mind. "At least your girl has a good appetite. I don't trust people who don't eat."

I heated at my embarrassingly healthy appetite as I followed West to the exit.

"Grandma," West called over his shoulder. "Can you give Edith a call and let her know what happened and that Miranda is on her way? I don't want her to worry."

I remained silent until we reached the bottom of the hill. "Maybe your grandma is correct. What if Bob bit Cindi, and she's hiding out because she's afraid she won't be able to see him anymore?"

West's gaze left the road for a minute. "Then, where in the hell is she?"

"I don't know, but I'll tell you who does. Those Schuster boys."

West pulled up to a stop sign and peered left, then right. "Hey, Shortcake. I'm sorry, but pizza is out today."

"It's okay," I said. "We had breakfast."

"Not exactly one of your aunt's fancy spreads."

"It was delicious." I rubbed at the reflux working its way from my stomach to my throat.

I ached to tell West that we would have pizza another day, but it was out of the question since I was going to pull myself together and let go of him. "I'm going to the press conference too."

"Good."

"Hey, West?"

He gave me a sideways glance.

"I'm going to read people's minds at this thing. I'm sorry. I know how you feel about it these days. But it's our best way of finding her."

"Yeah," he said. "You gotta do what ya gotta do."

"So, maybe—" I hesitated, then blurted, "maybe you shouldn't touch me."

"Okay. We gotta do what we gotta do."

"Exactly." I kept my eyes on the road and swallowed down every emotion surging through me as West and I headed toward the inn.

I would get over West—

Starting now!

Chapter 17

"I'm back, Aunt Edith. I'm going to get ready for the press conference," I called into the kitchen before hobbling up the stairs with Spot at my heels.

I scrubbed myself clean, applied makeup, and dressed in layers. I fed the rat and Princess Pickles and met Aunt Edith and Russ in the foyer so we could carpool to the town hall.

About four dozen people gathered in the room. I waved to my journalist friend Pat Grimwood. Propping his cigarette on his lip, he waved back.

The Westinghouse family, including a freshly shaven West, took up the first three rows. James Schuster stood front and center accompanied by Kramer, a few distinguished-looking men, and the Bellmount Police force. Dinky stood beside Winona, who sat hands in her lap, eyes focused on the floor. The town council scowled from a back corner. And finally, a non-glowing Cassandra Schuster posed board-straight.

Everyone who was anyone had gathered in that room. However, the Schuster boys were nowhere to be seen.

Aunt Edith, Russ, and I made our way to Brad, Liam, Tommy, and Keisha.

"Hey, girlfriend, what happened to you last night? And why are you limping?" Keisha asked before I had a chance to sit.

I lowered my sore body into a chair. "We went to Walt's camp to look for Cindi, and we got stranded there overnight because West's truck wouldn't start. Oh, and I fell a couple of times." I flashed Keisha a cheesy grin, then acknowledged Brad and Tommy with a less obnoxious smile.

James Schuster tapped the microphone and cleared his throat. "Hello. Thank you all for coming."

The hum of voices quieted.

"I want to thank the mayors of Greenport, Foxville, and Creekfield for joining us. I'd also like to thank our local radio, television, and newspapers for covering this multiple-county search for Cindi Westinghouse."

"You should be searching for Bellmount Bob," Jared Blackova yelled.

Grumbling erupted as the Westinghouse clan flashed choppers and bristled like a pack of starving wolves.

Apparently, Blackova didn't see the error of his ways because he kept spewing stupidity. "Bob is a local celebrity, and someone stole him."

Walt's bellow was audible over the chatter. "Someone kidnapped my kid, and you're worried about a damn animal?"

"Your kid probably stole Bob." Blackova's index finger traced vertical circles around his ear.

It took three Westinghouse men to restrain Walt as he lurched at Blackova. He was lucky that Grandma Westinghouse wasn't present. Had she been there, he would have been one bloody corpse. Kramer glared at Blackova through slits as she tucked Cindi's journal under her arm.

I palmed my forehead. What was West thinking? Ghosts? Glowing teenagers? Ol' uptight Bonnie would never understand.

Once Walt was secured in a seat, one of the men in the Fraternal Ring called out, "With all due respect, mayor, Bob brings half a million dollars of tourism into town every year. We need to find him. Have you checked in Creekfield?"

The room hummed.

Schuster raised a hand. "Quiet down, please."

As the buzz grew, Kramer stepped to the mayor's side and pulled her shoulders back. Her intimidating stance did nothing to quiet the crowd.

Schuster cleared his throat again. As the noise escalated, he left his podium to stride to the door, where he switched off the light. The room darkened, the crowd stopped talking, and Cassandra glowed like a firefly.

I gasped and turned to Brad, who gaped at the mayor's wife.

Schuster switched the light on. "Now that I have everyone's attention."

The crowd leaned forward, tilting dozens of ears toward him as he projected his voice and traveled to the podium.

"Our priority is finding Cindi Westinghouse." Once he was behind the microphone, his voice bounced off the walls. "She is a twenty-one-year-old high school student. The last time she was seen was at approximately six fifteen a.m. at Pinkie's Steeple during groundhog festivities. My office is releasing a photo to all media outlets. She was wearing a blue coat, pink mittens, and a purple hat, and she was carrying a pink backpack." He gazed at his wife. "Cindi was under my watch when she disappeared, so I will be using all resources within my disposal to find her."

Cassandra didn't flinch at his admission of guilt. Instead, she held her chin high. However, she no longer glowed.

If I were a superstitious woman, I would have fallen on my knees and prayed that the witchy mother didn't snack on her son's friends. I massaged my chest as the remnants of Grandma Westinghouse's breakfast alerted me to their presence.

Schuster swept an arm toward the Westinghouse family. "Once Cindi is in her family's custody, we will find Bob. He is a beloved member of our town, and I won't rest until they are both safe. Lieutenant Bonnie Kramer with the Special Crimes Division will be leading the search. I will open the floor for questions."

A half-dozen hands popped up. The mayor pointed to Pat, but Dinky interrupted, "Isn't Lieutenant Kramer in homicide? Does that mean you think Cindi was murdered?"

Bonnie Kramer stepped in front of Schuster and leaned over the microphone. "Let's get something straight." Her angry gaze perused the crowd. Once she had intimidated four counties, she said, "Homicide is part of the Special Crimes Unit, but there's no evidence to suggest Miss Westinghouse was harmed. I'm involved because this may be related to the murder of Phil Nowak. And I'll tell you what else." She growled in Blackova's direction. "Watch what you say because Miss Westinghouse is a personal friend of mine."

Blackova huffed. "If she's your friend, is that a conflict of interest? Should someone else oversee the investigation?"

I missed Kramer's response because Russ let out a few coarse words as Aunt Edith's, "Oh my, heavens," echoed in my other ear.

Dinky cleared his throat. "I'd like to hear from Creekfield's Mayor White. What do you have to say about your little stunt during my Miss Bob contest? You ruined it, and those hot girls were disappointed."

I supposed Keisha meant to whisper, "This is a fucking nightmare," to Tommy, but she had missed the indoor voice lessons in kindergarten.

Winona had also been absent during the How to Whisper class because she was across the room, and I still heard her say, "Aunt June, I'm sorry. Even though Richard is sexy, he can be a jerk."

June's body caved forward and her head landed in her lap, as she sobbed uncontrollably.

As Dinky and Officer Kline squared off in some sort of testosterone staring contest, I fought my desire to leap over the seats and shake sense into Winona. Richard, the dork of a DJ, was about as appealing as a cracker dipped in mouse saliva.

Schultz jabbed his finger at the crowd. "If this is some sort of Creekfield prank, I'll personally beat someone's ass." Following his outburst, he hitched his hands in his waistband and pushed his hips forward.

"Finally, the fucking sheriff has said something worthwhile," Russ declared.

Russ wasn't much better than my best friends when it came to voice modulation. Mainly because he chose to ignore etiquette. He said what he meant and meant what he said, and whispering wasn't a habit he engaged in. How he and my uber-polite aunt remained a couple, was a mystery to most Bellmountians. Although, I suspected that the saying, "Opposites attract," fit them to a tee.

Despite the boisterous crowd, Schuster quieted the room. "Mayor White, would you like to address this?" He ushered one of the official-looking men to the podium.

"Boo! Boo!" The crowd chanted as the middle-aged White moved to the center of the room.

He wiped his brow with a handkerchief before shoving it into a coat pocket. "There has been a long-standing rivalry between Bellmount and Creekfield. Our beaver handler, Kip Stone, and Bob's handler, Phil Nowak, had recently become friends. They both knew that a bit of healthy competition made the day more fun, but the pranks were getting out of control and they wanted to work together. Kidnapping does not fit with the spirit of the day, and I assure you that our cheer squad had nothing to do with this. In fact, Mr. Stone and I have let them know their prank was inappropriate, and they offered to join in today's search. Our sheriff has already orchestrated a search party." He snatched the handkerchief from his pocket and dried his brow. "My niece has Down Syndrome." He frowned, shook his head, then moved away from the microphone.

Schuster motioned to Pat. "P.T. Grimwood, do you have a question?"

"Two. How can we help with the search? Any breaks in the Nowak murder?"

With an inclined chin, Schuster deferred to Kramer.

"No new information in the Nowak murder. As for the search, I'm leading a party starting at Pinkie's

Steeple. I've called in my best detective, and he's shepherding the group meeting right outside this building. Two canine units should be here within the hour. We'll find her if I have to call in the entire state force. Sheriff Shultz will divide you into two groups, and search parties will commence in forty minutes. That gives everyone a chance to dress warmly and get something to eat because we have a long day ahead of us. The dogs should be here by then."

A half-dozen hands rose into the air, but the mayor ignored them all. He took a deep breath and handed the microphone to the gloating sheriff, who assigned us to groups, willy-nilly.

Kramer shook her head but didn't interfere. Although jurisdiction, rules, and politics were at play, the lieutenant liked Shultz even less than she liked me.

After we were dismissed, I cornered Mayor White, held out my hand, and dropped my shield. "Dr. Miranda Albright. Thank you for your assistance."

He took my hand.

I stared into his eyes. "Cindi is one of my dear friends."

Despite my best effort, I wasn't able to discern any of his thoughts.

"I'm sure we will find your friend, Dr. Albright," White said, his eyes warm and his concern genuine. "Please excuse me. I am heading home to oversee how the search is going on our end." His shoulders slumped as he walked away.

Why in the heck, after a lifetime of my oddities, had my body taken that moment to be normal? Was I losing my ability to read minds? Regret settled in the pit of my stomach.

West was assigned to the group starting in town, as were Tommy and Liam. Winona, Keisha, and I were relegated to Kramer's party.

I excused myself. "Please don't let me throw up Grandma W's cooking," I begged the great conductor in the sky as I raced to the ladies' room.

****

I was surprised—and ecstatic—to exit the ladies' room and find West waiting for me. He placed his hand on the small of my back and guided me toward the exit sign.

He opened the truck door and handed me a stack of papers. "Before I gave Cindi's journal to Kramer, I ran to the store and made two copies. I thought you might want one."

"Thank you. That was a great idea."

"What can I say? I'm the man. He tugged on one of my ringlets. "Boing!"

My breath hitched. How in the heck was I to display discipline when his touches thrilled me and he did such thoughtful things? I was just about to give up on my Get-over-West plan and wrap him in my arms when a vehicle pulled in beside us. I instantly recognized the 1986 unmarked cop car.

Apparently, so did West. "You've got to be shitting me?" He moaned.

A handsome man with strawberry blond hair, blue eyes, and a rugged scar through his eyebrow stepped out of the car. "Hey, Red. Hey, Westinghouse. Sorry to hear about your cousin. Lieutenant Kramer asked me to lead the search party from the west end of town," Sergeant Sean O'Sullivan said.

"Hi, Sean," I said. "That is awesome. We need all

the help we can get."

West shuffled his feet and let out a long, painful sigh. "Everyone's inside."

Sean gave a firm nod, then strolled into the building. I tried not to sniff at the air as he walked away, and I did not watch him retreat because he had a beautiful backside. I was just inhaling spicy masculine cologne and observing like any living, breathing female with hormones might do.

West cleared his throat, and my gaze settled on him. The truth was that even studly Sean O'Sullivan exuding testosterone out of every pore did nothing to take from West's sexual allure. I wanted nothing more than to reach for him, pull his ear to my lips, and tell him that I wanted to make love to him forever and ever.

No! If you care about him, let him go! the wind whispered.

"West?"

"Yeah, Shortcake."

"We are going to find her."

He held his breath and closed his eyes for a second. He opened them on an exhale. "I guess we better get back inside."

"Okay," I said.

I would get over him—starting now!

Chapter 18

Winona and I piled into Keisha's cute red car, then drove to the inn to prepare for the day. Russ offered us his arctic gear since he had no need for it. He and Aunt Edith had been stationed at the town hall where they were to help Brad set up a medical tent and man the telephones. Before we dressed in layers, Keisha wrapped my foot in a bandage. Even though my ankle was an odd shade of purple and resembled a balloon, neither of my friends asked if I wanted to sit the search out. Good thing, because relaxing on my hindquarters wasn't an acceptable solution. That, and since I was constantly injuring myself, resting until I healed, would mean I never got out of bed.

While the girls were talking to Aunt Edith, I placed Cindi's journal into a folder and wrapped Princess, my bejeweled semi-automatic in a blue towel. I shoved them both into my old backpack. Then I piled apples, cookies, and flashlights on top of the hidden contraband, and we made our way to Pinkie's Steeple. By the time we got there, Kramer had gathered the troops and was spouting directives.

About three dozen volunteers were to form a long line that started at the top of the steeple. We were to spread out and head down the mountain, making our way through the woods. If all went as planned, half of us would meet up with the crew assigned to Sean. The others would head in the opposite direction toward Creekfield. Heated school buses and hot drinks awaited us at various roundup points. Eventually, we would be shuttled back to our cars, and hopefully, be able to celebrate that we had found Cindi. A helicopter flew back and forth over the entire area, and when she was safe, a long white flag was to trail behind it.

Meanwhile, goofy Clive lurked and leered.

"Hey, Winona," Clive said once he finally approached.

Winona wrapped him in her arms. "We're going to find her."

A wad of gooey tobacco stuck out from between his teeth. "Mom's falling apart, and Grandma's on the warpath."

Winona sighed. "I can't believe this happened."

"Over my cousin and ready for me to show you a good time?" Clive knocked his shoulder into mine.

I stumbled.

"Oh, sorry." He steadied me.

"Be careful, Clive. Miranda hurt herself last night at your dad's camp," Winona said.

"What ya doing there?" Clive asked.

"She and West were looking for Cindi," Winona answered for me.

"Shit," Clive said. "West took a girl to Dad's camp while my little sis is missing?"

Keisha grumbled something about inbred hicks under her breath.

Even though I was certain she referenced Clive— she adored West—I glared at her.

"Can I search with you all?" Clive asked.

I tapped a finger to my chin and looked to the

clouds for a solution. Luckily, I found a win-win in the middle of a feathery wisp. "Clive, could you do me a favor?"

He had the same crooked smile as West. Except West possessed a mouthful of perfect teeth and kissable lips, and Clive, after almost thirty years of hard living, appeared to be rotting from the inside out.

"Sure," he said.

"Could you tag along with those men over there?" I pointed to the Fraternal Ring, taking notice that Greg was amongst their group. "Put some heat on them. See what you can find out about why they aren't getting along."

He assessed the men before turning back to me. "What do I get in return?"

Winona put her hands on her hips. "For Pete's sake, Clive."

"You get your sister back," I said.

Clive scratched his crotch.

"I'll tell you what you're gonna get if you don't help out," Keisha said.

Clive's gaze traveled Keisha's length. "You gonna give me my reward, beautiful?"

Snow crunched beneath her feet as Keisha clomped toward him and stuck her gloved finger in his face. "I'm gonna kick your balls up inside your ass if you ever stare at me with that lecherous look again. Now get over there and spy on those men like a good brother."

Clive clenched his fists at his side while a growling Keisha met his gaze.

I steepled my hands. "Please, Clive."

Winona cut her gaze from Keisha to me to Clive.

"You better go listen in and tell us everything, or I'll tell Grandma you were visiting Freida's brothel again."

His lips quivered. "I'm gonna go since you're being bitches, and I wanna find my sis." His shoulders caved forward, and he shuffled away.

It had only taken flirtatious pleas, a threat of bodily injury, the loss of paid sex, and the fear of Grandma Westinghouse to get Clive Westinghouse to leave us alone and infiltrate the Ring.

Three minutes after pawning Clive off on a glowering specter and a group of middle-aged rodent-lovers, Kramer hollered into her megaphone, "Stay safe!" Then she dismissed us into the wild.

****

Keisha, Winona, and I called out Cindi's name as we trampled down the hill. The sound of a man screeching Hitlerish-sounding words at a barking dog, a helicopter propeller whirling, and "Cindi" echoing off the surrounding surfaces had us a bit on edge, so the three of us were silent for the first thirty minutes. The longer we walked, the farther we got from the other scouts, the more we adjusted to the ominous situation, and the less nightmarish it felt.

Keisha formed her hands into a megaphone. "Cindi Westinghouse!"

No one answered.

Sighs all around.

Winona halted to dry her eyes with her big blue mittens.

I pulled up beside her and swung my backpack off my shoulder. After taking off my gloves, I bent to rummage around and retrieved two of Aunt Edith's jumbo chocolate chip cookies. "Here." I offered

Winona the largest one.

"I'm not hungry," she said.

Keisha lunged for it. "Good. More for me."

Winona grumbled and grabbed the other.

Keisha smirked.

Greg Grainey appeared out of nowhere, his complaints oozing before his body even finished forming. *"Thanks for dumping Westinghouse on us. He never shuts up."*

I'd have pointed out that the ghost was quite loquacious himself, except I didn't want Keisha and Winona to think I was talking to the trees. I did a double take because Greg was decked out in a puffy red coat that had a million pockets and bright red matching boots. The fashion-conscious ghost leaned against a tree and posed like a male model.

"You having a picnic while I'm out solving your case?"

I shoved the rest of the treats into the outer section of my pack and grunted.

"What's wrong, Miranda?" Winona asked, her mouth full of the cookie she didn't want.

"I have to go to the bathroom. I'm going to go over there for some privacy." I swung my finger over their heads.

"Mmm. Good cookie." Keisha smacked her lips.

"Do you have any more?" Winona reached for my backpack.

"I'll get them," I said, ripping it from her reach.

Winona's eyes widened, and she pulled her hand back. Keisha narrowed her eyes and grabbed for it.

"You packing heat?" Greg asked.

I yanked my backpack from Keisha's grasp,

handing her the bag of cookies. "Share." Next, I made the uncouth pronouncement, "I have to pee," before taking off for a thick patch of trees. I let out a huff of frustration because Greg hadn't followed me, and my entire farce was so that I could converse with him in private.

The fool stood still, staring at Winona, Keisha, and the cookies.

I tapped my foot.

He played with Keisha's braid.

I rolled my eyes.

He rooted in a pocket.

"For crying out loud, what in the world does a ghost need so many pockets for?" I grumbled. If I had needed privacy to do my business, Greg would have been in my face. However, when I needed him, he was shuffling his feet and watching my friends eat baked goods.

Squatting to form a snowball. I fought with my bruised muscles and groaned in agony. Once I straightened, I flung it at Greg. For the first time in my life, my pitch met an intended target. Even though it sailed right through him, understanding dawned in his eyes. Unfortunately, my plan wasn't well thought out because it also upset my friends.

"What the hell?" Keisha said, wiping snowball guts from her arm.

"Miranda, this is no time for goofing around," Winona hollered.

"I'm sorry. I thought I saw Clive." I turned my back to them and hurried off to a secluded spot, Greg at my heels.

"Some helium with that red balloon?" I said once

we were alone.

"Some vinegar with that piss?" he fired back.

We engaged in an ill-tempered staring contest that I won when Greg broke eye contact to say, "Why are you in a mood? You should be chipper. You got laid last night?"

My cheeks could have melted the snow I stood on. "Augh. My body and foot hurt, and I'm cold. I'm getting more worried about Cindi as time goes on. And Winona and Keisha argue all of the time." I didn't want to bring up the fact that I was depressed because I was forcing myself to get over West, so I dismissed the rest of my rant with a hand wave.

"Hey! Get this. I can't stay in the Schuster estate," he said.

"What do you mean?"

"I mean, I pop in, and a second later, I'm standing at the end of their front lawn, all confused and dizzy."

"I don't understand."

"The damn house kicks me out. Ejects me. Flings me a quarter of a mile away. I tried three times. I finally gave up. It gives me vertigo, and it's hot as hell."

"No way." I punched at his puffy arm in disbelief. Although I could touch Greg when I concentrated, this particular jab went right through him causing me to wobble off balance. I steadied myself. "Me too! That's why I was covered in vomit yesterday."

Greg grimaced.

"Did you hear people's thoughts?" I asked.

"Nope. I was there half a second each time. If that."

"Crazy. What is going on with that house and the Schusters?"

"No idea. But I can tell you that Blackova is a mean SOB. He is throwing fits and insisting the kid stole the groundhog. He seems capable of killing someone if you ask me. I think he's trying to make the kid look guilty. I'm going to snoop around his apartment later. Apparently, he lives on the third floor of the lodge."

"Do you think he could have her there?" I asked.

"I wouldn't put it past that creep to stash her somewhere," Greg said.

Winona's "Miranda, you okay?" carried over the breeze.

"I'm okay," I yelled back.

"Why are you talking to yourself?" Keisha called.

I cringed before projecting my voice. "Give me a minute." Then I whispered, "Do you know why the Fraternal Ring isn't getting along?"

"It seems that when Nowak died, there was a power struggle over who was to take his place," Greg said. "Howard Greene was the group's choice, but another one of the guys thought he should be in charge since he has been waiting for his turn since 1976. Also, Greene detests Kip Stone from Creekview. Although who can blame him?"

"Hmm, seems everyone looks guilty."

"Everyone but me—for once." Greg grinned.

"Miranda?" Winona called again. "Do you have diarrhea or something?"

I sucked in a breath.

Greg screeched, "Yessss!" in a high-pitched girly voice that sounded nothing like me.

I flung my fist and made contact with Greg's insulated, red bicep.

"Miranda," the normally intrepid Keisha screeched. "Hurry up! Did you hear that? I think there's a bobcat nearby."

"Why did you yell like that?" I asked my trouble-making ghost.

Greg was still chortling some kind of maniacal shrill when he disappeared.

****

Hours later we had warmed ourselves in a school bus, sipped at some hot chocolate, and received a report indicating there was no new information. We again marched along scouring the woods. Daylight had faded, and flashlights lit up the winter landscape like fireflies flitting on a summer's eve.

"Do bobcats eat people?" Keisha asked.

"If you're carrying lasagna," Winona said, as matter-of-factly as if she had been discussing the weather.

My lousy humor had escalated following Greg and his stupid ghostly howls. I grunted. "I'm sure there are no bobcats in these woods."

"Don't tell me, your great-great-great-third cousin five times removed died of a bobcat mauling involving Grandma Westinghouse's pasta," Keisha said.

"You think you're so smart, Keisha," Winona said. "You got it all wrong."

Keisha positioned herself in front of Winona, bent forward, and rolled her hand a few times before presenting it palm up. "Oh, excuse me. Then pray tell, enlighten me, your royal dingbatness."

"It was my aunt's sister's son," Winona said.

Facetiousness entwined itself in Keisha's stance, tone, and words. "So your fifth cousin three times removed?"

While Winona held up fingers, counting how many times removed the unfortunate victim was, I slapped at my cheeks to get the blood pumping and my circulation going. It wasn't my fault that I asked, "Was that the person who got attacked or the person who made the lasagna?" The blame for my unfortunate inquiry lay entirely with my frozen brain.

Winona's flashlight blinded me. "The meatballs were as big as baseballs."

"Light! Eyes!" I yelled.

"What in the hell does the size of meatballs have to do with anything? And who puts meatballs in lasagna?" Keisha asked.

Winona lifted both palms to the sky. "Everyone puts meatballs in lasagna, and I'm guessing they smelled good."

"Okay. We're done now. Conversation over," Keisha said. "Mistake to even bring it up. I just hope a damn bobcat doesn't eat my face."

"Wait," I said, securing my spot in the conversation. Once they gazed at me, I tried to trace Winona's family tree. "Did your aunt's sister's son live?"

The fire in Keisha's pupils singed my red brows to oblivion right before she used a gloved two-finger tap to rap Winona on the noggin. "Isn't your aunt's sister's son your cousin?"

Winona rested a mitten across her lips. It took her forever to consider Keisha's appraisal and finish her story. "Well, Wyeth, he was the one carrying the pot, saw a bobcat coming toward him so he said, 'Here kitty, kitty. Want a meatball?' And the cat said—"

Winona made cat paws, lifted her chin high, and let out an ear-exploding, "Meeeooowww!"

Keisha jumped and clutched at her heart. "Damn. I hate cats, lions, cougars, tigers—"

"Meooow," Winona screeched again. "Then the cat leaped right on him." Winona hopped about like a bunny as she made angry cat sounds. "Wyeth dropped the pot, and the meatballs rolled all over, and the blood and the tomato sauce all looked the same."

"Blood," Keisha croaked, bringing her hand to her mouth. "Dear God. Did the bobcat eat lasagna, meatballs, and your cousin?"

Winona frantically nodded up and down for a solid five seconds before changing directions and shaking her head back and forth. "Wait a minute. I don't think it was a bobcat."

Keisha's eyes bulged. "Oh, my God! Was it a mountain lion?"

Winona's gritted teeth turned into a grimace. "I might have my stories confused. It might have been Great Uncle Albert's old hound, Sherlock. You know, the dog that solved crimes?"

"Wait a minute. So you don't know anyone who was eaten by a bobcat or mountain lion?" Keisha asked.

Winona frowned. "Nope."

"No jaguar or cougar maulings?" Keisha asked.

"I'm pretty sure it was Uncle Albert's hound, and he was chasing a kitten and knocked Wyeth over. You know dogs chase kittens all the time."

"Then why was there blood everywhere?"

"Hmm," Winona said. "Might have just been tomato sauce."

"How in the hell do you confuse a bobcat with a

kitten?" Keisha asked.

"'Cause you make me all nervous." Winona's mittened hands flailed. "And I'm worried about Cindi, and you're the one who said that noise was a bobcat."

"We didn't hear a bobcat!" I bellowed.

"How in the hell do you know it wasn't a bobcat? Have you ever heard a bobcat?" Keisha asked.

"Yeah. How do you know?" Winona said, turning on me with an accusatory mitten. "They have bobcats in the big city?"

I stopped walking, and a sturdy wall of Winona Brickhouse Westinghouse plowed into me.

"Ouch," I grumbled. "FYI, I'm tired of telling you guys, Harrisburg isn't a big city."

"They have bobcats there?" Keisha asked.

"No. We don't have bobcats!"

"Then it's probably a big city," Keisha said.

"There are no bobcats in Bellmount either," I muttered under my breath.

Then the three of us stomped along, stewing in our misery until Winona rubbed at her belly, declaring, "I'm hungry for meatballs."

"Me too." Keisha licked her lips. "With lots of garlic. Yum."

I would never in ten trillion million years confess, but I craved a big hunk of lasagna and about three baseball-sized meatballs.

****

"Cindi. Oh, Cindi," Keisha called out before asking, "Girlfriend, what are you hiding in your bag?"

"Nothing. I just wanted all the cookies for myself." I formed a megaphone with my hands. "Cindi!"

Winona shone her flashlight in my eyes again.

224

"That's not nice."

I stuck my hand in the light beam as if swatting might remove it from my eyes. When that didn't work, I covered them with a hand. "I was going to give you guys the apples."

"Apples?" Winona wrinkled her nose and blasted me with her death stare.

"Winona, please stop shining that thing in my eyes?" Then, due to my temporary condition of my-friend-is-a-spaz blindness, I tripped over a branch, fell onto my knees, and let out a resounding, "Fudge!"

The girls were beside me in an instant. Winona illuminated me as Keisha picked me up and brushed me off.

"You okay, Miranda?" Winona asked.

I gritted my teeth. "I'm fine but stop shining that thing in my eyes."

"Don't change the subject. You were about to tell us why you are lying like a pathological psycho about what's in your backpack?" Keisha and her fib o'meter reminded me.

"Fine," I grumbled. "John Gibbons confiscated Cindi's clue journal when no one was looking."

"What are you talking about?" Keisha asked, holding a tree branch up for me to walk under.

"Yeah, what are you talking about?" Winona asked.

My recent tumble caused a cramp to shoot through my calf. I stopped walking to let it calm down. The girls stood by my side as I wriggled my foot about.

"Did you guys notice that Cindi's journal was left in the groundhog cage?"

"What?" Winona said. "Where is it now?"

"West gave it to Kramer. The thing is, I thought maybe Cindi left it as a clue to her whereabouts. So West and I studied it. We even showed it to my friend Alina."

"Why would you show it to her?" Keisha asked.

Dumb Miranda, I chided myself as I searched for something other than because she sees ghosts just like Cindi. "Because she is good with breaking codes," I lied.

"Cool," Winona said.

"Then why are you trying to keep us out of your stuff?" Keisha asked.

I bit my lip and exhaled. "Because I have a copy of it in my bag."

Keisha narrowed her eyes. "Why didn't you want us to know?"

I shrugged.

"You sure you don't have your diamond gun in there?" Keisha asked.

Winona's eyes grew ten sizes in less than a second. "Oh, Miranda!"

"I have a permit now, guys. I just didn't want to deal with this." I pointed at their gaping mouths. "Can we get back to Cindi?"

Keisha refocused herself with a full body shake. "You think she left it as a clue?"

"At first, I thought so. I even convinced West of it. But now I'm not so sure."

"Then how did it get in the groundhog cage?" Keisha asked.

Winona turned to me, shone the light in my eyes, muttered "Oops," then directed it above my head. "Miranda, it has to be a clue. Why would someone else put it there? She knows we're detectives and she wants us to find her."

"Get it through your thick skull," Keisha said. "We aren't detectives. I'm a college administrator, Miranda's a professor, and you're a waitress with bad taste in men."

Winona let out a long, painful moan.

A second later, Keisha hollered, "If you shine that damn thing in my eyes one more time, I'm gonna shove it up your ass."

"You don't have to be so mean." Winona's voice cracked, and she sniffled.

"Although sometimes you say something that isn't totally asinine," conceded Keisha. "I agree. My instincts are telling me that Cindi left it there for us."

In her excitement over Keisha's half-compliment, Winona lost control over her limbs. Her lack of coordination was the final straw in our fruitless search. Keisha grabbed the flashlight from her, shook it in Winona's face, then hurled it into the dark.

"Hey, you almost knocked me out with this thing," yelled someone right before Sean O'Sullivan appeared in front of us, Winona's flashlight in his hand. "Should have known it would be you three trying to smash my skull with a Flexlight."

I rested my hand on my temple. "Cindi's not in these woods, is she?"

"Nope," Sean said. "Good thing, because if she were…" His gaze settled on Winona, and he placed a hand on her shoulder. "It's a damn good thing we didn't find her."

That is when it hit me. We hadn't been scouring those woods for a live Cindi. We had been searching for a frozen corpse. My cramp increased in severity. I cried out in pain, then sat down in the snow, cradling my head.

"Miranda needs to get off her injured leg," Keisha said. "And a bobcat is chasing us."

"Or a hungry mountain lion," Winona added. "Since we don't have meatballs, he's probably trying to steal our cookies and apples."

Sean placed one arm under my legs and the other around my shoulders and lifted me from the ground.

Winona sobbed as Keisha's cooed words of comfort to her. Meanwhile, Sergeant Sean O'Sullivan held me against his warm chest and carried me to a heated bus.

Chapter 19

When my alarm went off, I ignored my exhaustion, dressed quickly, and headed to the kitchen to see if there was news on Cindi. One look at Aunt Edith's taut muscles, and my heart dropped to my feet. I drank two cups of coffee and ate one bite of toast before driving to campus. Unfortunately, I had no desire to stand in front of my students and pretend that everything was okay. According to Grimwood's front-page article—*Local High School Girl Disappears Along with Beloved Groundhog*—surpassing the forty-eight-hour mark rarely resulted in the missing person turning up.

It had been almost 8:00 p.m. when we returned to the town hall the evening before. Clive stood on the portico, a red cup in his hand. He filled us in, explaining that he had backtracked to the lodge to "have a chew somewhere warm and was rudely tossed out like smelly trash."

"Damn," Keisha said. "Can't you give up the booze and tobacco for a minute?"

"Well, they didn't have to act like I was robbing the damn place. I just wanted to get warm. Fucking fancy-pants ski lodge," Clive said.

Keisha huffed.

"Clive's correct, Keisha," Winona said. "They should have let him get warm."

I was too tired to take sides in the argument.

However, Clive's comment struck a chord with me.

West had also returned to the town hall before us. Although we stared at each other from a distance, we didn't have a chance to talk before he took off into the dark. The consensus was that West was hell-bent on finding Cindi, even if it meant he froze to death.

The only positive thing that happened was Brad had cradled my foot in his hands and rubbed it until the swelling went down and the ache eased. His pain management methods left me with a warm floaty buzz, so once I stumbled up the three stories to my turret, I hit my pillow like a lead anchor.

My morning lecture was void of passion or energy. After boring my students to death, I made my way to Lincoln's office with Cindi's journal in tow. I sat across from him, spreading the photocopied pages out so we could compare and contrast them. I gave Lincoln a quick rundown on what I had deduced from the artwork, highlighting the themes of animals and ghosts.

Lincoln pointed to the shape that looked like a crescent moon. "Is this the one Weston thought was the outhouse?"

"Yes," I said. "But there's no evidence that she was ever there."

Lincoln tapped on the picture that sat closest to him. "This is the one that fascinates me. Probably because I heard the story firsthand of this ghost who asked for a cookie."

I came around beside Lincoln so that I could peek over his shoulder.

He looked at me from his periphery. "Have you double-checked her school?"

"It was closed over the weekend, and I have no

idea if anyone searched there. Tommy and West visited her teacher. She didn't seem to know anything."

"This picture seems significant to me. Why don't you visit her school?"

"I think you're onto something. Plus, I think Jimmy Schuster is in that picture, and I know the brothers are up to no good. And Lincoln, I don't know if anyone has methodically searched the lodge. We've triple-checked the mountain, the surrounding woods, and the town, so I have no idea why the lodge hasn't been as thoroughly gone over. Cindi's brother was actually thrown out. Although I find him reprehensible, it did strike me as odd that as cold as it was, we were never given the opportunity to go in and get warm." I shook my head. "I can see Shultz bungling this. But Kramer isn't incompetent. She has an attitude, but she isn't a screw-up."

Lincoln ran his thumb and index finger through his beard. "That does seem odd."

"I know. Right?"

Lincoln and I stared into space until a knock at the door interrupted our silent contemplation. A red-eyed, mascara-less Winona entered. Although her ponytail was typically perfectly positioned, it stuck out of the right side of her head, adding to her frenzied look.

"Hi, Winona. What are you doing here?" I asked.

She approached the desk and rummaged through Cindi's papers. "I don't know. I guess I'm feeling helpless. West showed me the pictures. I know there are clues in them, so I'm trying to figure out what they mean. West says this one is from school." She pointed at the same one that fascinated Lincoln, then held up the one with the moon. "I think that's a house, not an outhouse. Cindi once drew a castle for me, and it was tiny, kind of like this. I think she just draws front doors."

"That's interesting," I said. "A front door under a moon, maybe?"

Just then, Keisha barged in, calling out, "Clive the pervert is probably behind it."

"Behind what?" Winona asked.

"What do you think?" Keisha rolled her eyes. "Cindi's disappearance."

"Huh?" Winona asked.

"Don't be ridiculous, Clive may be a goof, but he didn't kidnap his own sister," I said.

"What do you know, Miranda? You are naive and gullible," Keisha shot back.

"I most certainly am not. You are always accusing some innocent man just because you don't like him."

"What crawled up your bum and died?" Winona asked Keisha.

"Ladies!" Lincoln removed his spectacles and rubbed his eyes. Once his glasses were situated back on his face, he spoke with a gentle tone. "You are all stressed and taking it out on each other. The best thing you can do is make yourselves useful. Go check out her school and give the ski lodge a good going over. Miranda, I'll teach your afternoon class. And Keisha, I'll take care of whatever's on your desk before I head home."

Keisha exhaled. "As usual you are correct, Lincoln. Girls, I'm sorry for being such a bitch."

"Me too," Winona said, wrapping her arms around a grimacing Keisha.

"Me three." I smiled at my friends. "But Lincoln,

Dean Johnson won't be happy."

"I'll handle him. You girls get going."

I gathered up the papers, placed them into my bag, and kissed Lincoln on his cheek. "My lecture notes are on my desk."

He swung a finger toward the door.

"Thank you," I called, peering over my shoulder to shoot him a smile before I exited.

"They're going to have a special place in heaven for you, Lincoln," Keisha said before following me.

Winona didn't join us right away. "Lincoln, I need a psychologist because I'm having man problems."

Lincoln sighed. "I have one piece of advice for a young woman with man problems. If he isn't treating you like a queen, dump him on his ass."

Keisha leaned back into the office to call to Winona, "Yeah, flat on his ugly pale ass. Girlfriend, let's get going because we are going to find that little cousin of yours if we have to tear this entire town apart."

****

Keisha drove us to the outskirts of town and up the long winding drive to Pinkie's Steeple. Although the resort was open, there were only a few cars in the parking lot. Unfortunately, that meant it would be more difficult for us to remain incognito. The three of us stood in the parking lot, staring at the European-style building.

"What's the plan?" Keisha asked.

"I got one," Winona said.

Keisha groaned.

"Go for it, Winona," I said.

"Okay. Keisha is going to distract that grumpy

manager. Then Miranda and I are going to sneak up to the third floor and search his apartment."

"How in the hell am I going to distract him?" Keisha asked.

"Keisha, you are going to position yourself all sexy and show him your leg. Run your hand up your body like this." Winona stuck her hind end out, caressed a hand from her jeaned calf to her bodacious hip, ran her tongue over her lip, closed her eyes, and moaned.

"I hope to hell you don't do that in front of that boyfriend of yours. You look like your crap is stuck inside your colon," Keisha said. "Besides, I have on skin-tight leggings. How am I going to show leg?"

Winona straightened, thrust her shoulders back, and her chin out. "You have a better idea?"

"Hell ya! You got that girly-gun of yours, Miranda?"

"Augh. Yes, but we aren't taking a gun in there." It wasn't that I was against scaring the bejesus out of a murderer with my firearm. I simply didn't think handing it over to Keisha or Winona was a good idea.

"Miranda, what do you think we should do?" Winona asked.

I thought. And thought. And thought…"Keisha, why don't you tell Blackova you need to talk to him about reserving the lodge for your upcoming wedding?" I finally said. "While he is talking to you, Winona and I can look around."

Winona brought a hand to her mouth and gasped. "You're getting married?"

"Seriously, are you brain-damaged?" Keisha asked. "Did you miss the part where we talked about distracting him?"

Winona's face still resembled that of someone straining on a commode. "Oh, I get it now. That's a good idea, Miranda."

"Yeah. Great cover," Keisha said. "And just for the sake of finding Cindi, I'll plan a fake wedding to Tom."

Tommy? How interesting.

"Fine," I said. "Let's go."

Sandwiched between a grinning Keisha and a still bowel-obstructed-looking Winona, I climbed the steps to the lodge.

****

I stood with my back pressed tight against the wall. Winona held her breath and pulled in her belly as she tried to disappear into the bricks. Positioning herself closest to the entranceway, Keisha held a finger to her lips to hush us before leaning forward and peeking around the corner.

"Is he there?" Winona asked.

"Shh," Keisha said.

"Well, is he?" Winona asked again.

Keisha stepped back and swung around to press her back into the wall beside me. "Nasty looking dude with messy black hair and glasses?"

"Yes," I said.

Keisha leaned close to my ear. "I recognize him from the press conference."

"What?" Winona said.

"Shh," Keisha said.

I lifted my chin and pressed into my toes to reach Winona's ear. "Yes. He's there."

Keisha peeled her backside from the wall to stare around the corner before peering over her shoulder at us. "He looks pissed."

"I wanna see," Winona said.

"He always looks angry," I said.

"I wanna see," Winona reiterated.

I pointed to the ground, then held my finger to my lips before squishing my head under Keisha's arm so that I could check out the scene. Understanding my meaning, Winona crouched down on all fours and peeked from under me. The three of us gawked around that corner, taking in Blackova, red-faced and swinging his hands around. He appeared to be reprimanding a young girl working at the snack counter. Unfortunately, we were about as subtle as a shiny crown on a mud-covered leper.

"Can I help you ladies?" someone said.

I jumped and gasped. Keisha let out a resounding, "Holy shit," and Winona screamed, "Eek!"

"Sorry, didn't mean to scare you," Howard Greene said.

"Hello, Mr. Greene." I said.

Keisha glared at him. "Scared the shit out of us."

"Sorry," he said again.

"I'm just checking out this place for my wedding reception. I want to make sure it's up to snuff even when management thinks nobody is looking. I'm having a classy affair, with pink and white roses, violins, and champagne. And my cake is three tiers." A dreamy-eyed Keisha held her hand to her heart.

"Great place for a wedding reception. Any news on that missing girl?"

"Nothing," I said.

"I don't get it," he said. "Just disappeared into thin air."

"Any news on the hog?" Keisha asked.

Mr. Greene's face turned a deep shade of crimson, and his irises disappeared as his eyes turned into slits. "You mean Bob? And no. It's a travesty. I've started training one of the babies to take over the lead prognosticating job."

"What can you train a groundhog to do?" Keisha asked.

Howard Greene's previously narrowed eyes popped wide, and his brows hit his hairline.

"You can train them to do a lot," Winona said.

Keisha flashed Winona a hand.

"My Great-Grandpa Westinghouse once trained—"

Keisha held up her thumb and index finger, stuck them in Winona's face, then snapped them closed.

Winona licked her lips. "Trained the ground—"

Keisha's fleshy clamp opened, took hold of Winona's lips, and squeezed.

Winona swatted Keisha's hand away and puffed out at warp speed, "Trained a groundhog to ride on a skateboard!"

"You're full of shit," Keisha said.

Winona put a hand on her hip. "Tell her, Mr. Greene, groundhogs are smart."

"Huh?" I asked, seeing as how West and Greg, both with more worldly experience and common sense, had explained the opposite to be true.

Mr. Greene wore a combination of sad lips and confused eyes.

"Okay," Keisha said, hand in the air, hair tossed back, eyes narrowed. "I'm gonna say this one time and one time only. If you put a carrot on a skateboard, then plop a rodent on it, and push it, the animal isn't actually skateboarding."

"It wasn't a carrot," Winona said.

Hissing, Keisha again snapped a thumb and index finger trap, hushing Winona. "If you put a meatball—"

"It wasn't a meatball."

Keisha scowled.

Green rubbed his nose. "I gotta go. Nice talking to you ladies." He addressed Keisha. "Good luck with your wedding, miss." Then he dashed to the exit.

"You two upset him with your bickering," I said. "And I'm sure all of this commotion has alerted Blackova that something is going on out here."

"Mr. Greene's kind of weird," Winona said.

"He was perfectly normal. He's upset about his pet. I'd be devastated if anything happened to Spot, Princess Pickles, and—" I scrunched up my nose and grunted, "—the rat."

"I agree with her." Keisha thumbed toward Winona. "That dude acts all nice until you bring up lice-infested rodents. Then he gets touchy."

Winona shivered. "I hate lice. They make your head itch so bad. One time my Great Aunt Sally's potbelly pig—"

Keisha jammed her finger into Winona's nose, putting an end to the tale of Great Aunt Sally's insect-infected swine.

I motioned for the girls to lean close. "Keisha, keep Blackova on the first floor for about fifteen minutes. Then ask to see the restaurant on the second floor. Stay there for about twenty minutes. Meet us at the car in thirty-five minutes."

"Will do." Keisha stepped toward the entrance.

"Wait a minute," Winona said. "We need a signal to communicate with each other."

Keisha stopped short. "To communicate what?"

Winona *tsked.* "You're a terrible detective, Keisha. If someone is onto us, we need a way to alert each other."

Keisha's eyeballs rolled to the back of her head, and my squinty peekers about imploded.

"Keisha, if you think he's going to find Miranda and me call out—" Winona lifted her chin into the air and mouthed, "Cock-a-doodle-doo."

Keisha whipped her head so fast her chin reverberated. "What the flying fuck?"

"Do it really loud so we can hear you. When we were kids and snuck into Grandma Westinghouse's cookie jar, I used to yell 'Cock-a-doodle-doo.' Then West would know Grandma was coming, and he'd run off with the cookies before she caught us."

"I'm pretty sure West was just making an ass out of you," Keisha informed her.

"Naw." Winona's lopsided ponytail swung with indignation.

"Did he ever share any of those pilfered cookies?" Keisha asked.

Winona's answer was the largest pouty face in history. I grabbed her forearm and guided her to the stairwell as Keisha headed into the main room to corner Blackova.

Operation Cock-a-doodle-doo had commenced.

****

The second floor consisted of a humongous restaurant and a ginormous ballroom, a kitchen area, men's and women's restrooms, and an office. Besides a maid, a waitress, a chef, and about half-a-dozen individuals partaking of stinky shrimp cocktails, the second floor was empty. Fortunately, all the doors were unlocked. Unfortunately, Cindi wasn't in any of those rooms.

We climbed the stairs to the third floor, where there were a few more offices, storage closets, one unlocked lavishly decorated hotel room, and two locked doors.

I knocked on the first. "Anyone home?"

There was no answer.

Winona knocked on the second, "Cindi, it's Winona. You there?"

No answer.

Winona and I glared at the door.

"What if she's in there with her hands tied and a gag on her mouth, and he's feeding her stale bread and water? She might not have a blanket or clean underwear. She could be freezing." Winona wrapped her arms around herself and shivered. "You know kidnappers do things like that to torture captives."

"We need to get in there," I said.

"Want me to break down the door?" she asked.

"Good grief. No."

She sighed. "Okay, but I'm strong enough to do it."

I played with a ringlet as I tried my hand at simple physics—Winona's build versus a wooden barricade? She just might be able to… Insane! I sucked at math, and she would kill herself. Although she could probably take out a football team. I exhaled and dropped the strand to rub at my weary eyes.

"We need to get the keys from the maid on the second floor. I saw them sitting on her cart."

Winona's hazel eyes turned golden. "I'll steal them. I've never stolen anything. But this isn't really stealing. It's detective work."

"No. You wait, here. Lay low and make sure no one notices you. I'll be right back."

I retraced my path to the second floor, waited for the maid to leave her cart outside the ballroom, confiscated the key, then sprinted back to Winona.

"You get it?" Winona asked as I approached.

I held up the keychain in victory. Bending at my waist, I panted out, "Piece of cake."

"Wow! Your face is red, and you're sweating."

"I ran," I gasped.

Winona's voice took on its big-sis bossy tone. "Boy, you're in bad shape. You should take Tricia's aerobics class again."

Using my forearm to move her out of the way so I could open the door proved pointless. It required a bulldozer hitched to a semi to move Winona Westinghouse an inch.

****

The first suite we searched looked precisely like the unlocked one, except two open suitcases overflowing with clothing sat on the floor, and cosmetics littered the bathroom counter. Cindi was not in the room. We locked up and headed to the last door in the long hallway.

"This has to be Blackova's apartment," I whispered as we entered the room.

Blackova kept an immaculate abode. Everything was in its place, and it passed the white glove test with flying colors.

I checked the bathroom while Winona looked under the bed and investigated the closet. We rendezvoused in the center of the room.

"She's not here," Winona said.

"Let's check his personal things for leads." Applauding my brilliance, I rifled through the papers on his desk.

Winona rooted in the top dresser drawer, halting her search for a short second to ask, "What are we looking for?"

"I'm not sure. Anything that indicates he took Cindi. Her backpack is still missing. Be on the lookout for it."

"Eww!" A handkerchief dangled from Winona's outstretched hand.

I gagged. "Gross. Who uses those things anymore?"

"At least it's clean," she said. However, her face remained twisted into a grimace as she poked about.

I opened the desk drawer at the same time that I heard a faint "Cock-a-doodle-doo." The biggest problem with the bird call being, Winona hadn't moved her lips, and to my knowledge, no roosters were staying at the lodge.

Winona gritted her teeth. "Miranda."

"Fudge. We gotta go." I whispered.

Winona and I darted to the door, and I placed my ear to it.

"Cock-a-doodle-doo. Cock-a-doodle-doo," came from the other side. I grabbed Winona's hand and dragged her to the bathroom. It was no easy task because she fought me the entire time, repeating at least seven hundred times, "What's going on?"

"Shh," I ordered. "Move it." Once we were in the bathroom, I locked the door.

A fist pounded on the main door. "Open up!"

"Crap monsters. Kramer," I whispered.

Winona's mouth formed a big *O*.

We squished together, both placing a cupped ear to the door, straining to hear what was going on on the other side.

Winona's teeth chattered. "They are in the room now and are gonna break down the door."

My heart dropped to the first-floor eatery as butterflies pounded at my chest.

"See. Not here," said Keisha's muffled voice. "Let's go."

A second later, the locked bathroom knob moved. Like a terrified child, I wrapped my palm around it and held it in place.

"Hey, Sweetcakes," Kramer called. "Open up. I know you're in there."

Winona dove for the shower, clanging and banging as she hid behind a white shower curtain.

"I heard that," Kramer said.

"I didn't hear anything," Keisha said.

"I'm pressing charges," a disgruntled male voice hissed.

"Oh, no." Winona slipped and her behemoth body tumbled out of the shower, landing with an earthshaking *splat!*

She lay face up, wrapped in white fabric, her eyes as big as the toilet seat her head had smashed into. The curtain rod she had demolished stuck out of the commode, a piece of torn shower curtain hanging from its tip.

"Sheesh." I tried to help her stand. Unfortunately, my foot caught in the oversized shower curtain, and I tumbled forward.

I landed with my face smothered in Winona's generous bosom and her knee jabbing my gut. I whimpered. At least I hadn't impaled myself on the surrender flag sticking out of the toilet water.

As Kramer, Blackova, and Keisha entered that bathroom, I peered over my shoulder and groaned. A key swung from Blackova's skinny fingers, smoke oozed from his ears, and a frown plastered his ugly mug.

Boy-oh-boy, Keisha couldn't have looked more horrified if we were big cats.

Kramer, on the other hand, sported sparkling eyes and a growing grin. Then she chortled as she propped herself upright on the sink.

Like a pregnant walrus stuck on its belly, while wrapped in mildew-resistant polyester and suffocating in Winona's ample cleavage, I asked, "Could you help me up?"

"I leave you two alone, and look what happens." Keisha grumbled.

Once I was on my feet, Winona popped up.

"I'm okay," she called out. Seeing as how a second later she teetered backward, she wasn't okay in the least.

As I stood there scarlet-faced, and Winona wobbled about from her toilet seat concussion, Lieutenant Bonnie Kramer, of the Bear County Special Crimes Division, guffawed and slapped at her thighs until her eyes watered. Hopefully the woman fractured a rib and bruised her quads.

"See, told you we needed a signal," Winona said as her pupils spun about in their orbs.

Keisha leaned close to me. "Girlfriend, I bet you wish you had that girly gun on you about now."

Chapter 20

The three of us were quiet as we drove to Bellmount High. The introspective time allowed me to contemplate why Kramer had sent us on our way with an odd gleam in her normally intense eyes. After all, it was our second break-in in the past few months, and she should have thrown the book at us.

Keisha voiced her misgivings. "Does it seem odd to anyone else that we aren't sitting in jail right now?"

"I think it's because the lieutenant likes me and knows we're good detectives," Winona said from the back seat.

Keisha choked.

"After we go to the school, we are taking you to see Brad," I informed Winona. "In fact, I'm not sure why we let you talk us into taking you with us when you need a doctor."

"I'm fine," she insisted. "I never get hurt."

"You look like you're stoned out of your gourd," Keisha said. "Of course, you always have that dumb-ass grin and big goofy eyes."

I tapped Keisha's forearm, using our brief eye contact to give her a go-easy-on-Winona plea.

Keisha looked into her rearview mirror and sighed. "Are you warm enough back there? You need the heat turned up?"

"I'm sweating a lot," Winona said.

"Okay," I'm turning it down," Keisha said.

We rode the rest of the way in silence.

****

We waited in the high school office while a secretary wrote up a mouthy student who had been smoking in the bathroom.

"I knew a kid like you in high school," Keisha told the boy.

He glared at her.

"Dead. Rotting in a gutter by the time he was nineteen," Keisha said.

"Whatever, lady." The boy grabbed his pink slip and headed toward the office exit.

"Rats ate his eyeballs," Keisha called to his back.

He stopped for a second, looked as though he was going to respond, shook his head, then pushed on the exit door.

"Want a job here?" the secretary asked Keisha.

"She already has one harassing the students at Bellmount College," I said.

Keisha and the secretary both chuckled. Meanwhile, Winona stared off into the distance.

"You okay?" I asked Winona.

She bobbed her head up and down.

"Does she need to see the school nurse?" the secretary asked.

"Absolutely," Keisha said.

"No," Winona said. "I'm just dizzy. My cousin is Cindi Westinghouse."

"Oh," the secretary said. "They found her yet?"

The three of us muttered soft nos.

The secretary frowned. "Boy, everyone here just adores Cindi. She's a huge help. She stops by the office every morning and runs mail to the teachers for me before school even starts."

"She's a good kid," Keisha said.

I leaned over the counter to make out the name tag encircling the woman's neck. "Ms. Long, we thought maybe we could talk to her teacher. We know Miss Myers saw her right before she disappeared."

"You have to wait until school is over. She'll be helping the kids onto the buses in about fifteen minutes." Ms. Long pointed us in the correct direction, wishing us luck.

We situated ourselves on a bench in the back of the school, where vehicles picked up the students. Exhaust fumes and noisy engines enshrouded us.

I exhaled. Condensation formed a cloud that slowly evaporated. "When does Bellmount warm up?"

Keisha snorted.

"June," Winona said.

I burrowed my mittened hands deep into my coat pockets.

"So," Winona said, breaking the silence, "they sat together on the front porch, and she drank lemonade and rubbed the oil 'round and 'round on Oliver's back. She said she loved him so much it didn't even gross her out that they were almost as big as peas."

Keisha groaned.

"Winona, if something is the size of a pea, it means it's small," I said, in my metaphor-explaining voice.

"Oh, no way. These were humongous and gross. Plus, massages always put him to sleep."

"Damn hickish men and their disgusting growths." Keisha cringed. "Making women rub them. Not me. No way."

Winona didn't acknowledge Keisha's comment since she was busy perspiring and spouting nonsense. "But Mr. Bacon was super jealous, so he climbed the steps and bonked Oliver in the head, waking him up."

I took off my mitten, rested the back of my fingers on Winona's sticky forehead, put my filter into place, and played nurse. "You feel warm, but maybe it's because I'm freezing."

Winona swatted my hand away. "I'm hot because of all the cars, vans, and buses."

"Not sure if people with concussions get fevers and hallucinate," Keisha said. "Might just be her Polish blood making her sweat like that."

"I'm half Czechoslovakian," Winona said. "Besides, schools make me nervous, and when I'm nervous my deodorant doesn't work. And how did you know that Oliver had a concussion?"

"Hard to tell if this tale is the result of the bonk to her brain or she's in normal storytelling mode," Keisha said.

I suspected Winona meant to roll two eyes, but only one moved, making her look like a googly-eyed stuffed animal halfway through being upended.

"Well, Oliver woke up and chased Mr. Bacon all around the yard. 'Round and 'round they went." She enthusiastically circled her hand in the air. "Then he crashed into a fence post and knocked himself out cold."

"Huh?" Keisha murmured.

"I'm confused. Who ran into the fence post?" I asked since I wanted to distract myself from the stressful situation and the arctic conditions.

Keisha took a deep breath and let it out slowly,

punctuating it with a dramatic sigh.

"Well, first, Oliver hit it. *Splat!* Then Mr. Bacon ran into him and flipped into the air." Winona looked toward the skyline, and her finger made a few loop de loops. "He did three somersaults. Then, *boink,* he also got knocked out cold. He was on his back with his feet in the air."

"There is no way this Mr. Bacon did three somersaults," Keisha said.

"Yes, siree Bob," Winona said. "And he landed right on Oliver's head. Then poor Oliver was brain-damaged for the rest of his life."

"That's awful," I said, picturing one of Winona's forefathers lying supine in a field.

"Yes, siree Bob. It's God's honest truth. So brain damaged that every time he tried to pee, he took a step backward then fell over."

"Huh?"

"At least the lice were gone." Winona's mouth formed a firm line. "Well, they were gone on Oliver. Great Aunt Sally could have cared less about Mr. Bacon. She was really mad at him. Said he was 'the worst blasted swine' she ever had the displeasure owning."

Keisha leaped from the bench. "You did not just seriously waste ten minutes of my life telling me an absurd story about a disabled insect-infested hog."

Winona rested a hand on her heart. "Pigs can be just like children, guys."

Keisha groaned. "Only if you're a flipping yahoo from the boonies."

Winona didn't have a chance to defend her relations because the final bell rang, and students dispersed like ants sniffing watermelon. Once the crowd thinned, a tiny woman, surrounded by a group of teenagers, exited. She assisted the students into various vehicles, smiling and waving the entire time.

Keisha and I descended on the teacher. Winona took her time weaving to us.

I waited until the last of the students were taken care of to ask, "Are you Miss Myers?"

The woman turned a darling pixie smile on us. She was so diminutive that my five-foot-three frame towered over her by a good two inches, and she was seriously dwarfed by Winona and Keisha's stretch.

"Yes. I am. Can I help you?" Her youthful voice was as adorable as the rest of her.

Keisha thumbed toward Winona. "This is Cindi Westinghouse's cousin, and we're her friends."

Miss Myers nodded and gave the three of us a once over. "Please tell me you have found her."

I shook my head. "No."

A tear slid down Miss Myers' cheek, and she turned away from us to wipe it away. "I'm sorry. My students are like my children. I've been terribly worried. Her classmates asked so many questions today, and I was unsure what to tell them."

My students were older and more independent, and if something happened to one of them, it would break my heart. I placed a comforting hand on her shoulder.

"We understand you were one of the last people to see her."

"That's what I've been told. She had just gotten off stage with Chad and his family, and she ran over to hug me. I told them both how proud I was."

"Can you tell us anything else?" I asked.

Miss Myers wiped at the liquid dripping from her eyes before turning to Winona. "I was just about to call your brother."

Winona blinked a half-dozen times.

"She doesn't have a brother," I said.

The teacher's teary eyes clouded over, and her brow furrowed. "Two men came to my house. One was the park ranger. He's my postman's son and is super nice. The other man was—" Her sad eyes brightened. "Anyway, he said he was Cindi's cousin."

"Tommy and West," I said.

"Yes. Isn't West your brother?" she asked Winona.

"No. He's my cousin. I have a sister. We have lots of cousins. There are a lot of us Westinghouses."

"Oh," Miss Myers said. "I was going to call him and give him this." She reached into her coat pocket, retrieved a folded note, and handed it to Winona. "I went through Cindi's desk and locker, looking for anything that might help. She keeps herself organized. That's the only thing I didn't recognize as schoolwork."

Winona unfolded the paper and moved it in and out, attempting to focus her eyes.

"Can I see it?" I asked.

Winona handed it to me. "It's just a bunch of letters and hearts."

"Hmm." Letters and hearts.

"Let me see." Keisha ripped it from my grasp. "The letters D R G R D N G Y M Y and lots of hearts. Looks like one of those silly Valentines to me."

"Keisha, read the letters to me again," I said.

I closed my eyes and pictured the letters while Keisha enunciated, "D R G R D N G Y M Y."

I opened my eyes. "Doctor Gordon—I think Cindi

wrote his name. She has a huge crush on him."

"I thought she had a crush on Gibbons," Keisha said.

"She has a crush on Jimmy Schuster," her teacher said. "He's such a nice boy. So popular, and he goes out of his way to look out for Chad and the kids in my class. In fact, he eats lunch with them a few times a week instead of sitting with his team."

"G Y M Y must be Jimmy," I said. "This must be her boyfriend list."

Winona shook off her funk to grab the paper. "Grandma Westinghouse will beat her hide."

Miss Myers flashed Winona a hold-on hand. "It's quite normal for young girls to get crushes. I don't think we need to make a big deal out of this with her grandmother. Mrs. Westinghouse can be a bit..."

"Terrifying," I said.

"Hey," Winona said.

Miss Myers shuddered. "Speaking of the Schuster boys." She pointed at a van across the parking lot. Jimmy was in the middle of loading a wheelchair into the back.

"I'll be right back." I charged across the parking lot, calling, "Jimmy! Hey, Jimmy!"

I made it to the van and clasped my heart. "Hi. Do you remember me? I'm Liam's cousin and Cindi's friend. We've met a few times."

"Sure," Jimmy said. "Nice to see you again."

"Since you were the last person to see Cindi, I thought I could ask you a few questions."

Jimmy plopped a pile of schoolbooks onto the carpeted floor, swung two backpacks on top of the wheelchair, then slammed the door closed. "Well, I gotta take my brother home. He gets pretty upset if he doesn't get home right away."

I inclined my chin toward the boy with his face plastered against the window. "Chad looks more curious about what we are talking about than upset. So maybe I could ask you both a couple of questions."

I took off my mittens, slid them into my pocket, and rubbed my hands together to warm them. No need to startle a teenage boy with my icy grip.

Jimmy's smile faded, and his facial muscles tensed. "I've gotta get Chad home, then get back here for basketball practice. Coach gives me a few extra minutes to take care of family matters, but he gets pretty angry if I'm really late."

"I'll make this fast."

I waved to Chad. His head tilted to the side. Then, his wrist and fingers curled as he waved back.

"Sorry. We've gotta go." Jimmy opened the driver's side door.

I reached for him intending to hook my lie detector up to his wrist. It was a carelessly awkward move, but I was desperate.

He pulled away. "What are you doing?" Heat radiated from his body, and for a brief moment, he glowed red.

We both jumped when Chad slapped the heel of his hand on the window.

"I tried to tell you that you were going to upset my brother. He is shy and scares easily. Please just leave us alone. We don't know what happened to Cindi, and Chad is very upset about it."

For a moment, I felt guilty, but a second later, it turned into an odd weary feeling. I pulled my shoulders back and lied my butt off. "I was just going to shake your hand."

"Sorry," he said, once again amicable. "I'm just trying to look out for Chad. There have been so many people hounding him with questions."

If I asked him why he glowed, I'd out my abilities, so I held a pretend bubble in my cheeks. My moment of hesitation gave Jimmy Schuster time to hop into his van and peel out of the parking lot. I hobbled after them, trying to catch one last glimpse of Chad. It was a lost cause, and Winona was correct. I was in terrible shape. Plus, my quick movements reminded me that my foot was injured. I shuffled back to the women.

"Is everything okay?" Miss Myers asked.

"I think I upset Chad," I said.

"Chad is normally a bit shy around people he doesn't know," she said. "But he warms up quickly. He was reticent today and barely spoke. I think this entire thing has him very upset. He didn't even want to go to lunch. He ate by himself in the classroom. He normally wants to eat with his brother or his friends. It's not like him at all."

"Hmm," I said.

"I think we have everything we need," Keisha said. "We have to take Winona to the doctor."

My heart skipped a beat. Keisha had just called Winona by name; Winona was indeed in bad shape.

"Thank you, Miss Myers," I said.

She wiped away tears. "Please let me know what I can do. I'm losing my mind waiting."

"Okay," Winona said.

She smiled at Winona. "I know this is an inappropriate question considering everything. Is your cousin West seeing anyone?"

I gasped.

Keisha snorted.

"West dates lots of girls. Why?" Winona asked.

Miss Myers bit her lip. "He was very nice, and he's so dreamy. Do you think I could still give him a call even though you have Cindi's note?"

I also bit my lip. He didn't see *lots of girls* anymore because I messed him up with my weird psychic abilities, ghosts, and dead bodies. Let him go, Miranda. She's so sweet and would be good for him, my common sense whispered. I opened my mouth to say, "Call him." However, it stuck in my throat and came out as a grunt.

"West is a horny hound dog. Stay far away from him," Keisha said. "Rumor is he has half-a-dozen STDs."

I think Winona meant to bring her hand to her mouth, but she hit herself in the chin.

Miss Myers covered her gasp by placing a tiny hand across her pretty pink lips.

"Oh. And in case you're wondering, Tom Little treats women like shit. Stay away from them both," Keisha said.

"Keisha, Tommy's sweet—"

Keisha's hand landed on Winona's mouth. "Concussions. People say the darndest things."

She grabbed Winona and dragged her to the car. As strong as Winona was, she wasn't able to wriggle free. Keisha pushed the driver's seat forward and used a waving hand to indicate that Winona should crawl into the backseat.

"I don't have a concussion or a fever," Winona

said. "Grandma will kill Cindi and West both, and that was a terrible thing to say about Tommy."

Keisha shoved Winona's bulk into the backseat as Winona chattered on about Cindi's "boyfriends" and West's "diseases." Once Keisha had Winona caged, she pinned me with her gaze. "Girlfriend, you can thank me later for keeping her away from that crush of yours. A bottle of the finest chardonnay you can get your hands on oughta do it."

As soon as Cindi was found, I'd buy Keisha whatever she wanted.

****

Keisha and I sandwiched Winona and steadied her on the walkway leading to Brad's Arts and Crafts style office. Nasty Nurse Crane stood sentry over the waiting area and grunted at us in greeting.

"She smashed her head on a commode and needs to see the doctor immediately," Keisha said.

Before coming around to the front of her desk, Nurse Kane made sure her ramrod was firmly wedged between her buttocks. "He isn't here, and I'm trying to get the office cleaned up. Another doctor arrives later this week to help out, and this place is a mess."

Since I was accustomed to the unpleasant woman, I ignored her. Keisha and Winona took in their surroundings.

"It's not messy," Winona said.

Keisha's face contorted into a half-annoyed, half-confused grimace betraying her thoughts on Nurse Theresa Kane's overly officious manners.

"Not messy? *Pfft.*" Kane gave Winona the once over, then barked, "Sit down."

Winona obeyed, collapsing into the closest chair.

The nurse stuck her nose an inch from Winona's and stared into her eyes.

"When will Brad be back?" I asked.

Theresa Kane's muscles tensed even more. She straightened and then cut her gaze from Winona to me. "Brad? Show some respect. You mean Dr. Gordon."

I didn't have the time or the energy to fight a battle of wills with the woman. Therefore, I simply rephrased my question. "When will Dr. Gordon be back?"

She planted herself in Winona's space again and held up an index finger. "Follow." While Winona's eyes tracked, the nurse said, "Dr. Gordon had to run to the Victorian hotel to treat an injury."

"The Bellmount Inn? Who? What?" I stammered.

Winona had enough difficulty focusing on the traveling digit when she wasn't in shock. The announcement of an unfortunate incident left her gobsmacked, gawking, and failing her medical exam.

"Yes. The Bellmount Inn. The caretaker was injured."

"Russ Jenkins?" I asked.

Nurse Cane propped a hand on her hip and crinkled her nose. "Yes."

"Is he okay?" I asked.

"If he were okay, Dr. Gordon wouldn't have had to drive over there. And I am sure he will be okay now that the doctor is there."

Keisha grabbed Winona's hand. "Come on. We have to go."

"Wait a minute," Nurse Kane said. "She can't go anywhere. Her pupils are different sizes, and she can't focus."

"The hell she can't. We're taking her to the doctor

because you're busy. You need to clean up this mess." Keisha swung her hand outward, showcasing Brad's immaculate waiting room.

The nurse's jaw firmed and her chin performed a sharp down to the affirmative, as sarcasm flew over her head.

"It's not messy," Winona said as Keisha pulled her to her feet.

"Nurse Kane, you better take care of organizing the books. They're arranged in alphabetical order. I think you might want to do it by color. It's a lot easier on the eye," Keisha suggested.

The nurse skimmed the shelving units. "Right you are. Finally, someone who seems to get what I put up with working here."

Keisha pursed her lips and nodded. As soon as the office door closed behind us, she let loose. "God damn crazy nut." Then she leaned close, and her lips cupped my ear. "Girlfriend, we need Bradley asap. I'm seriously worried about Winona."

****

Under normal circumstances, West's, Liam's, and Brad's cars in the driveway were a welcome sight. However, since I feared the worst, the plethora of automobiles scared the bejesus out of me. Keisha navigated around a ladder on its side and parked at a cattywampus angle. We beetled along the path to the front porch as fast as we could with our numerous injuries.

I flung the heavy door open. "Aunt Edith!"

After trotting down the hallway to greet us, Spot led our train to the library, where West leaned against the frame of the wide-open pocket door. Russ, Aunt

Edith, and Brad sat at the oak table, and Liam reclined in the too-tiny wingback.

I passed by West, inhaling his endorphin-inducing masculinity, to hover over Russ' shoulder. "Are you okay? We heard you were injured."

Russ held up a bandaged hand. "Not bad enough for all this fuss."

Aunt Edith *tsked.*

"He was in the garage working, smashed his finger to oblivion with a hammer, and then fell off the ladder," Liam said.

"I'm constantly telling him to be careful with that hammer," Aunt Edith said.

West chuckled.

"I'm fine. Aren't I, Doc?" Russ asked.

"Yes. You're going to be okay." Brad's slumped posture and bloodshot eyes indicated he had used his uncanny healing powers—unusual when people were looking on.

"Good thing Weston and Liam were here today," Aunt Edith said. "Their quick response probably saved Russ's thumb."

Russ waved his bandaged hand. "It wasn't that bad, Edith."

"It was bloody and mangled." Liam shivered.

"You're not working today?" I asked my cousin.

"Just took some time off to bring Mom a present I thought she'd like. Thank goodness since Russ got hurt."

"Brad, Winona hit her head. She's dizzy and very unsteady on her feet," I said.

Liam *harumphed.* "I guess my gift didn't help."

"What gift is that?" I asked.

"A good luck charm. The Schusters had this hex sign hanging above their garage. It's been there for years. Cassandra thought it was hideous and got into a fight with James about it. He claims it's a family heirloom."

"It's folk art. It's supposed to give you good luck and ward off evil," my aunt explained. "And this one is a lovely piece. I'm not sure what Cassandra has against it."

"I agree, Mom. And now Gina's pissed at me for accusing Cassandra of being a bitch. Cassandra insisted on new furniture. Then she wanted this fancy brickwork removed from her family home and embedded above the front door. Keep in mind; the masons worked on it in the middle of winter. I hate visiting right now. The boys are great, but the estate feels like a powder keg of stress. Old man Schuster is a tyrant, and suddenly, Gina's mother is so forgetful she can't remember where she left her marbles."

"Rumor is there are financial problems," Keisha said.

"Poor as church mice," Winona added.

Liam pressed the palm of his hand into his forehead. "James had his parents take down the hex sign to appease Cassandra. I thought Mom would love it, so I asked James if I could give it to her. That's what Russ and West were trying to hang."

"Having bad luck when you're trying to hang up something to bring good luck." Russ chuckled. "Crazy, heh?"

"Yep. Crazy," I mumbled. A bad luck hex sign, furnace-like humans, terrifying mansion, missing teenager, murdered man, and purloined prognosticator?

West's "Shit! Shit! Shit!" brought me back to the present. He grabbed my hand. "Shortcake, I gotta show you something."

"Wait," Winona called to our retreating backs.

As soon as I turned and took in her frowny face, I knew what she was going to say.

"West, you better behave because if I tell Grandma—"

"We gotta go." I narrowed my eyes at Winona, giving her my don't-you-dare death stare.

West sprinted, and I hobbled to the foyer. I struggled to keep up as I followed him down the stairs, across the front walk, and past the upturned ladder.

By the time I reached him, he'd turned a large circular sign propped against the garage so that I could see it. "Take a look at this."

"Crap monsters."

"I know. Right?" He pointed to the golden half-moon in the center of the medallion.

"They've got her there, West. I don't know why, but those boys kidnapped her, and she knew they were going to do it."

"Come on," he said.

I followed him to his truck. He assisted me onto the seat before climbing into the cab beside me.

"Since Cassandra is the devil incarnate, I bet she wanted to get rid of a good talisman," I said thinking out loud.

"The devil?" West asked.

"Well, something evil. Maybe she's a witch?"

West scratched his head. "Do witches exist?"

I shrugged. "Probably not."

"But ghosts and psychics are real? Right?"

"Yes," I murmured.

He put the key in the ignition and started the car. "You got your gun?"

I tapped on my backpack. "Yes. But I don't want to shoot anyone."

A smile fought its way through his taut features. "You had no problem shooting me in the ass once upon a time."

I cringed.

West spun his truck around and screeched out a battle cry as we took off for the Schuster estate.

Chapter 21

My survival instincts told me I wouldn't last five minutes in the Schusters' home wearing three layers of clothing. I took off my jacket and mittens and neatly arranged them on the seat beside me. I tried to lift my sweater over my head gracefully, but it stuck to my turtleneck, exposing my midsection. As if that wasn't awkward enough, my disagreeable hair tangled in everything.

While I wrestled, blinded by ringlets and wool, West caught a glimpse of my skin and hissed. Finally, I tugged myself free, tossed my sweater on top of my winter gear, and showered my garments with a heaping dose of contempt.

West grinned.

"I've been freezing all day, so the heat in there should feel good," I said.

"I don't want you to throw up again. You want me to go in by myself?" he asked.

I swallowed and shoved my fear of the energy-charged house deep inside. "No. I want to go with you. I'm prepared this time. Let's review the plan."

West perused the massive structure. "Hey, look there's a mountain behind the house."

"Yes," I said hesitantly since I wasn't sure what he was getting at.

"Cindi's one drawing looked like a house in front

of a mountain."

I palmed my forehead. "That's right."

"First, we'll talk to James. Then we'll ask to speak to his sons," he said.

"I will trip and stumble into Jimmy just as you say, 'Where's Cindi?' I should be able to read his mind and find out exactly where she is."

"Got it," he said.

I gave him a bittersweet smile. "That's what Cindi always says."

"Yeah." He sighed.

Before leaving the car, I indicated the patch above the garage door that hadn't been exposed to the elements. "Look. Now that I know it's there, I can see the outline of where the hex sign hung."

West leaned toward the windshield and peered upward. "Yeah. I see it. I don't remember noticing anything there when we were here Saturday morning."

"I suspect it was taken down between the time Cindi went home with Chad last week and before our visit Saturday morning." I skimmed through a list of reasons Cassandra might have removed the sign and why they were keeping a captive. "I bet the Schusters know about Cindi's psychic abilities."

"Do you think she told them?"

"Maybe. But I am sure she and Jimmy both see the ghost harassing her at school for her treats. Jimmy eats lunch with her class a couple of days a week."

One would think that having already visited the mansion, I wouldn't gawk, taking in every detail like an awestruck child.

"It seems Cassandra took the hex sign down and then had that embedded into the brickwork?" I pointed at the medallion above the door. "Maybe the hex doesn't agree with Cassandra and Jimmy's energy, and that symbol over the door strengthens them."

"Maybe, because nothing about this entire creepy-as-hell situation makes sense," West said.

"West, I'm convinced the house is intensifying my abilities. That is why thoughts are bombarding me and I don't even have to touch someone."

"Do you think it could do the same thing to Cindi?"

"Maybe." I bit my lip. "Do you still think Cassandra is beautiful?"

"Gorgeous. But too unnerving for my liking. These days I like my girls a bit more All-American and sweet with a big smile. Don't get me wrong, I still like me a nice rack." He stared at my skin-tight turtleneck and his lips curved up on one side.

I should have been happy that West referenced me—even if he was teasing. However, my unconfident self heard the "sweet with a big smile," and images of a friendly Miss Myers popped into my head.

A moment later, a grim expression changed his face from that of the fun-loving flirt to the tight-jawed cousin. He grasped the knocker.

Bam! Bam! Bam! echoed.

The mayor opened the door, invited us in, and led us into the throne room.

Cassandra was propped on a velvet settee, looking as smug as Cleopatra herself. She tilted her chin to West before turning a glare on me. As we stared each other down, I wiped the sweat from my brow.

"My parents and sister are out for the day. Is there something I can do for you?" James asked.

West's face puffed up until he resembled a blowfish. Then his cheeks deflated, and his angry voice bellowed. "Cut the bullshit, James. Where's Cindi?"

Oh, West! No! Our plan crumbled.

Cassandra didn't move a muscle, but eerie light beams emanated from her skin.

I tapped West's forearm and prayed that no one heard me whisper, "Do you see it?"

West stood legs wide, chest expanded, gaze fixated on James.

James' hands hung by his side, and his voice remained calm. "Look, I know you're distraught. I get it. If I were in your shoes, I'd feel the same way. I promise that my office is doing everything within our power, and I'm sorry we haven't found her yet."

"I'm not a fucking moron. Your sons have her," West said.

"Dr. Albright, I understand you showed up at the boys' school today today and harassed them," Cassandra said.

An icy chill skittered up my spine even as I burned from the inside out. Sweat dripped down my neck, landing in my cleavage. The edges of her face blurred, and three eyes blinked at me. Make that four psychedelic green eyes that morphed into five, then six. My knees wobbled.

Cassandra stood and glided on red stilettos, stopping three feet in front of me. I collapsed into the closest chair and gasped for air.

Even though my shield was in place, I was once again bombarded with others' thoughts.

What the hell is wrong with her? "Are you okay?" James asked.

Stay strong, Shortcake!

Please don't let Mom hurt her.

I would have sworn that as Cassandra moved closer, her fingers wrapped around my neck. However, she still stood two feet away. "I suggest you stay away from my sons. If you continue to harass them, you will regret it. I've already discussed this with our attorney."

Attorney? We haven't talked to him in months. Why don't I know about it?

What's that bitch doing to Shortcake?

"Cassandra," James said.

She lifted her arm and extended red-tipped nails in her husband's direction. "James." It seemed more reprimand than plea.

"We need to talk to your sons. Now!" West demanded.

"Jimmy is at basketball practice," James said.

West knelt by my side and rubbed my back. "Cassandra, whatever you are doing to her, knock it the hell off."

The normally even-toned James' voice took on a panicky tone. "What are you talking about? Cassandra hasn't touched her!"

West's harsh "Ask your wife. And tell her to stop fucking with my brain," mingled with Chad's internal thoughts that he didn't want to get into trouble.

Chad entered the room. "Mommy, please don't."

"Someone explain what's going on. The Fraternal Ring was here earlier accusing my boys," James said.

"Chad, I know you know where my cousin Cindi is. I love her a lot, and I don't want anything bad to happen to her," West said.

We protected her. Then she got sick, but she's

better now.

Sticky perspiration coated every inch of me; something invisible tangled about my neck choking me, and my lunch traveled up my digestive tract.

"Mom, Dad, I'm home." Jimmy strolled into the room, sat his gym bag on the floor, and grimaced.

My attempts to discern his thoughts were pointless. Bile filled my throat. I grabbed West's hand. "Outside. Now."

West looped my arm around his neck. Absorbing my body weight, he dragged me to the front yard and dropped me about six feet from the front door. Kneeling beside me, he massaged my sweat-soaked back as I regurgitated yellow mucus onto white snow.

"The garage," I huffed between ragged breaths. "I think she's in the garage."

West's arm was around me again. This time he picked me up, slung me over his shoulder, and took off running. From my upside-down position, I twisted to see James and Jimmy following us.

"Nooo!" Jimmy cried.

Cassandra stood on the front porch. Her arms crossed over her chest as the sky silhouetting her appeared to catch fire. Chad frowned from his wheelchair.

Like lightning searching for metal, my static-electricity charged hair reached for the porch that sunk farther from us. I swallowed my lunch as two figures came into view and chased after us.

West halted, set me on my feet, and then turned the knob. "Locked." He pounded on the door. "Cindi!" he yelled. "Open up! It's West."

Jimmy arrived a second after us, positioning

himself between West and the garage.

"Open the damn door," West demanded.

A moment later, James reached us, hunched forward, and placed his hands on his thighs. "Jimmy, where's the key?"

"Hand it over, kid," said a stern female voice.

Lieutenant Bonnie Kramer came out from around the corner of the garage and pushed past me. Her gaze laser-focused on Jimmy, she extended her palm.

Blackova followed her, his beady eyes murderous.

Winona hadn't quite nailed the truth when she said we were "good detectives." However, we were relentless, I was an odd freak with strange abilities, and even though we left a mess in our wake, we did solve crimes. Perhaps Kramer hadn't arrested us for the Blackova debacle because she hoped we might lead her to Cindi.

"Jimmy, please tell me you haven't been hiding Cindi in the garage while the entire county looks for her," James said.

Jimmy stared at his shuffling feet. "I can explain, Dad. This isn't what it looks like."

"Mayor, you didn't think to search your own property?" Blackova asked.

West frantically pounded on the door. "Someone open the goddamn door, or I'm going to kick it in."

"Key," Kramer demanded.

Jimmy sighed, reached into his letterman jacket's pocket, and dropped it into her palm as a police car pulled into the driveway and parked beside us. A gawking Shultz exited the vehicle.

Kramer used a tilted jaw to herd Jimmy out of her way. She perused the crowd, her gaze settling on me. It was a waste of her wrinkle-producing glare because I wasn't the one she needed to worry about.

"I'm going in first. Everyone else will stay on this side of the door. Have I made myself clear?"

West grunted, and I grabbed his elbow, anchoring him in place.

Shultz pulled his radio out of his cruiser. "I think we found Bellmount Bob and the Westinghouse kid."

"Keep them out here. I'm not bullshitting. Anyone gets past you, and it's your ass," Kramer warned the sheriff.

Shultz waddled toward us, pushed to the front of the crowd, and placed his King Bouncer crown atop his bulbous head.

Kramer cracked the door. "Deputy Cindi, it's Lieutenant Bonnie. I'm coming in." She squeezed through the crack, and the door clicked behind her.

"What's wrong? Why isn't Kramer letting us in?" West asked.

"She doesn't want you all to see a dead body. That last one was really bloody. Probably the same guy did this one." Shultz sucked on the side of his cheek and slurped saliva.

West freed himself from my grasp, preparing to throttle Shultz as Chad wheeled toward us. Jimmy placed a hand on his twin's shoulder.

From beside me came a stern father's demand. "Boys, explain."

Chad looked to his brother, and Jimmy bit his lip.

I hurriedly calculated the precise angle needed to fall onto Chad's lap and do a reading. However, it seemed pointless since the Schusters made me akin to my old hair dryer during a lightning storm—a surge of power, an explosion, and then a defunct burned-out appliance.

Still, I would have attempted my gymnastic stunt, except Cassandra glided toward us. Her flowy black pants, long chiffon tunic, and thick hair blew in the wind. A red stripe parted the fast-moving storm clouds that rolled above us.

Meanwhile, the guys mumbled some pretty creative combinations of cuss words while looking up at the sky.

Once Cassandra reached us, she raised a graceful arm. Long sleeves, dark hair, and loose fabric billowed about her. "Let me through."

A gigantic-pupiled Shultz opened the door and stepped to the side as a fuming Cassandra Schuster entered the garage.

My heart beat erratically and nausea churned. Something was terribly wrong. Why else would the Schuster twins hide Cindi from their mother?

****

Shultz's zombie-like state allowed the six of us to bypass him. The scene that greeted us didn't fit the nightmarish moments we had just experienced. The building was more a guest house than a garage. A blanket was spread out on a coach, afternoon cartoons played on the television screen, and photos of race cars and sports posters hung on the walls. Cindi, Kramer, and the witchy woman were nowhere to be seen.

"What the fuck?" West said.

I didn't catch Chad's statement until he repeated it. His chest puffed with pride as he announced. "This is my house."

"The boys stay here," James added. "Teenage boys

need some privacy. Although Jimmy has been sleeping at the main house the last few days."

Jimmy motioned for us to follow. "She's back here."

He led us down a short hallway to a bedroom, where Cindi stretched her tiny legs out on a twin bed. An angelic-looking Cassandra perched on the edge of the mattress beside her. Bonnie Kramer stood propped against the wall, and black rodent eyes peeked out of a cat carrier sitting on the dresser. The women's expressions mimicked girlfriends enjoying a tea party rather than a kidnapped teenager, a special crimes division cop with a bad attitude, and an evil creature of the night.

West practically knocked me out of his way as he pulled his cousin into his arms. When they separated, he placed a hand on each of her shoulders and stared into her eyes. "Are you okay? Did they hurt you?"

"I don't want Grandma to be mad. I fell over." Cindi held up a bandaged hand.

A baffled West narrowed his eyes.

"Bob bit her," Jimmy said.

"Why did you fall over?" West asked.

Cindi blinked three times. "I got hot. I threw up, and I was thirsty."

"Did you pass out? Do you have an infection from the groundhog bite?" Before she could answer, West turned to Jimmy. "Did you get her a freaking antibiotic?"

"The first aid cream has an antibiotic in it," Jimmy said.

I stepped from behind West. "Cindi, were you in the big house?" I pointed in the direction of the mansion. "Did you get sick when you were there?"

Cindi grinned. "Howdy, Doctor Shortcake. It is about time."

West's jaw clenched and his face turned a purplish red. "Cindi, this isn't one of Grandma and Winona's detective shows. We were scared to death. We thought someone kidnapped you."

Cindi stopped smiling to take off her glasses and wipe away a tear. "I have to tell you a secret." Cindi crooked her finger for me to lean close.

I placed my ear close to her lips, but her voice carried to everyone in the room.

"There are lots of ghosts in that house," she said.

West grunted.

Kramer held up a hand "Everyone calm down. Cindi wasn't playing a game."

"We didn't kidnap her." Jimmy vehemently shook his head.

"Then what happened?" Blackova's hands hung by his side as he clenched and unclenched his fingers numerous times.

An odd smile made its way across Cassandra's face as she ran a hand through Cindi's hair and eyed her as if she was a chocolate-covered truffle.

"We were keeping her safe," Jimmy said.

Cassandra's insincere, horrifying smile and her glowing child didn't fool me for a second. Since Jimmy was at Pinkie's Steeple on the day of the crime, giving off huge amounts of disconcerting energy, he had to be Phil's murderer.

"Seems someone should have protected Cindi from the Schusters." I glared at Jimmy. "What I don't understand is why you killed Phil Nowak."

Jimmy's jaw dropped.

"What?" asked James.

Cassandra's invisible finger reached out and jabbed me in the chest. I rubbed at my heart.

"I didn't kill, kidnap, or hurt anyone," Jimmy said. "Cindi said the guy who did it was after her at the festival, so we brought her here. Then she got sick. I didn't want—" he looked at his mother, shook his head, and frowned. "Also, she is afraid of someone who said hi to her, and she thinks she will be in trouble because she tried to carry Bob and he bit her. But she was just trying to protect him from the guy who said hi." Looking quite sincere, Jimmy gazed into his father's eyes. "Dad, it all just spiraled out of control. Once Cindi got better, I was worried about how much trouble we were in. I couldn't figure a way out that wouldn't make you look bad and upset Mom."

Jimmy Schuster left out the part that he and Chad were hiding Cindi from their mother for reasons he couldn't mention. Meanwhile, the fingers of fire taunted as they crept upward, landing on my neck.

"Cindi?" Once Kramer held Cindi's gaze, she spoke softly. "Is the person who killed the man at Pinkie's Steeple after you?"

Cindi's tongue made an appearance as she nodded. "I drew a moon fast so Doctor Shortcake, Winona, and the sexy snoop could find me."

"You did what?" The brilliant Jimmy Junior asked, obviously unaware that Cindi had left a trail of clues.

"Except for some strange reason, the moon is no longer hanging in front of this building," I croaked out between breaths.

"The moon?" James asked. "Do you mean the old

hex sign? We took it down a few days ago. Liam has it now."

The witchy palm pressed against my windpipe, and I gasped.

"Who is after you, Cindi?" Kramer asked.

Cindi looked at West.

"It's okay. Tell us," West coaxed, his voice gentle.

I expected Cindi to point to Cassandra. Instead, she looked at the ground and muttered, "Howdy."

"Howdy?" Kramer asked.

"I think that's the guy who said hi to her," Jimmy said.

I bent forward and forced air into my lungs as a satisfied smile consumed Cassandra.

Officer Kline stepped into the room followed by Howard Greene.

"Howdy, Cindi. Glad you're safe," Kline said. "Got your message, Sheriff. Luckily, I was close. I figured I'd call Howard so he could come get the groundhog."

Eureka! Everything became clear. Unfortunately I couldn't speak, and since everyone was gawking at the two men, no one noticed that my air supply had been cut off.

Howard's gaze landed on the carrier, and he squealed, "Bob!" He practically leaped across the room. He placed his face next to the groundhog's so that only a thin layer of netting separated their noses. "Oh, thank God."

Cindi's muscles tensed, and she pulled a blanket across her lap as a lovey-dovey Howard greeted his critter.

I was only able to gasp out, "How—" before

collapsing onto my knees.

West rushed to my side. "It's okay. I got you. Breathe." He caressed my cheek, as his gaze cut to Cassandra.

Cindi frowned as she tapped Cassandra on the forearm. "Don't be mean."

Cassandra's eyes glittered with ecstasy as she took her time releasing the magical hold.

"Howie?" I asked my voice gravelly.

Smiling at the groundhog, Howard Greene picked up the crate. Before I could ask my question, he rushed toward the exit.

Still on my knees, I reached up and caught hold of his arm as he passed. "Did Phil call you, Howie?"

"Yeah. Why?" He glared at my hand on his arm.

"Why did you kill him?" I asked.

He feigned innocence with a hand to his heart. "I would never hurt him. He was my friend."

I clamped my hand tighter as I used his body weight to leverage myself onto my feet. "You aren't going anywhere until you tell us why you killed Phil." Although I'd dropped my shield, the Schusters sucked at my energy making it almost impossible to read his mind.

He tried to tug free, so I dug my fingers into his sleeve.

"I'm trying to be nice, but I am going to press charges if you don't get your hand off of me," Howard said.

I fought through the energy blockade and at last: *Why in the hell did Phil get chummy with Kip Stone?*

"Why were you angry about Phil hanging out with Kip Stone?" I asked.

Although Howard remained stone-faced, his breath hitched a millisecond after I mentioned Kip Stone.

Cindi pulled the blanket from her lap, walked to Howard Greene, and tilted her head up to study him. She adjusted her glasses, then poked her finger into his chest. "You wanted to steal Bob. Grandma says you go to hell for lying."

"That's right, Cindi." I faced Greene. "It's pretty hot down there, and if the sweat dripping down your brow at room temperature is any indication, it looks like you will melt when they hold your lying keister over a flame." It was a pretty ballsy statement seeing as how even my hair was damp with perspiration.

Kramer emitted a half-laugh, half-grunt as she peeled herself from the wall and straightened. "Cindi, is this the man who killed Phil, and is he trying to hurt you?"

Cindi nodded. "Howdy."

"You mean Howie," I said. "Howdy is how your father and some other people say hello, and Howie is a nickname for a man named Howard."

Cindi pursed her lips and concentrated. "Howdy means *Hi*. Howie means *Howard*."

I'm not sure how many people muttered, "Yes." Although Howard Greene was not one of them.

Kramer removed the carrier from Greene's hands and handed it to Blackova. She grabbed Howard and flung him face-first into the wall. With a flick of her wrist, she had him secured in handcuffs. "Come on." She nudged him toward the door.

Too bad the guilty party was Howard Greene instead of Cassandra or the ill-tempered Blackova.

"You can't take me in. You have no proof other

than the word of a crazy woman." He stared me down. "And a dimwitted kid." He inclined his chin toward Cindi.

Winona and Keisha were correct. He was rodent-obsessed. And Cindi had hit the nail on the head; he was a mean liar.

Kramer gave him a shot between his shoulder blades, moving him a few inches.

"You people don't understand. I had to get rid of Phil. He was getting chummy with Creekfield. He wanted to stop the pranks. He was even going to give away our secret handshake and let them look at our pledge to keep the peace. I wasn't trying to steal Bob. The kid's confused. I was trying to protect him from those beaver freaks."

Cindi situated herself so that she was in his space and looked up at him. "You are really mean."

Kramer chuckled. "Hey deputy, did you see him do it?"

"The ghost told me *Howdy* did it," Cindi said. "And Howie said mean things to me when I got off stage."

West groaned.

"See what I mean? The kid is crazy," Greene said.

"What did Howie say to you?" Kramer asked.

"He was trying to steal Bob, and he said he wouldn't mind killing a weird kid."

Kramer slugged Greene in the back, and his body flew toward the door. "Sheriff, get statements. I'm taking this piece of shit in before I beat him to a pulp," she called over her shoulder.

Why would a woman who seemed so on the ball leave Shultz in charge of questioning?

Shultz hitched his fingers in his waistband and rocked on his heels. "Anyone see anything odd here today?"

"Odd?" Cassandra's cold stare had replaced her evil smile.

"Nope," West said, looking at me for reassurance. "Nothing. Why?"

Glowing humans. Odd lightning streaks running horizontally. A hypnotized sheriff.

"I didn't see anything," I said.

James sucked on his bottom lip as Jimmy and Chad stared at each other.

"The only issue was that Dr. Albright harassed my family, and my boys were protecting their friend," Cassandra said.

If I hadn't left Princess in the truck, I could have put a bullet right between Cassandra's evil green eyes. She may have been walking away from the murder/kidnapping situation scot-free, but I was onto her. She was so evil she made Shultz, the incompetent rat, look like a savior.

"However, there is no need to pursue a complaint against Dr. Albright at this time. I believe everything is fine." A thin cloud of red light surrounded Cassandra for a moment as she stabbed me between the eyes with one of her invisible weapons.

"Yeah," Shultz said, his pupils spinning like a top. "Everything is fine."

Blackova finally looked up from Bob's crate. "Actually, the kid's pretty sharp. She took good care of Bob."

Cindi grinned. "And he only bit me once."

****

As we sat around waiting to be questioned, Jimmy Schuster caught my arm, singed my skin, and pulled me off to the side.

"Hey. I just wanna be normal. I wanna play basketball, hang with my girl, and take care of my brother. You know what I mean?"

"Yes." Unfortunately, I knew exactly what he meant, and it appeared we were onto each other. Still, I needed answers. "Why do you glow sometimes?"

He shrugged. "I don't know. I try not to. Mom doesn't mind it though—being hot and doing whatever it is we do. Honestly, Mom and Dad didn't know we had her. I slept in the main house because I think I make Cindi sick at night."

"Why do you make her sick?" I wiped the sweat from my brow.

"I have no idea. But I make you and Cindi both sweat like crazy, and I think I make your hair stand in the air. I might be some kind of electron magnet. I can't control it around you at all. I can sometimes put up a shield around Cindi, unless I'm sleeping. But I had to work really hard to learn to do that." He sighed. "You won't tell anyone, will you?

Magnets? Electrons? Shields? Jimmy and I were alike.

"Why did your mom have the new medallion placed above your front door?"

He rubbed his forehead and moaned. "I don't know. It came from my Grandma and Grandpa Weiner's house. I know this sounds crazy, but it makes me give off even more energy."

"Hey, girly," Shultz called.

I turned from Jimmy to glower at the sheriff.

The cop whistled at me like I was a dog, and then curled his finger. "Your turn. Let's get this over with and get home for dinner."

"Of course," I whispered.

No wonder Kramer had left Shultz in charge of questioning. The woman may have hated my guts, but she was a genius.

Epilogue

Awkward doesn't begin to describe Liam's dinner party. In theory, it should have been a wonderful evening. However, things went awry the second a sexy-smelling Sean O'Sullivan showed up at the inn with a dozen roses.

"You don't have a Valentine's date? Cool. I'm starving. I'm going with you." Grinning, he climbed into The Tank beside me.

I had three valid reasons for not protesting too much. First, I didn't officially have a date. Secondly, I was forcing myself to get over West. And finally, since Sean wore his fisherman net sweater, he resembled a rugged male model.

Liam's second-floor apartment looked out over the Susquehanna River. He shared Aunt Edith's panache for decorating, adding Sherlock Holmes-style masculine touches to his Victorian decor.

West had spent the day chefing away in Liam's kitchen preparing *hors d'oeuvres*, chicken cordon bleu, rice pilaf, roasted asparagus, and a from-scratch cake topped with strawberries and homemade cream.

Not only was the menu to die for delicious, but Cindi was safe and sound, and Howard Greene was behind bars.

Even though I had done my best to banish the strange Schusters from my thoughts, I was reminded of them when Bellmount Bitch Gina Schuster greeted me at the door.

She snarled before melting at the sight of the splendiferous sergeant. He winked at her. Who would have known the horrid woman was capable of blushing? We followed her into the dining room, where Tommy, Perkypants, and Liam sat.

"Hey." Sean extended his hand to Liam. "I hope it's all right that I invited myself."

Liam had also inherited Aunt Edith's flair for hospitality. "Sure, Sergeant O'Sullivan," he said. "The more, the merrier. What can I get you to drink?"

"Call me Sean and a beer if you have one."

"Steal City bottles?" Liam asked.

Even though Sean preferred an Irish red, he grinned. "Perfect." He helped himself to the snack platter and made himself comfortable in an upholstered dining chair. "Hiya, Little," he said before popping a hunk of cheese into his mouth.

Tommy greeted him and introduced Perkypants, who acted like a simpering fool, fluttering her eyelashes. You would think the apartment wasn't full of attractive men the way Tommy and Liam's dates behaved at the sight of the testosterone-stocked cop.

Liam excused himself to the kitchen. He returned with another place setting and a condensation-coated bottle. A moment later, West peeked out the kitchen door. He didn't even try to hide his dislike of Sean—rolling his eyes dramatically.

Sean performed a goofy finger wave. "Hey, it's the bartender," he declared with a smart alec gleam in his eyes.

West slammed the door, returning to his meal prep.

My stomach gurgled as I spent the next thirty minutes listening to Gina brag and Perkypants guffaw. My nerves were so frazzled I even passed up pastry puffs and cheese.

Perkypants resembled a trained seal, clapping at the most insignificant of details. I lost what little diplomacy I had left as Gina told a story of being crowned Prom Queen and Perkypants yahooed and slapped her hands together. I grunted, then before saying something I would regret, excused myself. I was on my way to pull myself together, check on West, and find out why dinner was delayed when there was a knock on the door. Since I was the only one standing, I opened it to a smiling Miss Myers. A grinning ghost leered from behind her.

"Hi," she said. "I didn't know you were going to be here. I'm glad I know someone. West just called to invite me for dinner." Acting as though we were best friends, she leaned close. "I'm so excited that I got dressed in five minutes. Do I look okay?"

She turned in a circle. Perverted Greg focused on her behind as her pixie curls bounced about her shoulders. Finishing with a "Ta-da," she rested a hand on her hip.

Greg gave her a thumbs up.

Beside the word adorable in the dictionary was a picture of Miss Myers.

I nodded, showed her to the table, introduced her to everyone, and told her I'd let West know she had arrived. She lit up at the sight of Tommy and joined the party with an ease that made me want to bash my head against the wall.

Greg plopped himself in my chair, said hi to

everyone, and eyed the bottle of wine.

I gave Greg a don't-you-dare-pick-up-that-bottle look and then entered the kitchen. West stood staring at eight full plates.

"Are you okay?" I asked.

He didn't respond immediately. When he finally did, his voice rumbled. "How's your date?"

I exhaled a sigh that my father could have felt from four hours away. "Sean showed up at Aunt Edith's tonight with flowers. I wasn't expecting him. When I told him I had to go, he invited himself to dinner."

"Whatever," West said. "We aren't dating anymore, and you can see whomever you want. I just hate the guy. It took everything I had not to spit in his dinner."

I had had enough of the entire dinner party fiasco. I squished up my face until it hurt, then barked, "Now, that's mature. Besides, I'm taking a break from men for now."

"A break? What a load of crap. It seems you are into O'Sullivan. I mean, you make out with him at crime scenes; you show up at dinner with him, and he stares at you like he is going to throw you down, rip your clothes off, and bang the shit out of you in front of everyone." West moved closer and looked down at me. Anger infused the breath that blew across my cheek. "And let's be clear, you don't do anything to discourage it."

I lifted my chin to meet his gaze. "What do you care? You're the one who broke up with me. At least you don't have to deal with my freakiness anymore."

"Is Doc on his way too?" West asked. "Should I prepare more food?"

"Sometimes you're such a jerk."

His beautiful hazel eyes had shriveled to dark slivers. "Yep. That's me. The jerk with venereal diseases."

I gasped. "Keisha said that. Not me."

"That was a fun rumor. The best one yet. You want to explain why I had to tell a nice girl who has a crush on me that I don't have dozens of diseases before she agreed to be my date tonight?"

Ten million emotions knocked the wind out of me. I met his incensed gaze. "What are we doing, West?"

"Apparently, I spent all day cooking for your date, who looks down his nose at me, and my date who thinks I'm scum."

"Stop it. Sean is just a friend, and your date is here. FYI she's excited and thinks you're awesome."

"I better say hi to her." He tossed a tea towel into the sink and grabbed two plates of food. "Make yourself useful and help me."

The door slammed behind him.

Annoyance seeped from every one of my pores. "She's here thirty minutes after I arrive? Do you have her number on speed dial?" I asked my reflection in the toaster.

I leaned against the counter to think. Why had I shown up with Sean and picked a fight with West? Had I done something dysfunctional and Freudian in my attempt to get over West? I assured myself it was best for us both. However, the ache in my heart disagreed with the assessment.

I was about to pick up a plate when I noticed a single red rose buried in the trash cash. An embossed white card sat on top of it. Curiosity got the better of me, so I reached into the muck, wiped asparagus off the paper, and read: *Shortcake. Be Mine. West.*

I leaned on the counter again and willed my breath to slow. How would I get over the man if he bought me flowers and got jealous over my accidental dates?

I folded the note and shoved it into my back jeans pocket just as West entered the kitchen and frowned. "You may be a great professor, but you're a shit-ass waitress."

When he reached in front of me to pick up food, I grabbed him and pulled him to me. My lips crashed against his, and my tongue parted his lips.

He pushed back, shoving my backside against the counter. I threaded my fingers through his hair and tugged.

"Oh, West," I whimpered as I rubbed my emptiness against his hardness.

He pulled his lips from mine to cup my ear. "Fuck. I want you."

Clinging to him, I captured his sexy moans with my mouth.

The kitchen door squeaked, and Liam gawked. He stepped inside, made sure the door clicked into place, then shook his head. "Seriously, you two? Get your shit together. Your dates are in the other room. And we are hungry." He grabbed two plates and, with a sigh of disgust, left us.

A sweaty West backed away and ran a hand across his mouth. His eyes were bright, his cheeks were flushed, his hair was disheveled, and his breathing was labored. His gaze focused on mine, he opened his mouth to say something but stopped.

"Tell me what you want me to do?" I pleaded.

He shook his entire body violently. "For now, I want you to help me serve this food."

Loaded down, we headed to the dining room. West set a plate in front of Miss Myers and sat beside her. I handed Sean his, then stood waiting for Greg to move.

"What's wrong, Randa?" Tommy asked.

"There's a ghost in my chair." I was at my wit's end and figured no one would take me seriously.

West's forkful of chicken hung mid-air as he stared at my chair.

Gina Schuster rolled her eyes, tapped Liam on the shoulder, and whispered in his ear.

"Girl, you're a hoot," Perkypants hollered.

"Eh, as long as the spook isn't perverted or hungry, just sit on his lap," Sean declared between mouthfuls of food.

Since the spook was both a lech and deprived, I continued to stare.

Finally, Greg stood. *"Damn, you need to get laid. Westinghouse's cock isn't doing a damn thing for your disposition. Why don't you give the Irish barbarian a go?"*

I flung myself into my chair.

"I'm going back to Alina's. This dinner party sucks royally." Instead of dissolving, Greg walked to the door and passed through it.

"A total hoot," Perkypants declared. "Like you're really fighting with a ghost. I can't wait for Halloween."

I pushed my dinner around my plate as I listened to seven voices blab on and on. *Wha, wha wa wha wa....*

"Shortcake?" West's gentle voice interrupted my asparagus stock counting. "I worked hard. Try it and tell me what you think."

He held his breath as I nibbled.

"It's delicious, West," I said in all sincerity. "You are going to be a world-class chef someday."

West's smile filled my entire field of vision until Sean's quick movement distracted me.

He grabbed his bottle, and chugged the remainder of his beer. "What's for dessert, bartender?"

A heavy-lidded West seduced me with sweet words and fiery eyes. "Decadent strawberries and sweet-tasting shortcake, covered in homemade cream."

I doubt the double entendre was lost to the men in the room.

"Hey, shortcake for Shortcake." Perkypants pointed at me and giggled.

Sean O'Sullivan licked his lips. "Mmm, mmm. I love strawberries, and I'll take another beer to go with my Shortcake." He placed a hand over mine.

"Who needs beer?" West asked. "For dessert I just want my Shortcake covered in whipped cream."

Something tickled between my thighs.

I was getting over West.

Starting…

A word about the author…

Nicki Pascarella lives in Pennsylvania with her husband, daughter, and hyperactive Shetland Sheepdogs. When she isn't writing fiction, you will find her reading, Belly Dancing, or running 5ks with her furry partner.

****

https://www.nickipascarella.com/

****

If you enjoyed this story, leaving a review at your favorite book retailer or reader website would be much appreciated. Thank you!

Thank you for purchasing
this publication of The Wild Rose Press, Inc.

For questions or more information
contact us at
info@thewildrosepress.com.

The Wild Rose Press, Inc.
www.thewildrosepress.com